SIDELINE

*Judy + Bryan —
All the Best to you
both a great health a wealth.
Enjoy! All the Best
Gary*

SIDELINE

GARY LETT

AuthorHouse™
1663 Liberty Drive
Bloomington, IN 47403
www.authorhouse.com
Phone: 1-800-839-8640

This book is fictional. It is an account of situations and experiences as related by the author in a fictional matter. Any brand names or noted figures mentioned are registered trademarks by their respective corporation. They are not a part of this book or with the author.

© 2012 by Gary Lett. All rights reserved.

No part of this book may be reproduced, stored in a retrieval system, or transmitted by any means without the written permission of the author.

Published by AuthorHouse   03/17/2012

ISBN: 978-1-4685-6692-5 (sc)
ISBN: 978-1-4685-6691-8 (hc)
ISBN: 978-1-4685-6690-1 (e)

Library of Congress Control Number: 2012905068

Any people depicted in stock imagery provided by Thinkstock are models, and such images are being used for illustrative purposes only.
Certain stock imagery © Thinkstock.

This book is printed on acid-free paper.

Because of the dynamic nature of the Internet, any web addresses or links contained in this book may have changed since publication and may no longer be valid. The views expressed in this work are solely those of the author and do not necessarily reflect the views of the publisher, and the publisher hereby disclaims any responsibility for them.

Edited by: Elizabeth Wagner, Hattiesburg, MS

Graphics by: Andrew Moye of Votum Design
Hattiesburg, MS

Introduction

"Good morning, Coach Hayes. This is Grant Simpson from the Sports Channel, how are you doing? I hope I haven't called too early?"

It was a little early, but Coach Hayes didn't mind. He remembered Grant, a good kid. "No Grant, I'm into my second sports page already. I hope you have been doing well yourself."

"Well, Coach, I'm doing just fine, but listen, I want to run something by you. With the start of football season approaching we're looking to kick-off a new program here at the network. It's called *Looking Back*. We would love to profile you and get your insights into football."

"Grant, you already drinking this morning?"

Grant laughs. "Not that I know of, Coach. I'm pretty sure I'm serious."

Coach Hayes laughs, too. "Well, Grant, if you feel good about doing this then I'd be happy to talk with you. Is there anything specific you're looking for?"

"Coach Hayes, we've found that our viewers and the readers of our magazine love to glimpse the foundation of the person. They want to know what guys like you saw, heard or did that made a difference to them."

"I can understand that. I have an interest in that myself."

"I figured as much. All those game days you've visited our booth—you know everyone likes your insight."

"Grant, I've said it a bunch, you've heard me. You just have to take what you have gone through and make the best of it. There is no one big aspect—it's just putting all the little things together at the right time."

"Coach, those little things are what we want to hear about. My crew will come down to sit and chat. Hopefully we'll get to play a round or two in the process."

"Sounds good," Coach Hayes said. He went back to the paper, but he was also thinking of what he might say.

I will try and recall, to the best of my ability, what I went through during those early times in my life. Hopefully my words can also carry you back to this time, a time of fond memories. My story begins like this . . . .

PART I

The fans are making so much noise the players can barely hear. They don't mind too much: Death Valley on Saturday night is what college football is all about.

The LSU fans are some of the most loyal in the nation and they seem to live for game days. Many fans show up to tailgate and be a part of the atmosphere and never even make it inside the stadium.

The clock is winding down. Bobby Geroux, QB for the Tigers, is flapping his arms to quiet them so he can call the play. There's the snap, Geroux rolls right, and he's looking for Jordan to make his move. He lofts a long one and, "Crap, what was that," as the ball falls helplessly to the ground. I'd almost stepped on the biggest toad frog I'd ever seen

Game over. I didn't see how you could keep throwing passes to yourself and be scared of stepping on a frog. Sometimes you may have to dive to make the catch or get tackled from behind: you couldn't be scared of frogs then. You see, in the mid 1960's, being in north Alabama, your AM radio could pick up the broadcast of LSU football. Most other games were played during the day, but LSU usually played home games on Saturday nights. So you came to know the names of most of the players; you had the floodlights in your back yard and played right along with the LSU Tigers.

Back then, you didn't have the glut of games on TV and there were a lot more games via radio. I believe a team, at that time, could only be shown on TV twice during the year, not counting a bowl game. It was—and is—so unique to be able envision the game transform right in front of you, without ever seeing it actually happen. That trait, being about to envision the game, became a trait that would be so important to me later on in life. In fact, I think, this power of imagination, this power to envision, is a valuable tool for all athletes to grasp. To know what may transpire, to focus and realize that if a player makes a certain move then he can only turn a certain way—this is a crucial skill that can give you a rare advantage. Of course, I didn't really understand that back then, in my backyard on a Saturday night, playing along with the radio. I just loved the game.

Stuart, Alabama, my small hometown, sits on the outskirts of the larger city of Marion, which served as the shopping hub for the entire area and featured the region's main industries: steel and carpet manufacturing. Our town was one of those you might find featured in the pages of *Southern Living*. It was a friendly place, where everyone seemed to know everyone. It was home to nearly 3,000 people. In the surrounding area people knew it for its single traffic light on highway 15, running north to south in Alabama. Of course, they also knew it for the Rebel Drive-In. That little diner had the best shakes and malts I've ever had. And they used to cost all of 1 quarter. They were the perfect thing to go along with those burgers and hot apple or peach pies.

I grew up in the time when you basically had to entertain yourself. So that explains the solo football games. The main entertainment was sports. There were many different sports played in Stuart. In and about town you were up early to play before it got too hot and were active late after it cooled down during the summer months. The neighborhood was special because we had our own little cast for teams and games. All the same faces, all the time, but the funny part was this: we didn't really get tired of one another. I guess we figured if we didn't get along, then it was back to the carport—throwing the rubber ball against the wall, all by yourself.

My family featured my older brother, Stewart. As he got into school he hated his name. I always understood that: although spelled differently, his name was the same as our old town. My Dad, Coach Paul, always had to tell him that he didn't know he was going to be living in Stuart when he was born and if Granddad was around he could butt heads with him over the name. One thing I think finally helped that situation is when I heard Dad say, "Just be glad we didn't go with an ex-President Rutherford Hayes and you may have been called Ruth." Then I guess Stewart wasn't quite as bad. He was about 6 years older than me, so I pretty much knew him as Stew. What I remember most is his athleticism: he was a very good all-around athlete.

Dad was the high school coach so Stew was always around the games, playing and trying to do his part while Dad was coaching. He just had that special knack, the sort of knack some coaches' kids acquire. As Stew started into playing little league, I got to be the little shadow. It is funny, today, looking at the old black and white photos and seeing the little pip-squeak in the team picture being the bat-boy. Being that little pip-squeak teaches you something, though; you get the see how to do things and how not to do things. Every so often I was able to fill in, mostly right field. I even got to throw back a stray ball from time to time.

As I mentioned, Dad was the high school football coach. It also meant he coached the Jr. Varsity in basketball, helped with baseball, and during the summer managed the city pool. This city job was reserved for the coach and his staff, of one. It was a big job when you think about it; he took care of the facilities and fields and anything about town that was sports related.

My dad, Coach Paul, had attended Northeast Alabama University (The Owls) a Division II school in that part of Alabama about 40 minutes from Stuart. He played football and was very aware of situations. To be honest, I always swore he could read minds. He just had a knack of knowing what people were going to try to do and I think a lot had to do with his own experiences. Dad was always a step ahead of me when I went to asking questions or trying to weasel my way out of something. I wasn't too good on the getting out of something and it was just my luck that dad, being a high school coach and teacher, always seemed to have a paddle around somewhere.

My mother, Brenda Hayes, was always active and was sports minded herself. She liked bowling and other things. She also made sure everyone got to practice and really looked out after her kids. Really she was what you'd call nowadays "a supermom," the kind who always had a snack ready for us kids after playing. It fit well that she married a coach. With Dad always active with school activities, Mom watched over the backyard games. She had put up a little hitting device when Stew was about 11 to help groove his baseball swing. As for me, well, when I was in the early learning stages, Mom taught me how to hold the bat and swing—I thus learned to bat left handed thanks to her instructions.

After games there were the trips to the Rebel Drive-In to get one of their famous milk shakes. For me it was either a grape or peanut butter shake. And thank goodness we got to go whether we won or lost!

There was one little gadget that Mom could always amaze me with, the paddle ball. Surely you remember the contraption with the long rubber band attached to the paddle and the little red ball at the end of the band? Well, most of us almost put our eyes out hitting the ball everywhere or wrapping the band around our necks. Mom could flat out never miss with either hand—hitting it up, down, left or right. If you weren't careful and broke something with the ball trying to hit it, she would just turn the paddle over and sting your butt with it.

My sister Sharon was in between Stew and me. She was a typical coach's daughter; she was good at sports and, of course, she was a cheerleader. During the times we grew up there just weren't any organized sports for girls. So, she did her own thing of hanging out with friends. I also remember how she was always real protective of us. Thankfully, she learned a lot of Mom's cooking favorites.

The last part of the Hayes family was my little brother, Quint. Nobody except Dad had ever heard of anyone named Quinton, so Quint was always it. Later on it was always so funny when somebody would ask his name. "Quinton," you would say and after that you'd get a "do what" comment or weird look. Supposedly Quint popped up a little unexpectedly, so I guess Dad had to pull out all stops on his name.

Quint was a good little brother, always gullible, but it became my job to look out after him. He took it real well, all of the little jokes you played on him. He learned from Stew and me and it didn't take him long to learn that playing the baby brother card was a good way to get by. He took his lumps from time to time but he sure was a lot better than me at getting out of things. By then I guess Dad had gotten tired of the corrections and whippings he had given me. In the end, Quint paid attention to my shortcomings and learned what not to do. We all kinda followed the same path laid down by Stew with organized sports anyway. Stew would throw and do things with us but being older he didn't play in our neighborhood games.

Finishing out the Hayes family was me, Bob. I guess being the middle boy a lot of things fell my way. For some reason, Mothers always talk about this or that trait in kids. I thought I had good reasons for doing most things but my parents thought otherwise. I believe I was at least 5 years old when I realized my first name wasn't Dammit. My dad would come in from school or practice and he would find out something I had gotten into. As soon as he would see me, it was "Dammit, Bob." As I mentioned he always seem to have a paddle handy. I almost got to the point that when I saw him, I would bend over. I tease you, but the truth is I had a lot of mistakes to learn from early on. Of course, I wasn't never into anything real mean, like harming animals, just day to day stuff.

Try this one and see if you don't get what I mean. Stew had a great hobby of putting together model planes and cars, had them all over his room. When I was five I had come down with a case of chicken pox and just had to stay home and scratch a bit. That got a little boring, as you may imagine. Now, I had a pretty good imagination, as about any five year old would have, and I tell you, I got restless. With limited entertainment—we didn't have a lot of daytime TV shows and cable wasn't invented yet—my curiosity got the best of me. Thus I ventured into Stew's room and had races with his model cars. A lot of them had crashes. Then there were battles with the planes. Those things don't fly too well and the pilots had some real rough landings on the floor. I left the pile of pieces there for Stew to glue back together. I figured, he did it once, he could do it again. Of course, he did not agree with me. When Stew got home and caught a look in his room, I was racing down the hall to hide. I ran into the bathroom and locked the door. He tore up the door to get to me and I was the one that got my butt whipped. Imagine that.

Now, that rounds out the Hayes family. Coach Paul, Brenda, Stew, Sharon, Quint, and me, Bob, growing up and living in Stuart, Alabama, population 3,000.

There are a lot of little things that fall into place to make a neighborhood comfortable. During the early to mid 1960's, our residential area was laid out well for kids. Our house had a decent size backyard with a lot next to it. Mom's grandparent's moved onto part of the lot with a trailer and they seem to always have some of those small Dr. Pepper's in the fridge. People didn't drink a lot of cola drinks at that time; we relied on water during the summer and, at times, Kool-Aid. So, the cola drinks were a real treat. One neat thing about our backyard was that we had 2 basketball goals, and the rest was surrounded in back and to the other neighbor's side by a fence. Knowing that, you can imagine how lot of activity was able to take place in that yard. We hardly ever had to leave it. We lived on a dead end street which meant we didn't have to contend with traffic problems. You can imagine how good that was for bike races.

Next door to us was a huge, fenced-in backyard. This made it the place for many endless games of baseball At times kickball games were our choice—for these you would use baseball rules and you made outs by catching the ball in the air or by throwing and hitting the runner with the ball. Kickball was usually the early morning game, designed to give the early risers something to do before the lazy ones got stirring. Now, understand, the big yard belonged to the Townsends. They were a big family with four girls—Sara, Becky, Kathy, and Trina—and only one boy, Matt. During those years little Trina was an infant, Matt was Quint's age and they were the best of friends, Kathy was about a year younger than me and Becky about a year older, and Sara was Sharon's age. Quint and I hung out with the Townsend's the most. During that time Kathy Townsend was quite a good athlete. She played baseball right along with us and proved her mettle in games you'll hear about later.

In our neighborhood each and everybody was welcome. For instance, while Mrs. Townsend was serving up breakfast for her kids, it was not uncommon for her to look over and see 2 or 3 more mouths to feed. Now, Mrs. Townsend made very good French toast. It was something not offered at our house—I guess it just never got on our regular rotation. So, when she had the urge to cook that dish, Matt would let us know and we would stumble over for breakfast. None of the kids got turned away. This happened just the same at night, especially during the summer months. If you were watching TV and happened to fall asleep, there would be a phone call: one parent would let the other know that she would be minus a kid that night. It all worked out well.

Most of the activities happened at our house or the Townsend's, but around us we also had the Kerns with their son, Blake, and their daughter, Cindy. The Reid's household had two boys, Kelly and Greg. The Moore's had a son, Pat, and daughter, Patricia. This was a particularly popular stop off because they had some good apple trees in their backyard. The Watson family, with their two sons, Tom and Jimmy, was unique because they grew some sugar cane and strawberries. Can you believe that there were nights when those fields got raided by some varmints? I'm still glad Mr. Watson didn't ever use any traps, or some of us would have been hurting.

For me, starting out, my best buddy was Pete West. Pete's dad was a chiropractor that moved to Stuart and met my Dad, the head football coach. They formed a great friendship and Dr. West helped to take care of the athletes for the Rebels. He was also there to aid Dad in building up the athletic program. Pete and I were about the same age, just 3 months apart. Pete's older brother Curt became very good friends with Stew as well and our families did a lot of socializing. Dr. West got the nickname "Hands" due to his occupation and had a knack for fixing about just about anything. They lived about a mile from us and had a good pasture behind of their house. We also had plenty of room to roam.

Remember how I mentioned that Stew was better at getting out of trouble than I was? Well, here is an example. Dr. Hands had gotten a bull from someone. Who knows why. He had an idea to start the Stuart Rebel booster club by selling raffle tickets for the bull. This would help Dad and his program to build new bleachers and concession stands for the football stadium. The fundraiser was a big success, but it almost didn't happen. Before the contest, Stew and Curt were at the West's. I should mention that Curt had a new BB gun. I should also mention that Stew and Curt were getting good at picking off targets. While shooting by the fence Stew sees the bull, standing there grazing. Curiosity got the best of him. He looked at the bull and thought his ball sac might make for an interesting target. Well, the second shot hit its mark and that bull was seeing red everywhere. The bull took off and broke through the fence. You might be expecting disaster, but don't worry: the bull was found about a mile away and they managed to secure him for the raffle. All the parents just assumed that the bull got stung by a bee and left it at that. Only Stew and Curt knew it was a bee-bee. Dr. Hands went to his grave without knowing the truth about Stew hitting his target.

* * *

Pete and I were always around the fields or courts no matter what the sport because our dads were usually there as well. Growing up that way, we were always getting ragged by the older guys. It was all good natured and we both seemed like little brothers to all of the older high school guys. We got to be involved with their activities and one of the most important things was this: we paid attention to what was going on. So, for most of the games and practices all the players would be looking for Pete and re-Pete since we were always together at most of the events. The games in Stuart were serious no matter what and everybody took pride in being a Rebel.

Just a few hundred yards away from our house was the Indy field. It was a large baseball field with a cornfield for a homerun fence, a good backdrop for the hitters. A lot of the towns had good athletes who weren't able to go to college and enjoyed baseball as well. Stuart was no different and had a good group of guys. Coach Paul and Doc Hands helped run the concession stand to make money for the games. There were no lights which meant all the games were played in the afternoon. The concession was perched down under a big oak tree, out of the sun.

As the bat boy, I did a good job of retrieving the bats and loose balls and generally keeping things in order. While doing this, I paid close attention to the games, of course. On one afternoon, I remember, there was a particularly big play. The bases were loaded. Big O at the plate for Stuart. He hits a ball into the right field gap. The catcher stands up and flips his mask off. I didn't think much of this; I just picked it up with the bat. At that time I don't think I had ever tried on a catcher's mask and, curious as I was, I went right ahead and slid it over my head to look through. As I was gazing out from the bench, a scene unfolded around home plate. The umpire was looking over his shoulder and the catcher was looking like the mid section of a washing machine, turning in both directions. No clue. I see the catcher shrug his shoulders, surely thinking 'how in the heck can you lose a mask in the middle of a game?'

A lot of heads start to look at our bench and I got a strange feeling. Just as I looked around to see what they were looking at, the catcher walked over and asked if he can borrow my mask. I'm glad Dad was down at the concession stand because he may not have thought it was as funny as everyone else did. But that was the beauty of being at the games. As a lot of people say, you learn by doing. I never became a catcher, though. Too much equipment to keep up with.

During the summer months our group was outside most of the time. A lot of the houses didn't have central air conditioning and being active got you used to the weather. The middle of the days usually meant riding your bikes about 2 miles to the city pool. Dad ran that, watched over the concession stand, and kept the chlorine at the right level. That was the only pool in Stuart and there were endless games of tag and all the daring jumps from the 3 foot and 10 foot diving boards. It never got boring and we were too young to gawk at the girls in swimsuits, at least at that time. I did notice how a lot of the older guys, Dad included, always made sure that Mrs. Paulson was comfortable. They were quick to make sure she had everything she needed. Everyone said she had been in a couple of Miss Alabama pageants so I imagined she was comfortable being looked at—I didn't think anything about it, beyond that. Like brats, though, if any of the older girls or ladies got too close to the water they were sure to get splashed at. There would be a line of guys hurrying up the board to continue a chain of cannonballs, can openers, watermelons, but hopefully no belly busters. I can't recall anyone who got hurt, either. If you were too much of a pain in the butt or ran on the sidewalk or got in people's way the Lifeguards had enough control to make you sit on the edge for a period of time.

One summer, my sister Sharon was training to be a lifeguard. This was lucky, seeing as how it gave Pete and me the opportunity to act like we were drowning. She was to get us and pull us back to the edge of the pool. Dad liked the idea of throwing us off the high dive. When he did that, she would swim out to rescue us. Well, Pate and re-Pete would wait till she got close and go under; we were determined not to be grabbed by sister. It seemed fun to us, but Sharon, well, she didn't agree. After a few yells to Dad we finally let her tow us in. I figured we might need a favor at some point. And so, a lifeguard she became. I have to say, though, in all her training, we did rule out the mouth to mouth deal first and foremost.

The playing and swimming was some of the best all around exercise you could do for your body, I later learned. If we knew that it was healthy, though, we may not have done it.

The little league park was below the pool and there was even a lake to fish in. So, a lot of full days were spent at the pool. Pete's dad, Doc Hands was in charge of the little league program and we helped a bit chasing foul balls and watching games. There was always a chase for the foul balls because it would get you a free coke at the concession stand. For helping, we always knew we would get to pick a couple of our favorites from the concession stand at the end; one of mine was always the long and crunchy Chick-O-Stick. When I was 7 and 8, I was bat boy for the Red Sox, Stew's team and Pete was there, too, because his brother, Curt, was also on the team of 11 and 12 year olds. Those were the days that night games took up our evenings.

As I may have mentioned, our neighborhood games were played hard and honest. You always wanted to win, but there was no bragging or in your face if you lost. One of our players, Kathy Townsend, was a very good baseball player. In fact when she was 11, she tried out for one of our local little league teams. I don't know if you know this, but during the mid 1960's girls were not allowed to play on the boys teams. As the first couple of weeks went on Kathy kept her pony tail in her cap, practiced well and didn't stand next to the coach. As fate would have it she made the team only to get dropped when she didn't put her batting helmet on quick enough and her ponytail fell out. The coach felt bad but that was the way it was at that time. I could see that she was disappointed, but Kathy handled it well. This didn't change anything in the neighborhood, though; she was always a top pick in our games.

The fun part of our neighborhood was that everyone was always outside doing things or playing games. Whatever sport was in season, well, that was what we played. The neighborhood games were fun. They were just different than playing on the little league team or midget football. I can remember hearing my mom on the phone at the beginning of a football season. I remember hearing her say, "We have a game at home this Friday," and I remember thinking it was going to be played in our open lot.

We Learned How to Watch Games

In today's time, there are so many games on television. When we were growing up, you only got one game a week from Major League Baseball. In Stuart, Alabama, that usually meant we saw the St. Louis Cardinals on Saturdays. And, as you may imagine, that meant we got real familiar with that team. We learned most all the names of their greats: Musial, Brock, Torre, Simmons, Cepada, Javier, Maxwell, Shannon, Flood, and, my favorite pitcher, Bob Gibson. Watching some of the best of all time taught us how they performed their feats. It's not the same now. Now, with so many games, you find yourself just watching the outcomes rather than paying attention to how the players performed. Back then, we really studied that precious game of the week and it made a difference in how we played the game.

I remember at an early age learning to hook slide the way Lou Brock would do when he was stealing bases. By paying attention, you learned which foot to throw off of, among the many little details in sports. You saw the right way to square around to bunt and how to move the bat to get the ball to go down third or first base. Simple things like throwing to the cut-off man, not throwing behind a runner, bunting the ball down and using your base coach were just a few of the things you would pick up on. All of these skills were showcased and, by watching the major leaguers, we learned to play the game much better.

I have to tell you, I was so fortunate: I had the mumps during the World Series. Understand that, back then, most all the games were played during the daytime. That year my favorite, Bob Gibson, set a Series record for strikeouts. Wouldn't you know, I also had measles during the World Series. I was a lucky little fellow. Had I not been able to stay at home, I would have been one of the many walking around with the little transistor radio, keeping up with the games.

It wasn't only baseball that we watched. Watching football was special, too, especially when Dad was around. He would point out how different plays could be anticipated just by looking at the stance the players were in. As a kid hungry to learn sports, you filed that info right into your brain. This makes me think that the brain works pretty much like a juke box. You have the piece of information, that's the record, and it gets put into a special slot, that's the number, and when you pick what you want the jukebox scans until it picks the right one. Sometimes it can take a little longer to find the record and sometimes if you try too hard it seems to take forever. You just have to trust that it'll pop in the right slot eventually.

So, baseball was the Cardinals. In football, we usually got to see the Baltimore Colts. To this day I believe John Unitas was a master at quarterback. You watched how he threw the ball so only his guy could get it. Every game he had a whole arsenal of throws: hard ones over the middle, long rainbow arching throws, and in position for the receivers to run after they caught it. It was also fun because Unitas almost always had a few trick plays up his sleeve. I remember a halfback pass, a hand off and a pitch back to him, so he could heave it to Raymond Berry behind everyone, all the way down the field. After we saw a play like that, we would be out in the yard trying to pull it off. We would copy Perkins, Matte, and Richardson. And, then, talk about getting creative, the upstart American Football League usually showed a late afternoon game featuring the Chiefs, Raiders, Broncos, or Chargers. This league aired the ball out. The announcers were even more up tempo and gave a good account to their style of play. Their uniforms were even more colorful, especially the Chargers.

The same went with watching all the games. You saw how the best performed and how they managed to do it, not just the outcome of what happened. You picked up on the little things: how to hold your hands when catching the ball, how to tuck the ball into your body to protect it, how to get your feet in bounds with a catch. All of these little traits can be used at all times and also during special circumstances. These simple traits that you pick up can allow you to out perform players that have a little more raw talent.

Putting football traits to use in Stuart got off to an early start. Because Dad was the high school coach, he helped to pave the way, and Dr. Hands got a group together to start a midget football league. It was a good way of having something to do after school and also to copy all that you observed. Watching and actually performing the tasks took a little time and effort. Pete and I were two of the smallest to play because we were ahead of some of the others at our age—skill wise, at least. We'd just been around the game so much. Now Pete and re-Pete, we always came up with what we thought were good ideas at the time. For example, one day at practice we figured if we got good and dirty, our Dads would think that we really got after it in, that we were going all out. But, I'll tell you what, just like I mentioned earlier, Dad had a knack of being a step ahead: getting dirty earned me a whipped butt instead of a gold star.

We learned over a period of time and I'll always remember one play in particular. We were in a game and the visiting team broke their huddle with only the center and quarterback over the ball. The rest were lined up on the other side of the field and in doing so it made the center an eligible receiver. Pete and I already had it figured out and Pete took the center and, after the snap, I had a clean shot to tackle the QB since nobody was there to block me and Pete had the center under control. It's the sort of play that most don't figure out: QB dumps a little pass to the center and away he goes. That's why in neighborhood football you usually have to count to 3 before rushing the QB to give a little time for a play to take shape. This is the type knowledge you gain by simply learning to watch.

The other aspect of learning to watch is learning to follow the rules. By knowing the rules you can actually use them to your advantage. Especially in youth games, it helps to know the rules really well. Knowing little things like when you can pick the ball up in baseball and when you are down in football, these rules can help a lot. When you watch games on

TV with the instant replay, you'll notice that the announcers are always sticklers for the rules. They love a chance to try and catch someone off guard, making a mistake. Paying attention and listening can give you a big advantage because you can be sure someone else has made that same mistake before. If you see the others making a mistake, you can, of course, try not to make the same mistake again.

Learn and Know the Rules

A funny thing happened in the spring of 1965. When Dad was coaching his teams, I was always hanging around. Mainly I paid attention to the players I was most fond of, imitating their moves and techniques. Starting my season as a ten-year-old in little league gave this paying attention a new dimension; I learned about something called "the team concept." My new coach for the year was a good young man named Herb Gladden. His family didn't live too far from us and his oldest son Brett was in my grade. It was a good situation—all got along just swell.

Coach had a good manner of explaining things to us and we learned that it took all of us to win. During our first team meeting Coach Herb asked us, "Which is the most important position on the field in baseball?" Most said the pitcher, one said catcher, and somebody else cast one vote for first base. Then Coach Herb asked this question: "It's the last inning and we are winning 4 to 3 with 2 out and it is the bottom of the 6th. There is a high fly ball hit to the right fielder." He looked around at us, waiting for the light bulbs to appear over our heads. He waited another moment before asking, "What's the most important position on the field now?" It showed us that at some point each would get their chance, and that we had to depend on our teammates. Yes, the pitcher is the most noted, just like a quarterback, but to win it takes everybody playing together.

Winning Takes Everybody Playing Together

I have always remembered that example from Coach Herb. I played third base and was our third pitcher—I had quite a good arm for my age. As you may remember, one other unique aspect about my game was that I batted left handed. My mom was left handed and she's the one who showed me how to hold a bat and swing it properly. I don't know where it was written that left handed batters are good bunters. I guess being on that side of the plate you get a better chance to see the ball. And, then, of course, the drag bunt is a big advantage.

We were playing a practice game and I was brought in to pitch. I don't recall the total result but here is what stuck in my brain. There was a 12 year old up to bat, Danny Thomas, not the actor but a show off anyway, and he was ready to hit away against this 10 year old. Lucky for me there were a couple of hard hit foul balls. Somewhere in my mind I remembered seeing a major league pitcher throw up a little blooper. I remember the batter looked real foolish swinging and missing. I lofted a little rainbow arch pitch and, at the pace it was moving, you could just about read "Official Little League" on the ball. It may have been the first time a batter was out on 4 strikes because, as the ball got to the plate, Danny Thomas swung and missed twice trying to hit it. From that I learned to try and judge the right situation for a specific play.

Know When to Use a Specific Play

The team concept carried over when I was watching Stew quarterback the junior high team. I started paying attention to what the whole team did and how they all played together. It was special, even in junior high, playing football in Stuart. The town lived to support the football team. You could see the expectations put on Stew because he was the coach's son. He handled it quite well. He had a special quality about him and was able to get the rest of the guys to play together. For me, this enforced the importance of the team concept.

Coach Rex Reed was the junior high coach and he tried to follow the system my dad used with the high school players. At a small school this was enough to get the kids in tune and that set system made for an easier transition to the high school team. In past years if the Rebels were hit by some injuries, it was not uncommon to bring up a couple kids from the ninth grade to play with the varsity.

The basic offense was not hard to learn at all. Let me explain it to you: the center position, or hole, is 4, left guard 3, right guard 5, left tackle 2, right tackle 6, left end 1, and right end 7. The positions were numbered as well with QB 1, TB/deep back 2, FB 3, Wing Back 4, if left, and 5, if right. Therefore, if the TB went over the Rt. Tackle it would be right 26 power with him following the FB. And, of course, there would be various changes in regard to whether the wingback lined up tight or wide and, also, to which side.

```
  TE  T   G   C   G   T   TE
  1   2   3   4   5   6   7   8
                (1qb)
        (4wb)    (3 fb)    (5wb)
                (2 tb)
```

This is your basic hole or slot alignment to build the tailback offense with. With this kind of offense, we were able to move forward with the different plays and tack on what we needed with the formations. As we progressed we were able to have an easy check-off system for the quarterback with numerical plays and a call color, one of which was "live" to indicate a change from the originally called play, if the defense happened to alter their look.

Learn or Have a Specific System

At our house, this rule was practically stamped on our foreheads. Curt and Pete West knew it well, too, because they were always around us and Doc Hands. Playing in backyard games, Pete and I would call plays by the numbers. Curt was a tight end and, of course, Stew was the quarterback. Stew was real quick and a lot of plays were based around his natural talent.

Coach Reed liked to throw in a few twists and brought out quite a few trick plays from time to time. He would also play the scout, going to watch the next game's opponent for my dad. He kept a little notebook of the trick plays he saw from other teams and would fit them into our system. In those years he proved to be a good, young junior high football coach; a good guy to keep around. Well, he was helpful to keep around for other reasons as well: he was the varsity basketball coach. This helped keep a solid program together. Coach Reed didn't like a long season because it might get in the way of basketball. At Stuart most of the same guys that played football played basketball, too.

I can remember one conversation we had at the dinner table. As you can imagine, most conversations at our table revolved around athletics.

Dad brought up an example that worked so well for coaching, a strategy that allowed you to get the best reply from a player or coach. Once you got that reply, you were able to mold the answer into one that would help the players achieve. Dad's example came from Doc Hands. You see, in the early 60's chiropractic care was not mainstream. In fact, back then, a lot of the chiropractic doctors were thought to be quacks. But Doc Hands had a great manner and he was always giving examples regarding health care. He would say, "You need to treat what is causing the problem not the symptom," and "Chiropractic works like a garden hose—the garden hose won't work until you get the kink out."

Know How to Ask a Question

But, the best advice Dad got from Doc was this: when asked health questions by doubtful folks, Doc would reply, "What have you heard about chiropractic care?" Then he would be able to answer questions and give straight answers instead of coming across as too brash. Dad told us how he applied this example to sports. So many times when you're dealing with coaches and players, you're also dealing with egos. When the egos came out, Dad would ask the coach's assistant a careful question. Then the coach gets to think about the answer and becomes his idea as well, something that's a lot easier to agree with.

This logic also applied to Stew's tenure as quarterback. Dad told him, "You don't have to come across as being too brash all the time. You don't have to be a total know-it-all." Dad explained that if you took the more humble way, you'd get better compliance from your teammates and better bonding team wise. I've seen this so many times in my career: people can be giving 100%, but their direction may be a little off. That's when the captain has to jump in there and help steer the course and head things in the right direction.

Learn from a lot of Examples

After we ate, when the plates were out of the way, the salt and pepper shakers became the quarterback and the pulling guard. Two toothpicks became the receivers. Dad was telling Stew, "When I watched your game Tuesday, I saw you run this play a few times, and not very well. When you run I—right, roll right and cross, you get to throw to the receiver that's the most open."

Stew nodded, soaking it all in.

Dad kept talking. "Remember on roll right, the left guard is pulling to keep the defensive end from knocking your brains out or disrupting the pass. When you roll too fast the end has you dead on."

I could tell that Stew was starting to get the idea. He just kept nodding and Dad just kept talking.

"Ok Stew, the pepper shaker pushes to the right. The salt waits just a count to let the guard block, usually keeps the end out wide. The salt shaker stops and right in front and has its choice of receivers to throw to. But, if you get ahead you don't get that chance because the defensive end will see to that." Dad looked at Stew and paused before he went on. "What do you think about letting the other players do their job? That'll make your job easier and, plus, you look better in the process."

Stew had a weird look on his face; I could see the little light bulb coming on. "I get it now," he said.

That is how the team works on a specific play: the quarterback needs to know what the others are doing. As Stew sat there he actually thought it was his idea to stop and let the guard make the block for him, to make the right throw.

Dad had learned not to bring up too much sports stuff during supper. Mom liked to have a little family time without all those x's and o's going on. Aside from sports, we had a lot of good conversations about everyone and it helped us to know what everybody was into. But, there was only so long Dad could hold off. After desert, he might as well have brought out a chalk board to discuss things. We all enjoyed it, though.

Little Quint always brought up some good points, good points about mistakes. He was catching onto the games. Stew had thrown two interceptions and Quint asked very innocently, "Stew, why did you throw the ball to the other guys? Then you just have to try to chase those guys down."

That really made me laugh.

Now Sharon was a junior high cheerleader and her observation was this: "Thanks to Stew we get to do an offense and defense cheer on the same play."

Yes, it was hard to get anything past each other because we were always there watching and pulling for each other. I think sometimes we were only watching to be able to pick on each other later on. But, that, too, was a very good lesson: sometimes you had to take the bad as well as the good. Not every game or play is going to work out for you and there is always going to be somebody ready to chop you right down.

Mom, maybe we ought to call her Coach Mom, was always quick to point out the good along with the bad during these sessions. She believed in trying to balance effort out and throw in a little encouragement: "Stew, on the pass to Joe, you threw it well. That guy made a great play on you. Next time, like Dad said, you ought to arc the ball more, you know, and you'll have a better chance."

What Mom pointed out was a key idea Dad tried to instill in all his players and his kids, alike: learn from your mistakes.

Then Quint spoke up: "Dad if you are to learn from your mistakes then Bob should be really smart, huh?"

Before, when everyone was distracted by Stew's interceptions, I was getting ready to gently toss the last dinner roll to Quint, but after a comment like that, well, forget it. The toss had too much steam behind it and, with a good accurate throw, I nailed him right between the eyes. You can imagine what that got me: a couple of licks on the butt from Dad.

Learn from Your Mistakes and Be Able to Handle Criticism

At Stuart, not being a big school, you had most of the same guys playing all the sports. Basketball started the day after football ended. Likewise Pete and I spent our afternoons in the gym watching our brothers practice and kept up with the basketballs and chased down bad throws. We also got to shoot in-between breaks.

At the start of the basketball season, the Rebels were a little shaky on their skills. After getting used to running with a ball now you had to dribble the thing up and down the court. It did help at our house that we had a couple of goals with regulation size wooden backboards to play on. Curt, Pete's brother, and Stew and their friends usually played in our backyard on weekends and it helped with the transition.

Their ninth grade coach, John Mabry, loved the game and had been the volunteer coach forever, it seemed. He loved to win and instilled this love into the guys, no matter what. Well, that year the "what" came in the fashion of the junior high Blue Devils from College Heights. College Heights was the junior high that fed into the Marion high Blue Devils, which was the large city school next to Stuart. For three days before this game practically all our team did was take a couple of steps and pass the ball. Rebound practice meant that you had to screen your man, shuffle him back and get the ball after it hit the floor. The young Rebel team couldn't understand why until the "what" made its way into the Rebel gymnasium. Our fans and players had never seen so many from another team ducking to get through the gym doors and, what's worse, these were ninth graders! They were huge. Lucky for them their colors were not green for they would have heard the "ho, ho, ho, green giant" from that commercial on TV all the time. Coach Mabry had the plan to just hold the ball, don't shoot and just freeze it. The game plan was a solid 4 corner offense with no intention of shooting until the last five seconds of the quarter.

The first quarter ended with the Blue Devils in front 4 to 2. Into the second quarter a couple of their players just sat down and watched Stew and Curt pass the ball to each other nice and carefully. Donnie East, who was Stuart's tallest ninth grader at 6'1," looked like a midget himself against three guys at 6'4". Donnie put a good move on one of the big guys and hit a shot with two ticks left to tie the score at 4 going into halftime. Coach Mabry liked what he saw and it was the only chance we had to compete for the win and not just look good. In the past ten years Stuart had never beaten College Heights but this game had a whole different look. The Blue Devils controlled the second half tip and started passing the ball themselves. After a few minutes their patience ran out and they lobbed it into one of their giants for a commanding 6 to 4 lead. The Blue Devils tried a little pressure but the Rebels had some smart and quick players and got control of the ball and, before long, it was back to Curt and Stew passing to each other. As time ran down in the third quarter Curt threw it to Donnie, he faked, and passed to Stew, who was fouled as he shot. He made the first and rimed the next to trail 6 to 5. With only five seconds the Blue Devils were able to pass over the Rebels and hit a shot at the buzzer for a monumental 8 to 5 lead.

At the start of the fourth quarter Curt was able to sneak behind and make a steal then throw to Stew for a lay-up to close the gap at 8-7. The young Rebels were all on the feet, most other teams would have been in the face, of the Blue Devils and if the ball got close they were to foul and not let them get an easy shot. Then out of nowhere came a big arching hook shot, a shot like none of the Stuart fans had ever seen, came from one of the Devils and the score went up to 10-7. In the last minute, after a couple of good passes and fakes, Donnie East made a reverse lay-up to trail 10-9. The Rebels had to foul and with ten seconds left one of the big players—three of these players would eventually play basketball in the famed SEC—missed and the little Rebels did a good job blocking out. They got the ball off the floor, just like in practice. But, in practice they didn't have to shoot over 6'4" players, and the last shot from just past half court hit the front of the rim. The Rebels got beat 10-9.

The next evenings *Marion Journal* sport headlines read, "Blue Devils escape freeze." It was big news all over the area: the famed Blue Devils never won by only 1 point, especially 10-9 when they usually won by 20 or more. This was an example of a valuable lesson and those Rebels learned it: have a plan and play to it.

Have a Game Plan and Play to it

About two months had passed and it was time for the young Rebels to drive into Marion to play the Blue Devils in their big gym at Marion High School. As the season wore on the Rebels got into playing well and winning their last eight games. This time before the game all the Rebels did in practice was run, run, and run some more. For this game, Coach Mabry had to be out of town and head varsity coach Rex Reed filled in. The place was packed to watch another freeze game take place but the people didn't get to see what they paid for. Coach Reed told Pete and me to have the water ready and the towels cold. From the opening tip to the final whistle the Rebels full court pressed and ran the Blue Devils crazy—unlike any game they had ever been in, once again. This time the margin of victory was the same but the Blue Devils won 56 to 55. At the end of the game, while the players were shaking hands, the fans of Stuart knew their young Rebels had played their butts off and all rose for a standing ovation and cheers. Even the host Blue Devil fans applauded as the Rebels left the court. That was one of the joys of living in Stuart—having the support of the people. The supporters knew the two losses, by 1 point each, were very special and, although eleven years passed without beating College Heights, an asterisk could be placed by these two games.

The next day headline of the sports section read "WOW 56-55." If you didn't know any better, when you read the article, you would have thought

Stuart had won the game. Coach Rex Reed said it was all Coach Mabry's plan. The writer, Casey Toms, said he never had seen a more intense game, at any level. The young Rebels were willing to put everything on the line and, knowing from watching others that they could get blown out, they didn't. Stew tried to hide it when he saw me, but, that night, in the locker room after the game, I saw Stew cry for the first time ever.

Give Credit Where Credit Is Due

During the transition from junior high to varsity, athletics took on a whole new meaning. Although Stuart was always serious in sports, it was really serious business now. Most all the players were older and faster, but some were just right down mean. Stew and Curt worked out a lot together, throwing and catching. Of course, if it was late or early in the day, Pete and I would be there as well. In July, to help our brothers, we would ride our bikes while they jogged to get in shape. We figured it was better to be teammates with them than to be bugging them all the time. It was quite an honor to be seen with the older guys and to hang out with them. We learned to stay out of the way and pitch in as we could.

Fall football practice started at the beginning of August. As long as you liked 100 degree heat and no rain, the weather in Stuart, Alabama was just great on the first of August. So, practicing football was something you had better be committed to. What I remember about that time is how most of the guys were outdoors during the day. A lot of the players worked jobs outside and, without an over abundance of air conditioning, those boys seemed to tolerate the weather better than today's players do. About the time I was ten, I was pretty much a full-time manager—along with my side-kick Pete, of course. With our brothers about to begin their sophomore year, we were out there in the afternoon right along with the high school team chasing stray footballs and throwing and catching them as well. It was always fun to feel like you were a part of the team and some of the jokes that got played on us made us feel that way as well.

Pete had a question in the locker room one day when he picked up the first jock strap he had seen. One of the players, Ed Sanders, aka Fast Eddie, asked Pete to put it on. Fast Eddie explained that it was to fit over Pete's face, like a gas mask. He assured Pete that this device would actually help him get more oxygen. After Pete put it on, he was told to ask Coach

Hayes, my dad, if he had a size that would fit him better. I think Dad almost split his bottom lip while biting it, trying to keep a straight face in front of Pete.

A little later, I went tugging on Pete, to show him how a couple of guys were "properly" wearing the gas mask. We knew it was time to plan a payback. We had learned from our older brothers that instant payback was something they expected, but we also knew that, given our age difference and size, we wouldn't get to far anyway. There could be no harm in it. So we spent a day or two. We thought about spiking Eddie's juice after practice, but we weren't sure what to put in it that wouldn't kill him. The team needed Ed: he had the most speed and was the star receiver. Doing him in wouldn't do the team any good.

The next day on the way out to practice I rounded the corner of the locker room with Pete right behind, taking the footballs out, and the answer was right in front of us. There was Loco, the dog that was always hanging around the school, the dog who would eat anything. Presently, he was squatting down, taking care of his business. Pete and I looked at Loco and then at each other and said, "Bing, that's it." When the players get out on the field we'll just slide some of Loco's poop into Fast Eddies shoes. We made our way back and put an ample amount into both of his shoes. We wanted to be sure we would get him with either foot.

It was hard to control our excitement during practice. We would glance at each other and start laughing. Our plan picked up extra steam listening to Eddie during practice. It seemed Tina Sampson, a junior to be and cheer leader, was his main squeeze. It turns out that she had been in Panama City, Fl for a week. She was going to pick him up after practice. You see, Tina was a lot of peoples' favorite and some the players said she filled out her bathing suit real well, whatever that meant. Ed's attention span was getting smaller as practice went on and after he dropped a couple of passes Dad bopped Ed's helmet with his famous clip board—Stew had told me that this was enough to make your ears ring inside the helmet—and told Ed to shape up.

Dad and the other county coaches were able to get gallons of orange juice daily, thanks to the school board, for the players to gulp down after practice. This was before Gatorade, you understand. While the players ran their sprints, Pete and I gathered up the footballs and headed to the locker room, to get the orange juice ready. We couldn't wait.

Being the fastest player Ed was jogging while the others were walking and hollering for him to walk. They said Coach would make them all run more if he noticed Ed had that much energy left. Fast Eddie grabbed a cup of juice, looked over his shoulder, and waved to Tina as he headed into the locker room. Since he was inside, we had to tell our brothers to take a peek at Ed. We told them that they would like what they were about to see.

"What's up?" Curt asked.

"You're about to find out," Pete and I said in unison. We could barely conceal our glee.

Curt gave us both a funny look and shook his head.

No doubt he was thinking we were young and silly, but we knew he'd think differently soon enough.

And sure enough, the word spread quickly amongst the players. Eddie had jumped in for a fast shower, hastily dried off, and zipped his shorts on. He went to put his shoes on and Pete and I held our breath. Then we heard, "What the hell, dog shit?" and the other players all started laughing.

Fast Eddie looked up and saw two little heads going around the corner and he hollered at me and Pete. He shouted, "I'll kill you, you little brats."

Then Big Jim, who was the baddest lineman on the team said, "Slow down there, Ed. I think you already forgot about the jock strap." He grinned at Ed.

But Ed didn't listen and he didn't grin back. He made a straight line for the showers, to wash his feet, and everybody scattered to make room for him. Outside the locker room, just beyond this scene, is when, maybe, Pete and I invented the high five. We were downright proud of ourselves. Our brothers were glad we'd fought back, but I was scared to hear what Dad would say about this. But, my worries were for nothing. He just said, with a wry smile, "I see ya'll slowed Ed down a bit." Then he just shook his head and walked away.

There is a valuable lesson in this story. In sports, a player will sneak a late hit or jab in on an opposing player. But what's amazing is this: it's usually the player who retaliates that gets the foul or penalty called on him. You've got to keep your wits about you and remember that a good play is the proper way to get back at another player. For example, whenever Fast Eddie took a late hit from another player, Coach would call a stop and go with Eddie looking like he was going to throw a big block on the guy. Then Ed would zip past him and haul in a long pass. That's real revenge. And the same goes for baseball: when a pitcher throws a high and tight fastball that knocks the batter out of the way, the batter has to get up without dusting himself off and smack the next pitch for a home run. Sweet redemption is the greatest thing.

Don't Retaliate in Anger

The game is tied and there are just four precious seconds left on the clock. The Stuart Rebels have the ball on the 25 yard line and Bob Hayes lines up to attempt a 42 yard field goal. There's the snap, and the kick is . . . it's GOOD! Rebels win, Rebels win! All those times in our backyard, all those kicks, all those hook shots and baseball swings, they all had a purpose. Being a coach's kid, I learned that it wasn't enough to simply go through the motions. I learned that you had to practice with a purpose if you wanted to be any good.

Practice with a Purpose

After we got home from practice and had supper, we went out in the backyard to practice whatever sport was in season. The six foot fence between the Townsend's backyard and ours was ideal for kicking over. I would make it a game with Quint to see how many kicks he could catch. That way, I didn't have to chase them and, besides, Quint was ready to show he could do it. Kick after kick sailed over that fence and just about each one was a game winner. When Stew got home, we would also play a little game of set-back. One would punt the football to the other and you had to catch it and then try to kick it past the opponent, to get them back to their goal-line. He took it easy on me, not trying to just win. In doing so Stew, learned to control his punts better. This might have been how he got to be the best starting punter and kicker in the tenth grade has ever seen.

When I think about it, paying attention to the little details is perhaps the most beneficial element in all sports. So many try to look for or focus on the one big THING, thinking it will get them over the top, but it's about more than that. It's about the many little things that come together and make a big difference.

What it Boils Down to Are Little Things

My routine in the fall took on a new dimension. I woke up early, even on Saturday's. During the football season, the film was sent to the lab on Friday night after the games. It was developed and was ready early the next morning for Dad to review and analyze. Since I was up I would go with him. I liked to be his sounding board, the one he bounced ideas off of. Dad would point out things he saw on the film and tell me to watch as he hit the review switch, over and over. The other good part is this: we got to eat out for breakfast, just Dad and I. Even in the larger city of Marion, the city Stuart bordered, all of the folks in Paul's Diner knew who Dad was and not because they shared the same name. They wanted to know how the Rebels did. I would be eating away at my pancakes, enjoying all the comments.

I learned a valuable lesson sitting in one of the shiny blue booths below all types of sports photos. A man named Red Parker, sitting with a coffee cup and an unlit pipe, asked Dad how Ed Sanders did in the game. Coach Dad said, "Ed made some good blocks. You have to respect his speed. That speed opened up more room for us to run."

I took interest in that question and decided to give my view: "Dad, if Eddie did good, then why did you grab his face mask and yell at him a few times?"

That got a chuckle from the men drinking their coffee and this chuckle encouraged me to continue.

"I bet if you'd had a paddle on the sideline his behind would have been stinging the way mine does when you're angry with me."

After hearing that comment I think one or two about spit out their coffee from laughing too hard. Dad just said, "Finish your breakfast, son."

Mr. Red said, "Lil' Bob, you see any more good things like that you just let us know."

When we got to the car Dad explained how what happens down on the field during the game doesn't get told to everybody else. "Whether it's good or bad the coach should always protect his players and be like a parent to them."

Protect Your Players and Don't Air Out Your Dirty Laundry

The film was running and Dad said, "Cut back, Melvin."

"Why?" I asked.

"Look," Dad said. We were running a 28 sweep and Melvin, the tailback, had Ed in front of him, blocking on the outside and taking his man to the sideline. Dad pointed to the film. "Look," he said. "Melvin runs right into them thinking he is as fast as Ed. If he lets Ed block him outside and cuts back inside he has a long touchdown."

I didn't know what to say, so I just nodded.

The film rolled on and, pretty soon, Dad said, "Crap Curt."

I looked to see the ball bounce out of Curt's hands and fall to the ground.

"Look Bob," Dad said. "That boy is hearing footsteps." Dad showed me how the ball was being thrown to Curt, but when it got to him he would turn his head to see if he was about to get hit. I could see what Dad meant by hearing footsteps.

A few minutes rolled by and then Dad said, "Dammit."

My first response was to blurt out, "What did I do?"

Dad's face broke into a grin. He said, "I mean Big Jim. Look at that, why didn't he just hold up a sign."

"What do you mean, hold up a sign?" I asked.

"Big Jim's getting a little lazy when we're passing. He weakens his stance. It's a dead give away that we're going to pass."

I nodded, understanding just what he meant.

"Ole,'" went the next sound bite from Dad. When he mentioned, Stew I was all ears.

I asked, "What does he do wrong?"

"He steps aside and lets the runner drag him five yards before he gets him down, instead of hitting him head on." Dad shook his head.

I watched Stew on the film and knew he would do better.

Dad made a list of more corrections on his chart to show the players on Sunday afternoon when they all came watch the film. He then said to me, "Bob, if we keep making the same mistakes we won't stand a chance against the other teams we'll be playing. We were better than West Jones last night and we got by with a lot of mistakes. But, we are 1 and 0."

Review the Proper Fundamentals
and Don't Keep Making the Same Mistakes

The door to the locker room opened and in walked Dr. Hands with the assistant coach Gabe Thomas. The good part was Dr. Hands brought in a few sausage and biscuits, which didn't last too long. I made my way outside with my treat and a carton of chocolate milk. I strolled over to the gate of the field just outside, maybe 50 yards away. I was just walking around and something shiny caught my eye, a quarter, lying in the grass outside the ticket booth. "Finders keepers," I said to myself. I put the quarter in my pocket and explained it to myself: if someone is not careful they can drop a coin or two and never know it. I piddled around with my eyes open staring at the ground and suddenly I saw a dime. After a little time I had a total sixty-three cents in my once empty pocket. I walked around some more and went under the main bleachers. There I found a billfold that had exactly $100 dollars in it. I gave it to Dad and he called the wallet's owner, Mr. Strickland, to let him know I found it. About an hour later he stopped by to pick it up, shook my hand, and gently placed a $20 bill in my palm. After that, I had a new project for Saturday mornings after home football games.

Lunchtime Sunday came and Mom had a great spread prepared, as always. I knew strawberry pudding was the dessert because I got to lick the spoon before going to Sunday school. When we finished lunch, we watched some of the Colts game. After that, Dad and Stew were headed to the school for their team film session. I was thinking about this when an idea hit me. I ran to the bathroom and came out with two cotton balls. I rushed up to Stew and said, "Here."

"What are these for?" he asked. He looked very confused.

"When Dad starts letting you have it, watching the film, they may come in handy," I said.

"Do what?" Stew asked. He was even more confused now. He said, "We won 34 to 7."

I shrugged. "Yeah, but it would have been 35 if you hadn't missed the extra point kick and watch out for the bull." I started to laugh and when I looked at Dad, I saw that he was trying not to. Stew dismissed me with a wave of his hand, and they went to get in to the car.

That afternoon in the backyard, our version of the Colts versus the Lions took place. It was a good game and when we finished Mrs. Townsend has a big batch of Rice Krispy treats and lemonade ready. After that, we were done for the day. When we got to our house, Quint fell asleep as soon as the couch grabbed him. Sharon was already back from hanging out at the Rebel Drive-In and I filled her in on what Dad was about to let Stew know, at least about the mistakes from Friday night's game. When they made it back, Sharon had to make her little jab: "Stew, your ears look a little red," she told him.

"Butt-hole," he said, nearly seething.

I held my hands up to let mom know: I didn't say a word.

It amazes me how fast a thought can enter you mind and how quickly you can act on it. In those days, Pete and I were holding down two jobs—at least, in a way. We were playing on the Stuart Lil' Rebels midget team and we were being true to our brothers, playing on the varsity. Pete's brother Curt was the tight end and my brother Stew was playing safety and doing the kicking. It was logical then that, on the Lil' Rebels, Pete was playing safety and I was playing split end. Pete was a little shorter than me and not afraid of anything, but I didn't play split end for my blazing speed. I could catch the ball and knew where to run, but I learned speed doesn't come with the name. There was another Bob Hayes that played for the Cowboys and he was the world's fastest. I, on the other hand, was just playing the same position. During the younger years knowledge came in handy and being involved and watching a lot was my main advantage.

Our other job, when we were not having practice, was being the managers and on this job I was learning a lot from Dad. This particular job sometimes kept us out of trouble and sometimes got us into trouble. I believe Fast Eddie Sanders would agree to the trouble part. As a matter of fact Fast Eddie took a liking to us after we pulled off such a good retaliation. I think we had him scared when we mentioned the part about spiking his juice.

It was our first midget league game and not much was going on. I learned over the years that a lot of youth coaches' sons get valuable playing time, whether it is football or baseball. Jamison Taylor was our quarterback and his dad was the head coach. J.T. was a good guy that had moved into Stuart at the start of the summer. Most of us just really hadn't got to know him well. We had tried a couple of sweeps and dive plays and, after the second series, I had lobbied Coach Taylor for a chance to throw the ball. I knew I was open because the safety kept backing up and the hook was open. After I asked to be thrown to, Coach looks at me like I'm trying to get his job. Well, sure enough, when we went back in the first play was for J.T. to throw me a 12 yard hook pass. I took my split, took off on the snap, and saw #20, the safety, backing up. I turned in just like we practiced. JT was in the process of letting the ball go and I was looking it right into my arms. Then that sudden thought hit me: a couple of weeks ago I had watched a Colts game. Ray Berry ran a hook and Unitas hit him right in the hands and when he caught the ball, he took a step to the inside and then wheeled around back to his left. The defender only tackled air. As the pass got to me, that thought flashed to me and I made the same move. When I looked back over my left shoulder, #20 was lying belly down and I was off towards the goal line. I could hear Coach Taylor hollering, "Run, run" and I was thinking, "What does he think I'm doing?" My first official touchdown and I knew Mom would take me to get my favorite peanut butter malt when the game was over.

We won 12-6 and Pete made a last ditch saving tackle on the final play when the other team ran a reverse. He was smart enough to watch out for a special play. We had seen that play in practice the week before with the varsity. Dad was yelling at Stew to "Stay at home and do your job." I was slurping at my peanut butter malt and Pete was downing his grape shake and we were getting most of the 'great game pats.' It made us feel big when our brothers strolled over and gave us pats on the head.

At the varsity practice the following Monday, during warm-ups, Fast Eddie said, "Lil Bob, I heard you caught a TD Saturday."

"Yep," I said and a smile stretched across my face.

"What did the defender do," Eddie asked, "fall down?"

"No," I said, feeling genuinely offended. "I ran a simple hook pattern, gave him a leg and he got all air."

Eddie looked confused. "You did what?"

I knew from listening to the rest of the guys that Fast Eddie may not have been the brightest one on the team so I said, "I'll show you. J.T., our QB, threw me a hook. I knew the safety was backing up and when I caught it I made a jab step to the right and then turned back to the left and I was off and running."

Eddie had a strange look on his face. "How did you know which leg to step to?"

"You're kidding me," I asked.

He just shook his head and said, "I usually just hold on and wait to get hit."

I was shocked and also very proud. "When you're running at the safety, if he is more to your inside, you turn to hook, then step to your right. Then if he is to your outside, turn and jab step with your left leg."

Most Defenders Almost Always Go for the First Move

"Now who taught you that" Eddie asked.

"I saw Raymond Berry do it for the Colts." I shrugged, trying to seem casual. "It worked like a charm for me."

As the offense started, well, wouldn't you know, that was the first play Eddie wanted to run. They ran the hook to Eddie. He made a good hook move and gets ready to put a move on the safety with his right leg. But, 'bonk,' the ball hits him right between the eyes. Thank God for facemasks. Big Jim shouted at him: "That's the way to keep your eye on the ball, Ed."

My dad said, "Eddie, it'll work better if you catch the ball first."

Eddie made a sour face and then tried to smile.

"Eddie, that's one of the things I've been trying to get across to you," Dad says. "If you run the simple patterns, well, they will open up longer ones for you even better."

Our Lil' Rebel practice was going well. We were excited to have won our first game and I was hoping that Coach Taylor would have more confidence in letting J.T throw more passes to me. I took a quick liking to the accolades of scoring and the attention it got you. We were doing a little scrimmage and we did our version of the stop and go. I put a good move on Pete, playing safety, and made the catch for a touchdown. The next series J.T. threw me a simple hook, which I caught. I then turned to run and here came Pete running right at me. I saw him going low, jumped over him, and was trying to keep my balance. I tried not to fall but I stuck my left hand down and, then, heard a "pop." I rolled over to see my left hand pointing in an awkward direction. Pete came over, saw my hand and said, "Man, I don't think Dad would like to see that."

Coach Taylor got me still and I got carried off for the first cast on my broken hand. Now I was relegated to watching most of the season and doing what I could on the sidelines.

It was awkward dealing with a cast on your left forearm and wrist, but the attention it brought was kind of neat. While I was at the varsity practice, I explained the play over and over. Fast Eddie said, "Lil' Bob, I can't wait to use that little spin move in Friday's game."

That gave me a thought—a good one, I thought. "Eddie, since Dad has seen you working on that you may want to make a few catches and save the spin for the Dalton game. We should handle East Point pretty easy Friday and you'll have a great game with Dalton." Dalton was Stuart's biggest rival and I was proud to have such a good idea about the game

"With thoughts like that," Eddie said, "we just may have to move Lil's Bob on up to assistant right away."

I wandered over to stand with Dad, who was watching the offense run through a series of plays that he really liked for this game with East Point. I mentioned to him about throwing Eddie a few hook patterns to help set up some plays for the Dalton game. "All by yourself?" Dad asked.

"What?" I asked and I looked at him.

"You had that idea all by yourself?"

I nodded.

"To be honest with you," Dad said, "I like that idea." He made a note on his infamous clipboard and spoke out to Mitch Davis, the senior quarterback. "Mitch, run wing left, 64 hook."

Then that was where Fast Eddie was split out wide to the right with the wing back to the left. The defensive corner back guarding Eddie had to make that sure he didn't get beat deep, that the hook was open. Mitch took his drop and hit Eddie right in the hands. This time he caught it instead of letting it hit him in the face.

"Now then," Dad said, "run it with the hook and go."

Fast Eddie did the hook, threw his hands up, and turned to run at full speed. Mitch gave a good pump fake and took a step back. He lofted a long rainbow pass into Eddie's arms. Ed came back to the huddle and gave me a pat on the head.

Practice your Special Plays

One of the pre-game rituals, with the Rebels was that Dr. Hands got to the game in time to do a treatment on the players to help with their alignment and also to prevent injuries. He'd have a table set up and the players would lie down so Dr. Hands could do his adjustment. The players had their own versions of what to call it. For example, Doc would walk in, and Big Jim would say, "Let's get crackin' doc." Pete and Re-Pete would sit by the table, to see who "cracked" the loudest. Fast Eddie usually won because he was slender and didn't have a lot of meat on his bones, or at least that was my guess. It worked out well, according to Dad, for the team doctor to be a Chiropractor.

The game with East Point went well and the Rebel's won 28-6. Stew was able to make an interception and return it 70 yards for a touchdown. Fast Eddie caught a couple of his hook patterns and just turned for a few yards. The good part was nobody got hurt and it was on to the big rivalry of the year with the Dalton Bulldogs.

That Saturday at Paul's Diner, the pancakes were hot and good. Dad explained to the men that we had kept things pretty basic and our real test would come next week with Dalton. Mr. Red asked me if I had any new tales and I just shook my head. No, Sir. After eating, we were off to the field-house. Since we had traveled over to East Point, there was no searching for money at the stadium. Dad reviewed the film with me sitting there and, after awhile, the phone rang. He got up to answer it and I picked up the control switch. I hit reverse, because the players looked funny running backwards. When Dad was off the phone, I told him to sit tight and to just say "back," when he wanted to reverse. I would hit the reverse button.

In the second series, the Rebels start a TD drive. Mitch hits Eddie on the hook and I stop it and reverse it. "What?" Dad said.

"There it is," I said.

"There what is," Dad said. He was started to get annoyed.

I reversed the catch again. "Eddie has plenty of time to take his step, turn and haul butt."

Dad smiled. "We will see come Friday," he said.

Toward the end of the game I started getting a little bored. Mitch threw a pass to Curt over the middle for 20 yards, down to the 5 yard line. I hit reverse and Dad said "Whoa, what?"

"Look," I said. "Watch Mitch catch this ball one handed when Curt throws it back to him."

"Dammit Bob," Dad said. "Hand me that control." He was angry, but with a better tone in his voice than I usually hear.

As the film was being wound back onto the reel, I asked Dad if he was going to pull out the option for Dalton.

"Why do you ask?" he said.

"We hit the dive plays real good last night and if Dalton tries to squeeze down a bit we can hit them pretty good pitching the ball wide."

Dad didn't really seem to hear me. He just went into his office and pulled out the previous year's Dalton versus Stuart game. I decided to take a nap on one of the tackling dummies. The nap was going well until Coach Gabe came in to start planning the attack with Dalton. Then I decided to take a walk to the new 7-11 Quick Shop that recently opened across from the stadium. They had plenty of merchandise there, just enough to take care of your spare change. As I start to walk out and down the street I heard dad mention right 18 option and Coach Gabe says, "That play looks good."

The Thursday *Marion Journal* included the build up of Dalton at Stuart. They called it "the area game of the week." A lot of extra people made their way to this game because of the intense, and usually good natured, banter that went on for the year following it. We usually had dinner together on Thursday's at home since practice was usually a short walk through for the team. But this Thursday Mom had sandwiches ready early because of the pep-rally. Since Stew hadn't been on the varsity before I didn't really know what was going on. Quint and I asked a bunch of questions. Come to find out, there would be a big bonfire and the band, cheerleaders, even Sharon and the junior high squad, would do cheers. It sounded like a lot of fun.

"What about marshmallows," Quint asked.

"That's not the reason for this bonfire," Mom said.

"Quint," Sharon said, "they're going to burn a bulldog."

I was shocked. I looked at Dad and asked him if they are going to let them do that. I said, "Heck, I got my butt whipped for kicking our dog, but you're going to let them *burn* a bulldog?"

Sharon finally owned up to the fact that the bulldog is one they made up of wire and paper. Everyone got a chuckle because we were so serious.

Then Quint spoke up. "I was thinking that it's good they're not the lions or the tigers."

Sure enough, the scene at the pep-rally was fun and festive. With my cast on I couldn't do a lot of running and playing, not like some of my

Lil' Rebel teammates were able to do. After a bit the band stopped playing and everyone got quiet so Dad could talk for a few minutes. It was the usual coach stuff and he went on to introduce the captains. First up to talk was Big Jim. He scared me with what he said: "Ok you Rebels, this game is going to come down to the kicking game—I mean us kicking their butts."

Everybody cheered and I was just thankful that they we not going to depend on my brother for winning the game with his kicking. Fast Eddie stepped forward and said "Those dogs will be chasing us the whole hour of the game and the only place they will catch us is in our end zone."

Some of the players were laughing a bit and I saw Dad shaking his head. Doc Hands was standing by me and I ask what was funny about what he said.

"Well, Son, Eddie hasn't figured out yet that the game is 48 minutes and not an hour."

As we started to leave, a light bulb went off in my mind. With all of those people at the game, it going to be great looking for dropped money on Saturday morning.

Early in the game it didn't look good; the Bulldogs scored first. They were driving for another score, but their QB threw a pass over the middle. Big Jim knocked it up in the air and Stew came down with it. Then the Rebels ran 18 Option and it worked like a charm for 20 yards. They ran 11 Option to the left for 12 yards. This set up the wide side to the right and Mitch threw the hook pass to Eddie, he stepped right and swirled to his left, showing everybody why he was called Fast Eddie—44 yard touchdown. Now the game was tied.

The Bulldogs star linebacker, #33, Gary Patterson, was wreaking havoc and hitting Mitch about every time he threw. Our right tackle was not quick enough to block him and he was making most of their plays. Pete and I were running the balls in and listening to the barbs back and forth. #33 let Mitch know that he would have his head before the end of the game and on it went. Since we were running the balls in, we were on the line of scrimmage and that gave you a good view. I had been watching #33 and learning a few new words to call people and, after awhile, I looked at Pete and said "Watch this."

"Watch what?" he asked.

"#33 is going to stay and follow the ball," I said and I was right.

During the next play I told Pete, "#33 is about to rush and hit Mitch," and he did, just as the ball fell incomplete.

"Good guessing" Pete said.

In the locker room at halftime, the players were drinking their cokes and Dad looked at Thomas, our right tackle, and I knew just how he felt because he was hearing "Dammit" from Dad just like I did.

"#33 is killing us," Dad said. "You've got to move your feet and keep him from mauling Mitch."

"Dad," I said, trying to interrupt.

"No, I don't want a coke" Dad snapped back at me, not even looking to see that I wasn't offering a coke.

"Dad," I said again.

"What?" he asked, firing back.

"I know when #33 is going to rush."

"Do what?" Dad asked.

"Every time he starts to rush in and try to take Mitch's head off, he puts his right foot back to push off. When he stands his ground his feet are even, to go side to side."

"Are you sure?" Dad asked me and he seemed amazed.

Pete jumped in then, to help me out. "Coach, Bob showed me a few plays and was right on each one."

Dad turned to the chalk board and put the alignment up and told Mitch to check to the draw on the right side. He told Thomas to just nudge #33 outside and he would take himself right out of the play. That way, Dad said, if we had the dive called and if he was standing there check to the option, we would beat him to the outside.

The second half started and Mitch checked to the option and we gained 12 yards. We swept left and Joey Case, halfback, slipped going left, losing 4 yards. We were about to run the hook pass and Mitch checked to the draw. #33 zipped past Thomas at the right tackle and Joey took the hand-off for 20 yards. One thing Coach Dad usually did not do was pass on a first down. He called the hook and go pass to Eddie and they took the fake. Eddie hauled in the pass from Mitch for a 45 yard touchdown play.

In spite of this, it was a tough fought game. The Rebels held on to win 21 to 13. They also won the bragging rights for next year. The locker room was filled with a lot of Rebel yelling and cheering. Fast Eddie lifted me up and let me know I would get one milk shake for each of his touchdowns. Dad got the players to hush a bit and let them know they played a good and tough game. "Ok," he said, then, "I know this is going to cost me, but great job Lil' Bob." He grinned at me. "You spoiled a good game from Patterson #33 and helped get us over the hump."

Thomas, the right tackle, patted me on the back as well.

Look for Specific Player's Tendencies

I rode home with Mom and tried to tell her what I did to help but the explanation got too long. Quint was trying to explain that he scored a couple of touchdowns playing cup football and finally asked if the Rebels had won. I hit the bed thinking of pancakes in a few hours.

Paul's Diner was full of life that Saturday morning. Marion High had won a big game, just like Stuart had. One gentleman complemented Dad for taking care of the Patterson kid in the second half: "He's one of the best players I have seen in the county schools for some years now. That was a big win for your Rebels."

"Thanks," Dad said. "We had some good bounces but our kids played tough. I am actually more worried about this week with another good team."

"Dang Coach," Red Parker said. "Go home and relax for a day."

It took me a little longer to eat, being only one handed with my cast. When we got in the car, I asked Dad why he doesn't give Red and the rest of the men more information.

Dad just smiled at me and said, "Well Bob, if you do talk a little more, it's too easy to leave off somebody and, besides, some things can get taken the wrong way."

Be Careful Talking in Public

Dad had picked up the film on the way back to the field house and said, "Bob, I'm proud of the contribution you gave us last night."

I didn't say anything. I was too proud.

Dad went on: "Ol' Red was right about one thing—after a bit we'll just go back to the house, watch some of the college game, and then we will go for shakes."

After that we started watching the film together. Dad was taking some notes and I said "Watch this." I ran it back and forth a couple of times and I said, "Look at #33 there, goes his right foot back and down goes Mitch."

I kept talking. "On this play his feet are even and he shuffles to the other side when we run away from him."

About that time there was a knock on the door. Dad got up, knowing the door had been locked. He opened it and I heard, "Come in." Dad asked me to stop the film, just as #33 Gary Patterson walked in.

"Hi, Gary," Dad said, not even trying to hide his surprise. "How're you feeling this morning?"

Gary shrugged, "Not too bad really because I didn't get to do too much in the second half." He looked around. "Y'all worked on us pretty good after the half. Stew kept us pinned back with his punting and we couldn't catch Eddie."

My dad just nodded. After a second, he remembered me: "Gary, this is Bob who you may remember was the bat boy on the little league All-Star team." Gary and Stew had played on a little league team together and they got along pretty well.

"What happened to you?" Gary asked me, looking at my cast.

"I made a catch in practice and jumped over the tackler. When I was trying to get my balance, I fell the wrong way on my wrist."

Gary nodded. "Well, that was good thinking with the jump. I hope it heals up pretty quick."

I thanked him and Dad said, "Gary, Bob also was pretty good at the thinking part last night."

"What do you mean?" Gary asked.

"I'll just let Bob show you."

"Show me what?" Gary looked around again and Dad started the film back up. I told Gary that in running the balls in and out I was watching his feet with his stance.

"Look here," I said. "You are set up about to blitz and go after Mitch, the QB. Now this play you are about to slide sideways."

"Wait, now," Gary said. "Where do you see that?"

I explained and showed him how he dropped his right foot back to rush in.

Dad said, "Gary, I was trying to find some way to slow you down and Bob spoke up about what stance you were getting in and what you did. Then we had Mitch to just check to what you were about to do."

"Damn, sorry, coach" Gary said. He turned to me. "Well, Bob, you cost me some sleep last night but thanks for pointing that out." He laughed then and said, "Hey, Bob, you think you want to be our manager?"

About that time Dr. Hands walks in with Pete. He had treated Gary numerous times in the past and they shook hands and had some chit-chat. Gary said he had to run and Doc gave him a ham biscuit, since he always had a couple of extra. Gary patted me on the head as Pete and I walked outside. "Thanks, Lil' Bob. Tell Stew good game again."

Gary went on to sign and play for the Georgia Bulldogs.

"Come on, Pete," I said.

"Where we going?" he asked.

"To the stadium," I said. I explained that I was looking around after the first home game and started finding some money in the grass and around the concession area.

Pete reached down and said, "Here's a dime."

Then the treasure hunt began. I told Pete about the first time, when I got a $20 reward for finding Mr. Strickland's wallet. It would have been funny to have had a recording of our hunt. You would hear the shouts of "nickel," "found a dime," "got a quarter" and then, finally, Pete yelling out, "Bob, a $5 dollar bill."

Luckily we had an agreement that we would split the findings and I hollered, "You know how much stuff we can get with that kind of money at the quick shop?"

We were about done when our dads were ready to leave. They honked the horn and we came running. "Dad, $7.40 we found together," Pete said.

I said, "Pete found a $5 bill. He is ready for the next home game."

Then we were in the car, headed to the Rebel Drive-In and then home to watch some college football.

The rest of the year had a fade to it. The Rebels, I learned, lacked some depth and had a couple of tough losses. We did make it to the Charity Bowl game, though. This event pitted the top of the five Concord county schools against the second place larger school of the three high schools in Marion. Stuart was to play East Central to close out the season. I was told and the sports page confirmed it had been six years since one of the county schools, Dalton, had upset Marion in the Bowl game.

As the game wore on, the Rebels couldn't get a break and didn't match up well head to head. East Central tacked on some late points and won 24-6. It was a good year to finish 7and 3. I then learned a valuable lesson about the game. Since we were in the visiting locker room in the City of

Marion stadium, I wasn't doing some of the normal putting things away that Pete and I would do after games. Coach Dad let the players know how special each of them was. "You all played with pride, heart and it was an honor for you to represent Stuart the way y'all have."

I got to see what all this really meant to the players. All those handshakes, a few hugs and the pats on the head showed me. It wasn't about each individual; it was about the team.

It Is a TEAM Game

For me, that year, the great part was the Saturday mornings I got to spend with Dad looking at the films and trying to find the little things that help individuals fine tune their game. Most of that came about, in part, because I had broken my wrist and had to spend my time doing other things besides playing. The other plus of the season was that we had the bragging rights over Dalton till the next year.

It looked so cool on the TV set. It was a cool and rainy day early in December, another Saturday in Stuart. The game on the tube was the annual end of season battle between Army and Navy. The weather looked the same in Philadelphia, PA, except a lot colder. The players would get tackled and slide 5 yards in the water and mud. The ball was hard to hold on to and bounced around like it had a disease. We didn't care who won; it was just the only game to watch. Then #15 dove for a pass and slid a good 8 yards on his belly and Quint said, "That looks like fun." After a couple more plays went by, the three of us, including neighbor Matt Townsend, looked up and said "Let's do it," almost in unison.

"It" worked well, if only because our parents weren't home. Sharon was supposed to be watching out for us but was on the phone, talking away. After a quick knock next door to another of our neighborhood mates, Jimmy Moore, we were five minutes away from our own mud bowl game. We had washing machines at home and, since nobody was there to tell us we couldn't play in the rain, it was show-time. Our game started out fun and was filled with laughter. We collectively had the chance to make the diving grabs and my team, Navy, was winning. All was going well. That is, until a strange play happened. Matt was throwing a long pass to Quint. In the lower corner of the yard, Quint dove for the ball and make a big splash—he did a good belly slide himself. I turned to walk back the previous line for the next play and Jimmy says, "Quint, come on."

"Get your butt up," I yelled to Quint, in a harsh tone, but he didn't budge.

I jumped over and could tell he was having trouble breathing and told Matt to run and get Sharon. Where was Doc West when you needed him? Sharon came running and looked down, rolled Quint to his side, and started to hit him on his upper back. She then laid him down, held his nose, and breathed into his mouth a couple of times. Then she started to hit his back again, and, finally, Quint coughed and spit out some water. Sharon sat him up and gave him a hug. A lifeguard at the city pool for almost 2 years and the first person she had to resuscitate, for real, was her little brother in her own backyard. Quint had swallowed some water during his belly splash and got choked. I believe that was lil' brother's last day to play wide receiver. From then on he was the QB, for sure, on all the teams he played on.

Of course, that put an abrupt halt to the game. We put our soaked clothes in the washing machine and got cleaned up before our parents got home. We made all sorts of promises to Sharon not to tell Mom and Dad right away. Matt was to be spending the night with Quint and was there when the folks came in, bringing supper with them. We were eating some crispy fried chicken plates that were bought from the First Baptist choir fundraising dinner. Getting ready to sit Dad asked, "Bob, at Johnson's Western Auto, I heard a few plays of the Army and Navy game on one of TV sets, who won?"

I hoped he wasn't talking about our version of the game and I said, "Navy was giving them a good soaking."

"A good what?" he asked.

"They were ahead by about 20 points at the end playing in real bad rain and cold weather."

Mom started in then: "You don't get out in that weather or, like it is here today, unless you have to."

We all looked at each other and didn't say a thing.

The chicken legs were being gobbled down by all us boys. Mom looked over and saw that everyone had a glass of something to drink but Quint. She said, "Quint would you like a glass of water?"

That did it. Matt was first. He had a mouthful of chicken that went spewing across the table. Then, Sharon dropped her glass to the floor.

Luckily it didn't break. I almost choked on my slaw. Quint was just shaking his head side to side afraid to say anything.

Dad was the first to speak up, "What happened?"

"One at a time" Mom said.

I spoke up that we just had to go copy the Army and Navy game. "Dad you would have been proud of some of the plays we made out there today."

Dad caught on right away. "Ok," he said. "That's enough trying to butter me up, what's the secret?"

I explained that we had to have our go of the game on TV, and, yes, we were ready to clean up our mess, and Quint made a good effort diving for the ball. The part about the water splashing up and Quint not moving had Mom about freak out for a second, but she also knew that was all fine now. I reasoned after doing the talking and I let Dad know he trained Sharon real well. From my promise to Sharon, I said, "I think it would be good to let Sharon stay out an extra hour tonight." About that time, before the answer, Stew comes bouncing in asking what's for supper. He said right quick, "You've gotta be stupid to be out in that weather today."

Just about everyone starts to laugh and all Stew asked was, "What did I say?"

Instead of winter, spring, summer, or fall everything in Stuart seemed to move along from one sport's season to the next. I learned, when I was about town with Dad or Stew, that sports was the topic always mentioned first. Dad explained that this just goes with the territory of being a coach. "Pay attention when you are with Pete and Doc West you'll see how many times he gets asked about back and neck problems."

After a little bit of a rebuilding year for the Rebel football team, finishing 7 and 3, a lot of anticipation awaited the upcoming year. Stew had shown a lot of promise as a quarterback and all the other receivers had a year under their belts as well. Curt West had everybody's attention for playing tight end and linebacker. Pete and I were very excited about having two of the "stars" of the team for brothers. One thing that hadn't gone on with the Rebels, as far as I knew, was having the guys work out regularly. It was against the rules to have organized practice before August first, but having the facility open for workouts was fine.

When the workouts started, I also started seeing things I didn't know how to comprehend. I thought jumping rope was for girls. The backs and receivers started out trying not to choke themselves, but pretty soon they got the hang of it. Now I know that, once you learn to jump rope, it is a great agility exercise.

Jumping Rope Is One of the Best Over-All Agility Exercises

Players were doing other strange things, like taking big truck tires and flipping them end over end. Some were putting on harness straps and running while pulling tires. Dad said that natural strengthening was very important and, besides, we had very few weights around at that time. The players worked hard and were ready to go as the first of August presented itself. Pete and I were doing our best to keep up and do as much as we could. It was fun to see what we could do around the older guys.

The start of football season was getting close. Our Lil' Rebel team was doing well practicing with Coach Taylor. The stars seemed to be lining up just the right way and suddenly the week of first game had finally arrived. I was excited that Dad was letting me tag along to see a Thursday night game between Southfork and Collins. Collins was on the far side of the county and was set to play at Stuart next week. Because they were playing on Thursday, Dad got a chance to scout the game himself. We tried to scoot into the stands without bringing much attention to ourselves, sitting on the Southfork side, since we weren't going to play them.

Collins had a hot-shot quarterback, a Joe Namath comparison, named Lance Wells. He also wore #12 and white shoes. In every way, he tried to act the part. Collins marched down the field with a good mix of pass and run to score a touchdown on their first possession. There was something that caught my eye after a few plays, something that seemed a little different. I watched a couple more series and it was the same thing every time. Dad was talking about a couple of plays with Coach Reed, who usually scouts the visiting teams. "Dad," I said as I pulled on his sleeve.

"What now?" Dad said, shooing me away.

"Well, Dad, I bet Wells hands-off on this play," I said and, sure enough, he stuck the ball into the gut of #34.

Dad looked at me then and I said, "Now watch, he's about to throw a pass." And again, sure enough, the ball lands in the arms of #81 for a 15 yard gain.

Dad looked at me again and this time I said, "You wanna bet a coke on the next play?"

"Okay," Dad said and I knew I had his full attention.

"Pass," I said as Wells had the ball dropped this time by # 81.

"Dammit, Bob," Dad said. "What's the secret, and don't you tell Mom I called you Dammit."

I shrugged and said, "Popcorn on this next play." I was happy to up the stakes from the coke wager. Collins ran the ball as I said they would and Dad was getting antsy.

"Namath," I said.

"Joe Namath what?" Dad snapped. He'd had just about enough.

"Wells copies Joe, right? So this is what I notice: if he is going to hand-off the ball, #12 doesn't buckle his chinstrap. If he is going to pass he snaps it on." The thing is, I was right. He followed that routine for the rest of the second half as I watched, snacking on my popcorn and drinking my coke.

As we walked out the stadium in the mid-fourth quarter, Collins was winning handily. I heard Dad say to Coach Reed, "I've never worked-up a game-plan depending on a player buckling his chinstrap or not."

The Rebels opened in good fashion by beating Willmut High 28 to 6. The Saturday routines that went with the past season started as they had left off from the last game. I was up early in the morning with Dad, even though it was my only chance to sleep in. The pancakes and hot syrup at Paul's Diner were as good as ever. Mr. Red spoke to Dad as we left: "Pretty good start last night."

"Thanks Red," Dad said.

Red grinned. "Well, who's the victim next week?"

"Collins comes to our place."

"They've got that Wells kid at QB don't they?"

"Yeah we'll have our hands full."

I couldn't resist. "But, Dad," I said and then stopped myself. I know that tap on the top of my head means to be quiet.

Dad smiled and said, "Come out and watch us Red, you know you've got a ticket waiting on you." Then Dad shook a few more hands and had some small talk before leaving.

"Bob, Paul's Diner is not the place to start giving out any game plan or secrets with a game," Dad said without looking at me. We just kept walking to the truck.

There Is a Proper Time and Place for Everything

The Lil' Rebel football team was practicing hard. I'd been catching more passes because Coach Taylor knew I could hang on to them. I may not have outrun a lot but I knew where I was running.

On the Sunday night before Labor Day, the band booster club always had a big Bar-b-Que. It was held across from the city swimming pool which was on its last day to be open. School would be starting on Tuesday.

One of my good pals, Jeff Whitt, had his parents heading up the booster club for the upcoming year. Jeff's older brother Stan was one heck of a drummer and had some of the fastest hands I've ever seen. Jeff and I were trying to give it a go and last the whole night staying up while the volunteers were cooking the chicken and ribs. As some of the meat was grilled to perfection, it was transported up to the school lunchroom where it would wait to be served as plate dinners a little later. The meat was loaded in pans and placed in the back of a pick-up. Jeff and I helped escort it sitting in the back since we were going quite slow. Being boys we moved down to the tailgate and would let the tip of our shoes drag along the top of the pavement. I wasn't ready when Mr. Whitt stepped on the brakes and my feet got more of the pavement than they should have. The friction got me off balance and into the street I went. We were just moving at about 5 to 10 mph but, in the process of falling, I twisted my left ankle under me. I limped up to the lunchroom and noticed I had a couple of scrapes on my elbows and knees. My foot was starting to throb a bit and, when Mr. Whitt suggested he could drop me off at the house, I relented. Off to bed I went.

The next morning I had slept late, but didn't actually feel too bad. I stood up okay, but when I went to walk, I fell flat forward. My ankle was already black, blue, and swollen. I told Mom I had fallen, which I did, but I didn't get to the part about how I'd fallen from a moving pick-up truck. We headed to meet Doc West and he said I may have been better off had I broken it. I had to use crutches for the first time and it wasn't fun starting the school year in that fashion. The other part was another year of missing out on playing football after breaking my wrist the year before.

Be Careful Doing Outside Activities

It was finally Friday and I was ready to see how the Rebels would fare against that good Collins team and their star QB, Lance Wells. I had told Pete all about the chinstrap. With my bum ankle, he got to do all the running in of the footballs and I just held on to them. The Rebel defense started out a little cautious. Right on cue Wells was manning his chinstrap, just the same as last week at Southfork. Assistant Coach Gabe Thomas started to add a lot more pressure with the defense when #12 buckles his strap. Curt had a field day blitzing the QB and racked up 4 of the 6 total sacks. The Rebels kept the pressure on, almost shutting him out, but he got a late score against the defensive reserves, just before the Rebels won 28-7. Two of the touchdowns were set up by interceptions via Stew roaming the secondary at safety. In the locker room after the game Dad was letting the team know they had done a good job: "Okay, guys you know it is a Dalton week. So, have fun tonight, but get ready for a little walk-through Sunday at three."

Then Dad surprised me. In front of the whole team he said, "Wait, guys, my little scout here gave us a great tip and made our defense look real good. Give Bob a hand."

I had a smile from ear to ear and Stew patted me on the head. He asked what flavor shake I had on my mind. Of course you know what I said: "I'll stick with the peanut-butter this time."

Since this was the first home game of the season, Pete was staying over with me. We wanted to get an early start scanning the grounds at the stadium for some loose money. We arrived at Paul's Diner and the air was already filled with the warm smell of bacon sizzling. The Saturday morning experts were already drinking their coffee and second guessing the different coaches' decisions. Red stood up to shake Dad's hand and let him know he enjoyed the game and the free tickets. He said, "I didn't think you'd be able to handle that Wells kid the way you did, but I bet he has seen enough Rebels, now."

"Thanks Red," Dad said. "I had a good scouting report that held true to form." When Dad said this, he patted me on the head.

While they talked a minute or two more Pete and I dove into a good stack of pancakes. Ms. Sue served them up with our choice of syrup. Today I went all out and had boysenberry. Pete tried the blueberry.

Getting back to the field-house, Pete and I headed out to the ticket and concession area to start our search. I told Pete to continue on, that I was going inside to sit—my foot was getting too sore. I found thirty cents as I headed back in.

Dad got me a chair and a foot stool. He also gave me the control, since we were watching last night's game. "Bob," he asked, "Where do you get some of the ideas and tips you see players do?"

"I just pay attention watching and listening to the games on TV."

Dad nodded. "Well, watch and see if any of our guys catch your eye while you're at it."

It felt good that Dad trusted me. Coach Thomas was there early today and he chimed in. "Bob, if I ever get a head job, you are going to be my first assistant."

It was the week of the Dalton game and the pressure was reaching a high level. Both teams had won their first two games and were laden with good talent. The pep rally was fun, even though we leave off the marshmallows. Pete and I got to make fun of our brothers who both had to say something in front of the fans. The game was hard fought and the Rebel's charged back to score with four minutes left to nearly tie the game. "There's the snap, the hold, and no, Stewart Hayes' kick is wide right. Dalton stays ahead 14-13," shouts the radio announcer.

As we had seen and heard on Saturday's watching the Wide World of Sports, the agony of defeat was the real deal. You could have heard a pin drop on that short bus ride back to Stuart. All Dad said was, "Sunday at 3 pm and be careful." I was carrying the ball bag and walked by Stew, who was sitting in front of his locker. "Sorry," I said and he looked up. When he saw the tears running down my cheeks, he gave me a hug.

It Is Great to Have Passion for the Game, at Any Level

When I got up with Dad to Paul's Diner, there was something I didn't expect to see sitting in our carport. There were two tied up chickens painted Rebel yellow. "Dad," I asked, "Where did these come from?"

"I believe they may be for Stew." He said it was actually showing a little respect that they cared enough to razz him.

At Paul's there were a lot of tough luck greetings that morning. I told Ms. Sue I may have to try the oatmeal and toast this morning.

"Oh, now," she said. "I heard it was a good game."

"Not quite good enough," I answered, shaking my head.

Dad and Red talked a little bit longer and as we started to drive to the field-house I asked, "Why did you talk with Red a little more?"

"Well, he is on the Concord County School Board and understands a bit more. You know, he used to be a coach."

We drove up to the field-house and we both turned our heads toward the field. It took us a second to make out the image. Stew was on the field, with all the balls, kicking extra points. Dad and I walked out there. Dad said, "What's up?"

Stew looked at Dad. "Well, in basketball Coach Reed has us to shoot free throws when we miss. I hate that I let everyone down."

"Stop by inside when you get through," Dad said, walking back toward the field-house. He stopped and called back, "Come on Bob."

I had thought to stay and catch balls for Stew.

Dad had another idea. "He'll feel better and get tired quicker by himself."

The film started to roll and Dad made this comment: "They were all over Curt last night. That's the first game where he hasn't caught a pass."

A few plays went by and the film was rolling along. I clicked it back and forth a couple of times. "Dad," I said intently, "I think I see why."

"See why what?" Dad asked.

"Watch Curt," I said. "He's about to go out for a pass."

Dad nodded and watched.

"Now," I said. "You see the difference? In this play we are going to run the ball. You see, when Curt gets in a 3 point stance, he goes out for a pass. When he gets in a 4 point stance, it's a run play."

My dad just kept nodding and watching the film.

"See," I said. "The safety even starts to move over when he is in the 3 point stance." About that time the door opened and in walks Curt and Stew.

Dad looked at them. "Don't say anything guys, just watch this. I keep trying to tell you it can come down to the little things you do." He looked at me. "Show them Bob."

I turned on the projector and the film rolled. They were both amazed with my findings.

"No wonder I couldn't get any space," Curt said. "I might as well been holding up a sign. I won't do that again."

"Dad," Stew said. "We're going to stop by Doc West's office and be home in a bit."

"Y'all stop and pick up Pete and we'll all have some burgers and watch the Tennessee and Auburn game," Dad said. Then he added, "Stewart, have Doc to look at your hip."

Stew had a mean look on his face that has been shown to me on numerous occasions. Dad studied him for a second and then added, "No not because of the kick. From getting clipped. You're limping a bit."

"Okay, then," Stew said and he started to walk out the door.

"Curt," my dad said, "tell Doc to come over also when he finishes up."

"No problem," Curt said. Then he added, "Hey, Bob thanks a lot."

Both seasons were clicking along just great for both the big and little Rebels. My ankle still limited me, though, and I missed the opportunity to play. With only two games remaining, I finally get to dress out. Coach Taylor said he'd try to get me in for a play or two. The game wound down and we went up by two touchdowns with about four minutes to go. I went up and tugged on Coach Taylor's sleeve. I pleaded with him: "Heck, just let me kick off."

He succumbed to my repeated request and out I went. Just like I had kicked hundreds of balls in the backyard and at varsity practice, I teed the ball up. I then turned and measured my steps. I waited for the official's whistle. I dropped my arm to let the team know it was time to roll and I planted my foot right through the ball. All the safety could do was turn and watch it sail over his head as he raced to pick it up near the goal-line. The Lil' Rebels downed #17 on the 12 yard line. The coverage was a good feat for any team, especially in our league. As we went off the field Pete jogged next to me, slapped me on the helmet, and said, "It's about time you do something around here."

Coach Taylor walked by, too, and put his hand on my helmet. All I said was "I told you so."

"Well," the coach said. "It was good you proved it, too."

I asked, "What about next week's game, Coach?"

"Okay," Coach said, "you're on for the last game."

I couldn't wait to go and get my after game treats. Pete had intercepted a pass and run it back for a touchdown with some good moves, but everyone was delighted about my kick.

At the Rebel Drive-In we were downing our rewards. I had gone out on a limb and gotten a grape shake. Then up walked Curt and Stew. "I hear you are about ready to take my kicking job," Stew said. Curt said they got tied up in town and hates that he missed us showing off.

Pete smiled and said, "Just doing our jobs on the field."

I took another approach: "What were the girls' names?"

Coach Taylor was true to his word and I got to kick off in our last game of the season. We scored twice and it felt really good to get to play, in uniform, even if it was just for three kick-offs. Now, we just had to get the Rebels through the remainder of the season.

The last two games were crucial to win the County Championship. Dalton had suffered a couple of key injuries and lost two games. The Rebels hung on to beat Oak Grove 14 to 10 to go 7 and 1. That set up the last game for the championship with Warren High.

The breakfast was nice and warm and Ms. Sue served up my usual pancakes. Since we were winning again, I went back to my first choice. Dad was sitting and talking to Mr. Red for a bit and, after waiting a few minutes, we left to go to the field-house. The film was replaying the victory over Oak Grove and I knew most of Dad's thoughts were on Warren High. At least, that's what I thought. "Dad," I said, but he didn't answer. "Are you asleep?" I asked.

"No, just thinking a bit," he said.

"Dad, it was sure boring running the balls in and out last night."

"What do you mean, boring?" he said. He didn't like that word, I'd noticed.

"Pete and I like it when we get to throw more. That way the job is more fun."

"I see," Dad said.

"I think Stew, Curt and Rich, the wide-receiver, would like to throw and catch more. I mean, I'm giving you a hint from Stew."

"Okay," Dad said. "I get your point, but keep it quiet with them."

Later, after lunch, Stew cornered me at home and asked what Dad had said about opening up some more passes. 'We'll see,' is all Dad had said. I really didn't know what to tell Stew. "He seemed distracted, but you still owe me," I finally told Stew, reminding him of his little bribe to try and get some info out of Dad.

I found my way for Stew to pay me back. I had been at Pete's shooting basketball. When I got home late in the afternoon I learn that Quint was staying with Matt and Sharon was at Beth's for the evening. "Stew, I guess you're going out with Monica."

"Yep, going to a movie," he replied.

"I bet in Dad's car also," I said, but that time Stew didn't answer.

Home alone on Saturday night with Mom and Dad, I came up with a plan. There wasn't a lot to choose from on our two TV channels.

I got washed up real fast. Before Stew left, I went and hid down on the back floorboard of the car. I stayed real still, without a sound, and learned we were headed to the Riverbend Drive-In.

"What's showing?" Monica asked.

"The Good, The Bad, and The Ugly," Stew answered.

I was pleased because Clint, who used to be Rowdy Yates on Rawhide, was one of my favorites. I thought that if Stew didn't kill me, right off the bat, I'd be okay.

I knew that Stew looked forward to his Saturday dates with Monica because she was a cheerleader at Marion. With practice and games he didn't get to see her a lot. As they pulled to a park Stew said he would run to the concession stand. This was my moment of truth. "You may want to get an extra popcorn," I said, as Monica jumped a foot in her seat and gave a small scream. Stew couldn't think of anything to say and I was glad I couldn't read his mind.

I said, "Sharon and Quint were gone and I didn't want to watch Lawrence Welk with Mom and Dad. Plus, you owe me for today." I looked at Monica. "Hi," I said.

Stew glared at me. "I may owe you," he said, "but I don't owe you this much." He kept glaring at me. "Not a word Bob."

I was relieved, but I was also still thinking of practicalities. "Stew," I said. "Would you mind calling home and telling Mom and Dad that I am not in my room?"

After the movie Stew was thoughtful enough to drop me off at the house before he carried Monica home, if you can believe that.

To this day, that movie is one of my all time favorites and I guess the circumstances played a role with that. I didn't get killed, but Stew sure started checking the back seat before leaving the house.

The week went well and after a couple of series not much had happened for the Rebels. In the sideline huddle Dad told the offense, "Let's have some fun guys." He called for a fake and then Stew hit Rich all alone for a 65 yard score. On the next possession Curt caught a tight end screen and went for a 46 yard score. We had them so spread out then—Warren High didn't know what to look for. Final score 35-7 and Concord County Champions again. In the huddle after the game Dad addressed the Rebels. He said, "I don't know yet who we will play in the Charity Bowl, but if y'all trust me, we're going to kick some butt. We're going to be the first team to beat those city guys in a long time." He smiled at all of his players. "See y'all at three on Sunday." As the players went off the field I went by Stew and Curt and asked if that was more fun. Payoff would be good Sunday after practice.

We were having our breakfast when the top sports writer of the *Marion Ledger*, Casey Toms, asked Dad if he could join us. "Sure," Dad said. This is my middle son, Bob."

"Is this the little guy I saw boom a kick-off a few weeks ago?"

A smile painted my face from ear to ear.

"Yeah," Dad said. "He's been trying to take Stewart's job ever since."

Toms said, "My son was on the Eagles team that you whipped pretty well." "Well, maybe he'll get his shot in a few years," Dad said.

"Okay," Toms said, getting down to business. "What chance do you think you have playing Marion this Friday?"

"Slim and none," Dad said. "We're just going to give it our best and try to make a good showing for our Rebel faithful."

"But, Dad," I started to say.

He held up his hand to stop any more comments from me.

"Well Coach," Toms said, "Stew has had a really solid year. Has he had any offers come up yet?"

"Just a few requests and Curt West is in the same boat as well." It was clear that Dad didn't want to talk about this.

"Thanks, Coach Hayes," Mr. Toms said and he shook our hands. "By the way, Coach, any truth that this is your last game as Stuart's coach?" he asked.

My Dad said, "I've got Lil' Bob here and Quint coming up after this."

"I see," Toms said. "Good to talk to you again. See you Friday."

We started to leave and Mr. Red shook Dad's hand and said, "Good job the way you buttered Toms up with what you just said."

"Hopefully Marion will buy into it."

I was getting angry at Dad as we went to climb in the truck. "What do you mean slim to no chance?"

"Bob, I want Marion to think that all week and I hope we will get them good."

In the Sunday meeting Dad got up in front of the team and said, "We are not watching the Warren film. We've got a new attack to put in just for Marion. Like I told you after the game Friday, trust me and play your butts off."

Dad proceeded to display some roll out passes and misdirection plays we hadn't run all year. "This'll give us a chance to use our quickness against those bigger guys. Plus, we'll throw in a couple of plays to keep them on their heels."

The Charity Bowl had an over-flowing crowd with Stuart having only one loss and their coach saying they have no chance. The big Marion cheering section was singing out taunts against the Rebels one right after another. As Stew kicks off the Rebels made a good hit and the Stuart fans got to show their strong support. The Rebels charged fast and furious as Stew aired the ball out while on the run with Marion not able to catch up to him. It was 20-10 into the fourth quarter with the Rebels still fighting and winning. The Blue Devils loft a long pass for a 50 yard touchdown. As they lined up for the kick, Curt busted through to block it, to keep a 20-16 lead. This meant Marion had to score a touchdown to win.

As the clock wound down their strength was showing and they marched down the field running the ball play after play. With a minute to go the Blue Devils were first and goal at the 8 yard line. The Rebels made a couple of good stops and it was fourth and goal at the one with 20 seconds left in the game. At the time out, Coach Thomas looked at Dad and asked "Is it time now?"

"Ok listen up," Dad said. "I want 8 men side by side down and ready to fire off. Curt, as their quarterback puts his hands under the center's butt, holler go! Everybody hit fast and low."

"Won't we be off-sides?" Rob, the nose-guard, asked.

"Yeah, but they can only move the ball inches," Coach Thomas said.

"Curt, we'll do it twice and on the third time everybody shift left and if they don't jump, call time."

As the QB got ready the Rebels charged forward and the flags flew into the air. The same went for the second time. Then Curt gave the go-go signal and the whole line shifted left. At least three of Marion's players stepped back, getting a 5 yard penalty. Now it was fourth and goal from the 5 yard line. The Blue Devils tried their power sweep and Joe-Bob Davis, the off safety, took a dive over the top of a blocker. He took down the runner and staked his place in Stuart football history. The feeling was wonderful as all the Rebel fans poured onto the field.

After all the hugs, pats on the back, and Rebel yells the team started to file into the locker room. Even Mr. Red was there at the locker-room door. He gave me a pat on the head and Dad said, "Come on in, Red." Before closing the door Dad also noticed sportswriter Casey Toms waiting. He ushered him in as well.

"Quiet down guys, I've got a few words." He looked around at the team. "In all my eighteen plus years, I have never seen a group of young men stick it out the way you did tonight." He paused and smiled at everyone. "All of you have done everything Coach Gabe and I have asked you to do. I feel this is one of the biggest wins in Stuart history and y'all really earned it."

Dad looks over toward me then. He said, "Bob come up here." I walked up and Dad put his hands on top of my shoulders. He said, "Men I did not want this to linger on, but there is a reason this win was so special. I'm proud of you all and this little guy has been a big asset, as well, and probably helped us win a few games." He seemed to swallow hard, then. "But," he said and paused. He looked down at the floor. "But, I," he stopped again. Finally he said, "I'm stepping down as Coach."

I looked up to see a stream of tears rolling down Dad's face. "I'm not moving anywhere just going to work with Mr. Parker, over here, with the County Board of Education." The boys on the team looked terrified. "I wanted to tell you guys first and foremost and not for you to hear it from somebody else. After eighteen years at Stuart it sure is great to go out on top!"

The team all started clapping and there were a few "You the man, Coach," amongst them. The senior players walked up to him and it was a chorus of, "Thanks Coach." Then, at the end of the line, were Curt and Stew.

Curt hollered for everyone to quiet down. "It has been a great year and, Coach, thanks to Bob and Pete hanging on to this, since it was Marion's, here's your game ball."

More cheers went up as Dad held the ball up in the air. Then he embraced Stew with both arms. They were both trying to get the tears out of their eyes.

"See you and Bob in the morning?" Mr. Red asked Dad later on.

"We may be a little later tomorrow," Dad said.

Casey Toms finally got to talk to Dad and asked him about the goal line stand.

Dad said, "It was our only chance to try and get them off guard and they had three other plays to try to score as well. If I recall we held them on two other fourth down plays so they had their chances earlier in the game."

Toms then asked, "What makes coaching at Stuart so special?"

"Well," Dad said. "If anybody wanted to break into a house, Stuart is wide open right now because everybody in the whole town is here at this game." He thought a moment before he went on. "These guys play for pride and for the whole town and that is special. Toms, I usually talk to you afterward, but this is why I let you come in here with us after this specific game. I felt bad about misleading you when you asked the other day and now I hope you see why."

"Thanks Coach and congratulations again, I've got to go print this up," Casey Toms said, walking out the door.

You Have to Have Desire and Preparation to Go Along with Emotion

Outside the visitor's locker room, most of the Stuart fans were still there, making a big pathway for the players to walk through on the way to the bus for the ride home. Mom was standing there with Quint and Sharon. Dad hugged Mom and she said, "I've already heard you told them."

"Yes, the cats out of the bag now," Dad said.

"What cat?" Quint asked and he followed that with, "I'm hungry."

Then Sharon got a big hug from dad and all she said was "Can it be 12 tonight?"

Everybody starts to file out, all making their way back toward Stuart on cloud nine.

"REBELS WIN THIS WAR!" was the main headline in the *Marion Journal* on Saturday morning followed by the sub-heading, "Coach Hayes Saves his Best for Last." The byline read Casey Toms.

That Saturday night Doc West had our family over for a cook-out. Mom did her dessert specialty with a banana pudding and chocolate cake to go along with the steaks, potatoes, and bread. Everybody was quite full and still talking about the game. Then Sharon asked what was said in the locker room. Dad said, "Okay, I will lay everything out." He looked around. "I've been talking with Doc ever since Mr. Parker asked if I would be interested in an opening with the County Board of Education, starting in January, which meant a good pay raise."

"I had thought of moving up to principal next year but Brenda didn't think that would be fair to a new and younger coach coming in. And also, I felt it best to make this change before Pete and re-Pete here get to varsity."

Curt said, "Coach you handled everything well and nobody has said anything bad about you moving up to the Board."

I said, "Dad, is that why you had been talking to Mr. Red more this year when we've been at the diner?"

Dad smiled, "It's tough getting things by you, Son. In fact, we may have to move you up to coach." Stew said, "I agree," while Curt nodded beside him, "Bob has shown us a thing or two this year."

Then, finally, Quint weighed in: "It would sure surprise me if he helped at all."

Later on the conversation shifted. "By the way, Dad, what about a coach for next year?" Stew asked.

Dad said, "We already have a committee set headed up by Doc, Red Parker, and a couple more. We want to get someone in real quick."

Doc West set Curt and Stew straight. He said, "Boys, if I mentioned a name or two I bet his name would be posted at the Rebel within an hour."

Dad said it is about time to head home before these comments get too out of hand.

After a couple of weeks, there were eight of us having a good game of hoops in the backyard. It was a good and fair game with nobody calling too many cheap fouls. Pete's team got the bragging rights after this contest.

When we went inside to get something to drink, Mom had a big spread of food on the dining room table. "Look at this guys," Quint said.

"Hold your horses' boys, your snacks are in the kitchen."

I said, "Gee Mom I thought we impressed you pretty good with our shooting and you were going to feed us good."

Mom laughed and said, "I saw too many short bank shots you missed to come in talking like that."

"What's the deal Mrs. Hayes?" Pete asked.

"Your Dads' and a few more are about to stop by, so y'all better go wash up." "Who is a few more?" Quint wondered.

"Later," she said.

A short time went by and a couple of cars pulled into our driveway. "Must be somebody new since they are using the front door," Quint said.

We were all sitting together in the den. As grown-ups started talking, we heard some familiar voices: Dad, Doc West, Red Parker, Principal James, Reverend Starnes, and a couple more from the booster club. The voice we didn't recognized belonged to young man with the name Alex.

A few minutes went by after Reverend Starnes said a blessing before the anticipation got the better of us. Mr. Red Parker was first to see a couple of heads peak around the corner. "There's Lil' Bob," he said.

I said, "Hi Mr. Red. How are you this afternoon? You remember Pete West and Quint don't you?"

"Of course, where are your big brothers?" he asked.

"Mom says they're supposed to be here any time now but don't hold your breath."

Dad was talking to the young man we didn't know and his hands were busy, explaining a few things to him. We caught his eye and he waved for us three to come to him. "Boys," he said. "This is Coach Alex Sloan. He's now the new Rebel football coach."

We all looked at him.

My Dad went on. "Coach, little one is my youngest Quint. This is Pete West, Doc's youngest. And here is my middle one, Bob."

We all said hello.

Coach Sloan said, "Bob, I have already heard I may have to put you on my staff." "Staff?" I said back to him with a puzzled look.

"Anyway," Coach Sloan said, "I am going to be in need of a couple of good managers.

I said, "Well, we may have to turn it over to Quint since we'll be on the junior high football team."

"Do you have any boys Coach Sloan?" Quint asked.

"I've got two cheerleaders at the house almost your ages. Amber, the oldest, is 11 and Tara, the youngest, is 9. I am sure you boys will be meeting them before long," Coach Sloan said. "Anyway, you've got first call on my manager's job."

We looked up and saw Curt and Stew walking in. Doc West and Dad waved them over to meet Coach Sloan. I overheard the introductions: Coach Sloan first went to Georgia to play from Cobb County High, but wound up at a junior college in Mississippi for two years. He then played at Northeast Alabama for the Owls.

Dad said, "Before you two were playing for me Coach Sloan helped us for a year here at Stuart while finishing up his degree." Dad smiled. "He even played on our indy baseball team as well."

I looked at Pete and said, "I hope he wasn't a catcher" thinking I may have gotten his mask one time.

Dad added, "He's also been the offensive coach for East Central by way of Madison High."

"Great year, guys," Coach Sloan said. That was some effort beating Marion. We weren't able to."

There was a lull in the conversation and then Coach Sloan asked, "Stew, what have you heard from the schools?"

"I visited Memphis State and talked with a couple of other Division II schools. Some said they need to wait about grades, said they needed to hold on a bit."

Coach Sloan nodded at Stew and turned to Curt. "Curt, I hear you may be in line to go to West Point?"

Pete and I looked at each other, not really knowing anything about West Point.

Coach Sloan noticed our confusion. "Playing for the Army guys," he said.

We burst out laughing and Coach Sloan asked what was so funny.

"Well Army is really Quint's favorite team," Pete said with a big grin.

"There's a good story behind our version, some time ago, of the Army and Navy game. But, we'll spare you that for now," I said.

We felt good getting to meet Coach Sloan before everyone else did and, of course, the manager's job was ours if we still wanted it. But, we weren't ready to make that decision now. Now there were a lot of good snacks on the dining room table that Mom and Mrs. West had prepared, and it was time to get busy with those.

Spring couldn't get here fast enough. That meant baseball and we had a pretty good team returning. I was to be our main pitcher for Coach Herb Gladden. I had missed my opportunities in football, after breaking my left wrist the year before and hurting my ankle during the past season. Although the last two games were almost worth it, with my kick-offs and everything.

I was now seeing things from a different perspective, since I got to participate a little more. In practice we would be taking infield and Coach Herb would have the younger kids running the bases just like in game situations. It really helped to see and recognize what you were supposed to do when you had done it before. I had done the same thing a few years earlier, running the bases while the coach hit infield practice, but it had a better meaning now.

Practice Game Situations

Coach Herb showed me how to throw an off-speed pitch that scared a lot of right hand batters. The two long fingers were placed inside the narrow 2 seams and gently squeezed the sides of the ball with the thumb and ring-finger. You threw it over-hand and had to turn your wrist inside. In doing so you didn't have to twist the elbow or put undue pressure—this helped avoid injury. The target would be the batter's shoulder and, the pitch, if thrown properly, would spin down the middle of the plate. Having a good fastball was great for keeping batters off guard.

We were about a week away from opening day and we had a newcomer, Sam Bower, who couldn't hit a lick. Coach Herb's brother-in-law Glen White was our assistant coach. Coach Glen usually pitched batting practice and barked out instructions. Little Sam took a good practice swing and stepped into the batter's box. When the pitch came he stepped way back and didn't come close to the ball. "Don't step back," Coach Glen said, time after time. Some of us sensed the weakness in Sam and shouted out encouragement to no prevail. Coach Herb called for next batter and called Sam over to him. I was on deck and got to hear the conversation.

"Okay, Sam," Coach Herb said "what's wrong?"

"I, I saw my brother get hit in the head and . . ."

"I see," Coach Herb said, cutting the story short. "Bob," he said to me, then. "Why do you wear your helmet?"

"To protect your head so the ball won't hurt you," I said.

Coach Herb looked Sam right in the eye and said, "Little man, this is what you are going to do: when the ball is pitched you are going to step into it and hit it. You got that?"

Coach Glen said, "Okay, Bob," and then Coach Herb said, "Bob step back and Sam get back in the box."

You could see most of the guys in the field just shaking their heads.

"Okay, Sam. What you gonna do?" Coach Glen asked.

"Step into it and hit it," Sam shouted.

Coach Glen threw the pitch and Sam stepped, swung, and fouled it off.

"That's the way to get a piece of it," Coach Herb said as a smile hit Sam's face. Before Coach Glen threw the next pitch, Coach Glen went over it again: "What are you going to do, Sam?"

"Step into it and hit it," Sam said.

There went the pitch and Sam lined one between the first and second baseman. Encouragement came from all over the field, now, and the same routine of "What you going to do, Sam?" rung out before each pitch. After hitting the ball solid, Sam walked by and I tapped his helmet with my bat: "That wasn't so hard, was it Sam?"

Sam shook his head.

"Good job," I said.

"Thanks Bob" Sam said.

After practice we were about to leave and I said, "Coach Herb, good job with Sam—we're going to need him."

"Well, me and Glen, too, have got to tell you guys what we want you to do and not what not to do. We want you to catch the ball not try to not drop it."

"I *see*," I think, as I walk away.

Always Coach from the Positive and Let the Players Know What You Want Them to Do

Our opening day game was with the Lions. The first batter was my good friend, Jeff Whitt. He had told me in school earlier in the day that he didn't want to be a strike-out victim. "I'm gonna bunt when I get up to bat," Jeff told me. Sure enough, it was a fastball down the middle and I went charging in and almost caught the ball before it hit the ground. Good ol' Jeff was true to his word. We won 5-0 and I only gave up three hits.

After a couple of games went by, I was playing shortstop against the Reds while Brady Clark was pitching for our team, the Cardinals. Our next game was with the other top team the Stallions. Coach Herb would always kneel down and give one finger for fastball and two fingers for the off-speed pitch. Brady's pitch didn't have as much "bite" as mine, but was still effective. About the third inning, I looked over and saw a couple of the Stallion players watching from behind the Reds dugout. We got into bat and I went up to Coach Herb and said, "I see . . ."

But he cut me off and said, "I've already caught them out of the corner of my eye, but good job for noticing."

The Stallions and Cardinals faced off in the late game on Friday night. There was always a good turnout, with no school the next day, to see the two undefeated teams play. Coach Herb informed me and Brett, his son and catcher, that he would be giving the same signals. "But I . . ." I said.

Coach Herb cut me off again. "Settle down, Bob," he said. Then he went on, "Brett if I have my hand on my knee, it'll be a fastball. If I take my hand off my knee then it'll be the off-speed pitch. Some will be the same at first so let's have some fun."

The first batter started to step into the batter's box and I saw him glance over toward Coach Herb. He had one finger down and his hand on his knee. Brett set up outside and I threw a good fastball that #2 takes for a ball. Same signals for the next pitch but he swings and misses. Coach Herb then gives the two fingers and his hand off his knee and #2 fouls back the off-speed pitch.

1 ball and 2 strikes is the count and Coach Herb gives Brett the one finger and his hand off the knee. I threw a good off-speed pitch and the batter helplessly took it, for a call third strike. The coach said, "The pitch

was right down the middle," and the batter was trying his best to explain he saw Coach Herb call for a fastball.

By the fourth inning, the Stallions didn't have a clue. Brett was giving them heck behind the plate and my pitches were hitting his mitt. After a good off-speed pitch Coach Herb called time out to come and came to talk with me. Brett came to meet us at the mound and Coach said, "Guys y'all can't be laughing too much out there."

We got the best of them for this game and win 4-0, staying undefeated. I learned that there are two different things: signals and tendencies. It's a lot easier to change signals.

Be Careful Trying to Steal Signals

After the game, we got our free coke. I had seen Mom and Dad in the stands, but I hadn't seen Stew. It was always a pleasure to gain favor from your older brother. "That was a good game, Bob," Stew said. "Eight strike-outs and a shut-out is great, but what was so funny out there?" I explained the signal scene to them and Dad said, "Bob, you have to control your emotions both good and bad. Otherwise it can come back to haunt you."

"Okay, guys," Mom said, "that's enough coaching. Let's head to the house."

Control Your Expressions

The season was about to close and three teams were tied for first place. We, the Cardinals, had to beat a good hitting Kings team and the winner was to face the Stallions in the finals who had gotten the bye. Because of the tight tournament schedule the pitching rules only allow 6 innings per 3 days rest, so Coach Herb made the decision to pitch me against the Kings.

It was a great night for baseball. Stuart City Park sat just below the swimming pool with a little playground in between. Behind the right field fence flowed the winding Cove creek. It was just a good place for kids to have fun and to play—whether official games or the always challenging cup-ball games.

The game was about to start and we had a habit of having the starting pitcher go out on the mound and throw a few to Coach Herb, helping him gauge what to call. The Kings were out of their dugout swinging their bats and I was about to take the mound. "Wait a sec, Bob, I've got something for you," Coach Herb called. "When you get out there if I give you a thumbs up, I want you to sail a fastball over my head into the fence."

I started to say, "Why do . . ."

Coach stopped me in mid-sentence. He was always cutting me off. "Just do what I say," he said.

What I didn't think of was this: behind the fence were a couple of sheets of plywood that would help the ball not to stick into the fence. And when a ball came at a good pace or fouled back it made a very loud "WHAM." After a few pitches, Coach saw the Kings inching closer to get a good look at the opposing pitcher. He gave me the thumbs up and I sailed a fastball over his outstretched arm and, "WHAM!" as the ball catches everybody's attention. I saw all the Kings looking toward me and after a couple more pitches, we repeated the act. I was trying not to giggle and almost peed in my pants, holding back the laughter. Coach was yelling for me to hit the mitt. He let out a "That's awful," as I walked off the mound.

The Cardinals huddled up and hit the field. The first King batter gently stepped into the batters box and managed to swing at just one pitch before walking back to the dugout—the first strike-out victim. We managed to score 5 runs with little Sam Bower getting 3 hits and 3 RBI's by stepping into the pitch and making good contact. Coach Herb's pre-game antics paid off dearly. By the game's end, I had struck out 15 of the 18 outs and gave up just 1 hit for a 5-0 win.

A Little Gamesmanship Can Work Real Well at Times

Our success was short-lived. After a 30 minute break, we took on the Stallions and played pretty good ball, but nothing good becomes of it. Our well-hit balls landed in their gloves and we went down 2-1. Brett hit his first home-run of the year, but we fell just short of winning.

After Coach Herb talked to us, Dad said, "Great game pitching, just tough luck in that last one."

Mom didn't say anything, just squatted down and gave me a hug.

"It would have been great to have won that last one," I said.

"You played your tail off and all of you gave your best," Dad said.

I said, "I learned from you that the winning part is a lot better than having a good game."

"By the way, you really settled down when it came game time pitching," Dad said.

I almost laughed. "No, that was Coach Herb's idea to show them a few wild pitches since I hadn't pitched against them this year."

Dad had a big smile come across his face and said, "That's pretty good there," towards Mom.

Quint caught up with us and proclaimed that his team won the big cup-ball game going on close to the creek. "Nobody fell in the creek and I got on base every-time." He smiled at our parents and then turned to me. "Sorry I missed it," he said.

Winning Is the Bottom Line

As we were about to get in the car, when I noticed Sam was walking toward us with his mother waiting on him. "Sam," I said, "Have you had a shake from the Rebel Drive-In yet?"

"Nope," he said.

"Mom, will you tell Mrs. Bower we can drop Sam off?"

"Sure" she said.

I said, "Sam, this is my Dad, Coach Hayes."

My dad said, "Sam, that was some games you just played, especially that first one."

We pulled into the drive-in and Sam asked what the best flavors were. "Peanut Butter is my top choice."

"You're joking," he said, very serious. "I think I will stick to chocolate myself."

We sat outside on the concrete tables and Sam got his shake from Mom. "Thanks, Mrs. Hayes," he said.

Before he could take a sip I shout, "What are ya gonna do, Sam?"

Sam sighed. "Will I ever live that down?"

"Not for a few years, anyway," I said.

Dad sat down with us and I told him the stepping back story.

"That is pretty good coaching from Herb and I see it paid off real well. Just keep working hard Sam," he said.

"Coach Hayes, being new in town, it helped that Bob and Brett made me feel welcome. They helped a lot."

As the last of the slurps finally ended, we dropped Sam off and said goodnight. After two games, it didn't take long before Quint and I were fast asleep.

A Little Encouragement Can Go a Long Way

PART II

That summer was unlike any other we had experienced. Although everybody still called my dad Coach, he was enjoying his new job with the County Board of Education. But this meant he was no longer in charge of the city swimming pool since. That was now Coach Sloan's job. At least, Sharon still had her job as lifeguard and, sometimes, Stew filled in as well. We really trusted Sharon, ever since Quint's unusual water debacle.

The transition went quite well and it got to be fun doing little errands for Coach Sloan. At the pool he was always drawing plays and meeting everyone. Coach was human in the fact that he noticed Mrs. Paulson. Some things just don't change. Being coach at Stuart was a serious position because most everyone was interested in the Rebels and always had questions for the coach.

We were talking football one hot day and Coach asked me what I thought about the team coming back to be under him. I was eager to give my opinion. I said, "Coach, you've got to replace a few key positions and you may need to put more load on the backs without Stew at QB. You may be able to use some of the speed to our advantage with Will and Craig coming back. It is also very good your system is similar and spring training went pretty good."

Coach Sloan grinned. "Like I said, when we met at your house, I may have to put you on my staff. We may be able to catch some early teams by surprise since they won't have a lot to go on."

Know the Strengths of Your Team

A few days of the week, Pete and I would spend our late afternoons at the stadium with Curt and Stew working out: running, throwing, and kicking. Mr. Red Parker had the right contacts and Curt was going to play for the Cadets of Army at West Point. Stew, on the other hand, had narrowed it down to Northeast Alabama and Tillman University, just below Birmingham. During that time the major universities in the state, Auburn and Alabama would sign up most players, since they had the money and no limits on scholarships. Because of this, a player like Stew, even though he had been selected to play in the high school All-Star Classic, would often have to play the waiting game.

I remember hearing Dad tell Mr. Red that he felt bad pushing a player who happened to be his son. "But that's one of your responsibilities as a coach," Mr. Red had said.

But the waiting game ended soon enough. The answer came the next day at the city pool, of all places. Coach Sloan was behind the counter acting busy, when a tall gentleman, about 6'3," walked up. "Hey, Coach Dale, how're you doing? You ready to take a dive?" Coach Sloan asked.

"No," Coach Dale said, very seriously, "I made my way over this afternoon after we had a staff meeting. After talking to you the other night, I looked at a couple more films and you were right, the Hayes kid does the right thing too many times."

Coach Sloan looked at me and whistled for Sharon to take his place behind the counter. "I think you may be here at the right time."

Sharon got to the counter and I was all eyes trying to figure out what was going on, especially after this tall man has mentioned the Hayes kid. "Sharon, this is Coach Dale Clark of Northeast Alabama. Coach, this is Sharon Hayes, Stewart's sister and cheerleader for our Rebel team."

Coach Clark said, "Your dad has been a good friend and a heck of coach. How's Mr. Parker treating him?"

Sharon smiled and answered calmly. She said, "He says everything is going well, but football season isn't here yet.

"Okay, Bob, before you bust," Coach Sloan said when he looked at me. "Coach Clark, this young guy is Paul's middle son, Bob. I know you will get to know each other very well."

I smiled and shook hands with Coach Clark and I was amazed. I thought Doc West had strong hands, but Coach Clark's hands were the largest I had ever seen.

"Nice to meet you, Bob. I guess you were one of the ball boys I saw on film and at the game with Marion last year."

"You noticed?" I asked and felt about a foot taller. I didn't know this, but Coach Sloan had called Stew to come by the pool and just then we saw him driving around the curve to park his tan VW.

As Stew walked up, he heard his name being shouted out by Quint, on the high dive, wanting him to watch his so-called cannonball. Splash went Lil' Brother and Stew looked over to see Sharon and I staring at him.

"Stewart you remember, Coach Clark," Coach Sloan said.

"Sure," Stew said as the two shook hands. They make their way over to a table and they each had a coke.

"What is up, Coach Sloan?" I asked.

"I hope Stewart . . ."

"Call him Stew, Coach. Otherwise, he'll think he's in some kind of trouble."

"Okay," Coach Sloan said. "I hope *Stew* is about to become part of the Northeast Alabama Owls.

"Thank Goodness," Sharon said. "This waiting period has been eating at him."

After about 15 minutes, I saw Stew grinning as both stood up and shook hands. The two walked over to us and Coach Clark said goodbye to everyone. Finally he said to Stew, "I'll see you and your parents around six at Paul's Diner."

"Coach Sloan, Coach Clark says he talked with you and it got his curiosity up and helped his decision making," Stew said.

"I had talked with your dad and he felt uncomfortable asking where they were at with their decision about the QB. And time was closing in. I think you'll be a good fit. You may have to be a little patient, but I'm glad it is all settled now."

"It won't be far to see your home games" I said.

Sharon said congratulations and kind of gave Stew a hug, something I had never seen before.

Quint came up then, to get a score, per se, on his high dive attempts. He also asked who the tall man was. Sharon said that was Stew's new head football coach.

"Okay," Quint said. "Watch this before you go."

We all laughed.

"I see that Quint is excited for you," Sharon said.

Stew said, "Thanks, Coach Sloan, for your help."

"Well, you earned it. Just keep working hard with Curt."

In the *Marion Journal* the next day, there was a photo of Stew signing to play for the Owls. It was the first time in Stuart school history that two players had signed to play in the same year. Casey Toms went on to say that Coach Dale Clark was in his third year as head coach at Northeast Alabama. Coach Clark had played for "Bear" Bryant at Kentucky and was a promising player, sure to play pro-ball, until he blew out his left knee in the Wildcats' last game of the season. He worked as a graduate assistant while finishing his degree. Then he moved on to Western Kentucky for five years, serving the last two as defensive coordinator. At thirty-one years of age he had become one of the youngest head coaches, at any level, in the country.

When Toms asked him to evaluate Stew, he said the usual spiel about being an incoming freshman—it was always tough and he has quite a bit to learn. But, said Coach Clark, being the son of a good high school coach would be a plus.

Being only forty minutes from the Northeast Alabama campus provided Stew the opportunity to workout a few days of the week with some of the other team members. A few he had played against before, so he wasn't as isolated as Curt would be at Army. Stew had a knack not to draw too much attention to himself and his position being a QB, especially when there were going to be about five or six in all. Coach Clark had said that he would have a couple of transfers to come in, along with the three from spring practice, but he wasn't pleased with their 4 and 6 record the previous year. Getting a head-start would be helpful.

Take Advantage of Your Opportunities

After a couple of weeks of practice, the *Marion Journal* had reports daily, with both Alabama and Auburn to read about. The *Journal* did keep people informed about the Owls and it was surprising to read a story about Stew in the Sunday morning paper. Casey Toms did an interview with Coach Clark and asked him how Stew was doing. This lead to the caption of "Diamond in the Rough." Quint said he would pay attention when they had a picture to put it into perspective. The coach said one thing that would be welcome was this: it is the first year that true freshmen would be allowed to play in a game. In the past, you either had to play junior varsity or just be on the scout team which was pure hell a couple days a week. Major colleges still had a couple of years to go before true freshman could play.

There was a lot of excitement in Stuart with the onset of football. The Rebels had a new coach in Alex Sloan, coming off a banner year. Most everyone kept up with either Alabama or Auburn and then hopefully Stew added a bit of interest to the Owls. The first game was up-coming and Northeast Alabama faced an afternoon game at Tillman University. This was the same Tillman University that Stew almost went to.

It was nice and toasty outside, around 90 degrees. Somehow, it was different watching a game knowing Stew was on the sideline. We were all there in support of Big Brother. Tillman got off to a great start after some Owls' mistakes and took a 28-7 lead. The Owls couldn't do anything on offense and scored on a blocked punt. In the middle of the third quarter Tillman kicked a field goal to lead 31-10.

I tugged at Dad's arm to make sure we saw Stew throwing the ball on the sideline. As the offense went out, so did Stew. The Owls gained a first down on two running plays and then, on the next play, he faked it to the half back, turned and lofted a long and high pass that #80, Bobby Snead, ran under for a 68 yard touchdown play—that was on his first collegiate throw. The extra point was missed but, at 31-16, there was a little excitement for the Owls. Stew didn't make any mistakes and, with time running out, he threw another scoring pass, making it 31-29. They had to go for 2 to tie. Stew rolled to the right and had to reverse back to the left, dodging two defenders. His pass bounced off the receiver's hand. Close but no cigar.

With no expectations and rebounding from that far behind, it was almost like Northeast Alabama had won. Stew gave out the right compliments to his teammates and was just trying to do all he could to help the Owls win.

Stew was able to come home for lunch the next day, Sunday, and Bobby Snead, a true freshman as well, came with him. Of course, Mom went all out for Sunday meal after THAT game. And, of course, the talk was about the game. Bobby said, "Stew, I've got to ask, on that first touchdown pass, where did you come up with that rainbow throw?"

Stew laughed. "Believe it or not when I was in the ninth grade, I had thrown a couple of interceptions, and Mom here had told me that I needed to put more air under the long throws. I saw you just getting ahead of the DB and wanted to let you run under it."

"I thought your Dad was the coach in the family," Bobby said and everyone chuckled.

Be Ready for Your Chance

All started to flow pretty well. By the fifth game, Quint and I were able to start watching the Owl games from the sidelines. Before the game, we were able to help retrieve loose kicks and throws, making us feel somewhat important. We got to see firsthand that the hits were harder, the players were faster, and we learned quite a few new words that would get us in trouble if we got caught using them.

As the season makes its way toward the last game, there was a specific play that changed the course of athletics for a specific person. If I hadn't seen it, I wouldn't have thought it was that big of a deal, but I saw it. Pete was with Quint and me at the game. Doc West was there with Dad in the stands. Mom had to be out of town with Sharon for a cheerleading competition.

During the first half, Pete and I were discussing the merits of playing football and basketball. Pete said he was more partial to playing basketball and seemed to stand out more in the games he'd played. This was coming on the heels of junior high football always going against the first team in practice and getting the feeling of being a tackling dummy.

The air was turning colder into the third quarter, being mid-November. Stew had the Owls on a drive and we young ones were watching about twenty yards downfield as the play happened. Bobby Snead ran an out pattern, nothing exceptional. Quint and Pete were talking with their hands in their pockets, staying warm. Stew had to hurry his throw and the ball sailed over the hands of Snead. "Watch," was all I got out of my mouth as the ball caught Pete right below his belt buckle. With his hands still in the coat pockets, all Pete could do was fall over sideways and curl up. Quint and I did our best not to laugh, knowing where he just got hit. One of the managers came over to pick Pete, who is still curled into a ball, up. He then took him over to the bench and to lay him on his side. Pete, at least, started to breathe again but was moaning pretty extensively. A few of the players on the sideline just shook their heads.

In the stands Dad said to Doc, "I believe Pete is down."

"Yeah, I saw that, but there's nothing I can do to help him right now."

"Poor Pete," Dad said.

After a few minutes the manager asks Pete how he feels.

Pete said, "You're kidding me?"

The manager replied, "I can give you a bag of ice to put on it."

Quint had tried not to laugh, but, now, the circumstances had gotten the best of him.

The Owls had to kick a field goal, in case you were wondering.

We helped Pete to his feet and he waddled instead of walked. The clock wound down and the Owls lost by 3. The manager came over and gave Pete the game ball. He said, "Well, kid, you deserve this."

After a few minutes Pete looked at me and said, "Bob that does it for me. It's now 100% basketball."

Quint said, "I can't wait to tell Stew."

The normal after-game conversations took on a different twist now. Quint started trying to tell Stew what had happened and warned him not to stand too close to Pete. The Owls, with that last game, finished the season 4 and 5. The worst loss was by 8 points. "A lot of would-haves, could-haves and should-haves," said Stew. That stuck in my mind.

That next spring football started to look up. I was in line to be the starting QB for the Rebel Junior High. Our spring training didn't last as long at my level. It did give us a chance to play together as a unit and we had a pretty good team all working together.

Coach Clark, at Northeast Alabama, hired a new offensive coordinator, Ken Duncan, from Alabama. He had been "Bear" Bryant's quarterback coach. Coach Bryant, being good friends with Coach Clark, felt he would like the fit and wanted to help his assistant to a new position. The Tide had changed their style of attack and, in doing so, Coach Duncan brought in a high profile transfer with him, named Thad Bishop.

One thing happened during spring practice for the Owls. The style of offense Coach Duncan fancied fit Stew like a glove. Plus, Thad just got out worked and out hustled. Coach Clark was glad of the effort Stew had put in, and the players grouped together like never before.

At the end of the semester, getting ready for summer break, Stew and Coach Clark were talking in his office. A beep came over the intercom, reminding him he was supposed to be in Tuscaloosa to meet with a couple of coaches. "Ride with me Stew," he said and off they went for a brisk two hour drive.

"Coach, you ever raced at Daytona," Stew asked.

"No, but if I get pulled over by a state trooper, and I tell him I'm on my way to see Coach Bryant, we'll probably get an escort." They got there in real good time without hurting any other drivers.

Inside the vast coaching offices at Alabama, Coach Clark was shaking a few hands and talking with a couple of the assistants he knew and had played with in the past. Stew said he was looking at a couple of photos on the wall and a deep voice came from behind him through a just opened door. "Son, come in for a minute and have a seat," Coach Bryant said.

Stew went in and sat down.

"Your dad is Coach Paul Hayes, right?" he asked.

"Yes sir, I'm Stewart, but now my dad's with the County Board of Education."

Coach Bryant said, "I had heard about that. It sounds like a good decision to me." "I've met him a few times watching games over the years and I liked how he coached his teams at Stuart. Coach Dale told me that you stepped up, took the challenge, and, so far, have kept your hold on the QB job."

Stew nodded. "I've tried," he said.

Coach Bryant went on. "I like my boys to be there when counted on. You know, what you do can speak a lot louder than what you say."

"Thanks, Coach Bryant. The system Coach Duncan installed is just an improved version of my dad's and I know it quite well. I mainly learned what not to do."

Coach Bryant nodded. "Stewart, you keep working and get those guys playing together and have a great season. Tell your dad I said hello and if you are down here and need anything, just give me a call."

"Thanks a lot for the advice." Stew smiled. "It was great to finally meet you, Coach."

As they walked out of the office Coach Bryant asked Coach Dale where the hell he'd been and they went in and talked for a short while.

Stew told me he had no idea that opportunity would happen and he was in tall cotton.

What You Do Can Speak a Lot Louder
Than What You Say

The ride back to the Northeast Alabama campus is not as brisk.
Stew said, "You didn't tell me Coach Bryant was who you were coming to see."
"I was glad he had a little time to talk with you, Stew. We talk a good bit, he and I, and I still get a lot of advice from him. When I was at Kentucky, he was like a Father to me."
"Stew, we have a good chance to do well this year. We have a good line on both sides of the ball and that will give us stability. I believe we will have more speed and Coach Duncan has good experience manning the game." He looked out at the highway. "I wanted to get firsthand knowledge from Coach Bryant to help our situation."
"What situation is that," Stew asked.
"I think the staff has got a good fix with contacts in our area with some ideal summer jobs for a lot of you players. Alabama does a good job of that and it helps keep them together in a good way as well. I wanted to make sure I had the right final approach."

Bobby Snead was terrible at doing laundry. That summer he was staying with Stew and Rod Yancey, the center, in a trailer off campus. There were quite a few more that had also gotten on at the Richton Pipe Foundry, and after work they would all get together and workout about three or four days a week. "Stew, I thought we were to get a cushy job. They are working our asses off," said Rod.
"I think that was Coach Clarks' idea," Bobby answered.
After a couple of weeks, Quint was away at church camp with Matt Townsend, and I got to go spend a week with Stew at the trailer. I got to hang out in the morning at a pool where Bobby's girlfriend, a cheerleader, was the lifeguard. At night it was interesting: the players got to the Old Hickory restaurant and just sign the ticket with their discount card. It was also funny how some of the orders, like a fresh strawberry pie, would make their way out in a to-go box. The guys, and some girls, ate well.

I got the chance to run, throw and catch with the Owl players and learned quite a bit. One afternoon I was on the sideline and Coach Clark sat with me watching the guys finish some of their drills. The coaches could watch but not be actively involved. "Are they working hard Lil' Hayes?" Coach asked.

"I see better timing and trust. That's something I haven't seen in a couple of years."

"What do you mean, Bob?"

I looked out at the field and then over at Coach Clark. "It seemed like players were waiting for something to happen instead of making it happen. I think they know and trust more. I think Coach Duncan's skills allow them to do more. He has an extra option or decision and it helps to get more involved in the play."

Coach Clark looked surprised. "Coach Sloan was right that you had some good knowledge about the game."

"Thanks, Coach," I said.

The annual opening game with Tillman University was here. I was enjoying my status as play holder for kicks in warm-ups when punter Kyle Hanson was kicking. Then I also liked be able to catch a few punts and kick-offs. I had the regular duty of running the balls in and out during the game. Quint would be there, too, holding them and helping to keep them clean and dry.

Some coaches were very skilled at circumventing the rules. At that time in college football if a receiver stepped out of bounds, on his own, he could then step back onto the field and catch the ball. Well, Tillman took that to a whole new level. Their team would line up along the sideline and the receiver would run off the field, run behind the players, and back on to receive a long pass from the QB. The receiver would be wide open and able to jog right into the end zone.

At the half, the game was tied at 14. Walking out of the locker room, Coach Clark called to me and said, "Lil' Hayes this half run the balls in from their side and if you see them lining up to run the lay-out play holler at Ralph, LB, and he'll know what to do."

"Gotcha, Coach," I said. I was always glad to help.

Into the third quarter the Owls went up by a field goal. A little later they were forced to punt. I heard, "All up after the punt," and sure enough on the second play the receiver came over to the side and the Tillman team was all in a line. I hollered at Ralph Morris, our middle linebacker, and both backers blitz and sack the QB as he was dropping back to make the long throw. The Tillman coaches started yelling and we got chased off their sideline. I got an assist that won't show in the stats and a pat on the back from Coach Clark. The Owls won their first by 4, beating a good Tillman team 24-20.

Another past collegiate rule was this: during a timeout only one player could come over to the sideline. Coach Clark started using me to carry extra instructions to the huddle. It helped to elevate my perceived status and made me a part of the team.

At practice Monday I told Coach Reed, "Have I got a play for you," and he listened. By the end of practice we were working on the lay-out pass.

Knowing the Rules Can Be a Big Advantage

The Stuart Junior High had won the first game by 18 points. We played a clean game and Zack Morris, who has become one of my closest friends, showed out with his speed scoring 3 times. Zack would just run as fast as he needed to and with the look of no effort at all. We had a second down and 6 from our own 40. Coach Reed called right 18 option. As the ball was snapped our full back went left. I took some steps back looking for room and Zack hollers, "Bob." I pitched it to him and he started right, then made a circle left, and cut back to his right, outrunning the defense for a 60 yard touchdown run. I filed this play, or better yet the process of this play, into my memory bank.

Don't Panic

I thought Dad pulled out all stops when it came time for motivating Stuart to play their rival Dalton. Coach Clark raised my level of awareness a lot higher. Coach Duncan had control over the offense and he was ready for, perhaps, the top game on the schedule. The University of Tennessee at Winston (UT-W) was ranked second in the nation in Division II. Last year they, finished ranking third in the AP Poll, scored a couple of times late in the game to rub it in on the Owls, and at midfield Coach was shaking his finger in the face of the UT-W coach instead of shaking his hand. Revenge was eminent.

After that game, due to some locker room renovation, the team had to dress at their basketball coliseum which meant getting on a bus for a short ride. The bus got full and I was sitting in a front seat and got to hear the best post game speech I have ever heard. Before the bus started Coach Clark stood up and pointed at each player and said, "In 365 days they are going to be toting their whupped ass back to Tennessee." He sat down and that was it.

Speaking with Conviction and Right to the Point Can Work Wonders

Playing for Kentucky, while in school, Coach Clark hated everything about any school from Tennessee, especially UT-Winston over the last few years. Tuesday evening Dad was talking to Stew on the phone as they did most weeks during the season. I walked by the kitchen and Dad had a puzzled look on his face. Suddenly he started to laugh. I heard him say, "Son, now you know how important this game is to Coach."

"What was so funny?" I asked Dad at the end of the call.

"Well," Dad said, "As you know Coach Clark hasn't beaten UT-Winston since he has been at NE Alabama. Stew was a little alarmed, as was his roommate Bobby about something."

"What?" I couldn't wait to hear.

Dad smiled at me. "After supper last night Coach had the trainer to give the players a vitamin C tablet with their meal. Turns out the next day when all of them went to take a leak, they all peed orange. Turns out it was a harmless kidney pill for an exam, but pretty dang funny to me."

Mom laughed. "Paul, I'm surprised you didn't think of that at Stuart."

The Rebel Junior High goes to 3 and 0 by downing Collins. My stats looked good with a couple of touchdown passes. But, the truth of the matter was that both were short swing passes to Zack, to get him outside, and he did all the rest with one for 54 and the other for 62 yards. Our defense shut them out. Dad said he liked what we did by playing within ourselves. He liked how we didn't make mistakes.

The warm-up for the Owls game was intense. The players knew this was their big chance to step up and show how all the hard work has paid off. On the field the routines stayed in place. I started to go hold some snaps for Rod Yancey, our center, and he instructed me to stand over to his left about 15 yards away. He put his hand on the ball and zipped a couple over toward me and then says, "That's good."

As the captains, Stew was one for this game, make their way to the center of the 50 yard line for the coin toss both teams were lined up behind their respective captains and the finger pointing was going both ways. Trust me, a lot of the players were not happy about some of the others Moms. I'll leave it at that. The fans feed off of the players actions and it was the loudest I had ever heard at that time from the fans.

The Owls kicked off and Carter Taylor made a big hit to set the tone for the game. 3 and out went UT-W and Stew took over and faked a couple of handoffs to the tail-back. He kept around the end for 12 and 16 yards. Then he dropped back to pass but ran a QB draw for 20 yards. Stew faked again and then hit Bobby down the sideline to go up 7-0.

At that time, I had never seen the velocity of some of those hits. At the half the Owls were up 17-10 on the #2 team in the nation.

In the locker room, when I was about to go out, Coach Clark called me over. "Lil' Hayes, after we return the kick, stall a bit in getting the ball back to the official. We want to get our offense out there in a huddle."

"Gotcha, Coach," I said, even more happy to help than usual. I knew better than to ask, but I was sure he was up to something.

Back in the game, Bobby Snead returned the kick to the right sideline. I started to walk to the official and I looked back at Quint who is holding another football.

"Wrong ball," I shouted to him. "Pitch me that one." I let the ball slip out of my hands and kicked it a couple of yards before picking it up. "Sorry Ref," I said and then I turned to Quint: "Dang it, Quint."

"What'd I do wrong?" he asked. He was trying to do his best, after all.

"Nothing, just watch," I said—we had their players attention.

In the meantime, the Owl's team was huddled up in the middle of the field waiting on my antics with the ref. The ball was placed on the right hash mark with the UT-W defense lined up at the ball. Rod Yancey jogged over to the ball—he usually broke the huddle first. He got there and the whole offensive unit, being in the middle of the field, turned and set real fast. Bobby Gross, the speedy tailback, caught the long sideways snap from Rod and turned to his left. He took off as the Owl offense all peeled to their right. It looked like a gate closing. With precision from the linemen, he coasted 74 yards for a long touchdown run. UT-W never knew what hit them.

Know How to Set Up Your Special Plays

Instead of doing what worked in the first half, Coach Duncan started running traps and short passes. He totally had the number #2 team in the country at his mercy. The Owls didn't let up and poured it on to shock them, 52-13. Coach Clark finally got his big win and a ride on the players' shoulders to midfield. He told the UT-W coach, "Hank, we're even now."

As I started to walk out, hoping to find Stew, the ref, side-judge, stops me. "Kid," he said, "that was some play you helped set up."

"Thanks," I said.

In the locker room the players were singing a chant: "We don't give a damn about the whole state of Tennessee, the whole state of Tennessee, cause we're from Alabama." Coach Clark calmed them down, but Quint and I were already soaked in all of the excitement.

"Where is Lil' Hayes?" Coach Clark asked. He had a ball in his hand and said, "Bob that was one fine act you two put on. You and Quint deserve this." We got cheers from the whole team and even a hug from Stew and Bobby. Walking out of the locker room Rod Yancey patted me on the back and I said, "Nice warm-up with your snaps. You'll be ready for the shot gun formation now."

As we were making our way outside the locker room, we looked up and Dad was grinning from ear to ear. "Yes, Bob, I watched and saw the whole play. You two did a good job," Dad said and he patted us on the head.

Coach Duncan stopped by to say hi to Dad and shook our hands. "Coach, I liked the way you kept the pressure on them. Too many try to sit on the lead and let a team like Winston back in the game."

Coach Duncan smiled. "Thanks a lot, Coach Hayes, and what about these two, huh? I see the apple doesn't fall too far from the tree."

Zack Morris picked an awful time to have the flu. The Junior High Rebels were to play College Heights Junior High, but our speedster was out. Coach Reed shuffled our backfield around. We had planned to run some misdirection at them along with some fake and go patterns but Coach said we will have to see what happens.

Thursday, game night was here, and it also was not good that it started pouring rain about 5 o'clock. Being undersized and sloppy with our footing, we were really against the odds.

We scored first on a hook and go. Our quickness allowed us to block a punt for another score. Toward the end of the third quarter, winning 13-8, we ran a post pattern, but when I was throwing the ball, it just slipped right out of my hand, into the arms of the middle linebacker. They scored to take the lead 14-13. With less than a minute left in the game, our left end was uncovered. I made sure he was lined up properly, dropped back and arched a long pass that Hoody Myers hauled in and raced for the winning touchdown. BUT, as the ball was in the air, I saw the official to my right drop a penalty flag. The referees got together and the call was that the left end was lined up off-sides. We went ape, to put it nicely.

We hollered at the refs, who were getting off the field as fast as they can. It seemed to me that I could have gone for any call but that one. Then to see the flag dropped with the ball in the air just added more fuel to the fire. I had seen my share of bad calls and had heard Dad chew out his legions of refs but the score remained 14-13.

On the short bus ride home, Coach Reed called me up to sit with him. "Bob, you helped to keep us in the game. Sometimes, especially on the road, you are going to get some calls against you. Just remember to try your best to not let it get to that point if at all possible."

"I hate it for our guys, Coach. We played our butts off against those bigger players and then had it taken away like that."

"When we are on the road, you won't see me holding onto the ball. We played winning football, let's just take our last two for the county title," Coach said.

Sometimes You Have to Take the Bitter with the Bitter

I came out of the locker room and Dad was there, holding a big golf umbrella and waiting on me. "That's just damn bad luck, Bob. I'm proud of the way you hung in there," he said as he rubbed the top of my head.

I got into the car and Mom handed me a peanut butter shake and a burger they just picked up. All she said was, "Sorry, Son."

"I know would've, could've and should've," I said.

"Sounds like you've been hanging around Stew," Dad replied.

The next afternoon Coach Sloan called me into his office. "Bob," he said, "That was some tough game you led last night."

"I'm sorry about the interception. Charley was open and the ball just came out so bad." I wanted to explain it to him. "I've had my share of throwing wet balls and you saw the one that went to Hoody, but the bad one just had a glob of mud and I hate it."

"No, Bob. I just wanted to let you know you kept everyone together with Zack out and I'm glad it hurts because it shows me y'all care." He looked at me and smiled. "I'm going to be counting on you in the next 3 years so hang in there and keep working."

"Thanks, Coach," I said.

Then Coach grinned. "This is the first chance I have had to talk with you, and I know that you know, so fill me in on that 'waterbucket' play the Owls used against UT-W."

I laughed. "I'd be glad to change the subject, Coach."

Two weeks later was our last game of the year and it was against Dalton Junior High for the Concord County championship. Both teams were undefeated in county play. Luckily, we were back to full strength and ready to go. What made this game unique in our area was that we started out playing against the same guys in little league baseball and midget football. In all-star baseball we were even teammates for a while. But it was always fun to try and whip each other's butts once we get on the field.

Dalton crowded the line to contain Zack, starting out, and we stayed conservative a little too long. We were down 8-0 at halftime. Coach Reed was going over a couple of changes when the dressing room door opened and then slammed shut. Coach Sloan stepped up and let us have it: "Don't even think about moving forward playing like you are. You've got the largest crowd behind you but still it kind of stinks out there. Now get your butts in gear!" We knew Coach Reed was our junior high coach but Coach Sloan was "The Man" at Stuart.

A Little Motivation Can Go a Long Way

We opened it up a bit and moved down the field. On the 20 yard line, going in, I pitched it out to Zack sweeping right and I carried out my fake to the left and nobody looked. Zack stopped and threw a pass that I caught for a touchdown and, with an option right for the conversion, we were tied 8-8. On our next possession we had a good mix of runs and play action passes, since they were still crowding the line, and we scored again, 16-8.

We were about to get the ball back and Coach Reed called for, Right 28 sweep, and then a jumble lay-out pass. After the sweep we broke the huddle and the flanker and tailback were both standing behind the fullback. I turned and hollered, "Zack you're out," and waved him off. We caught them watching us and I took the snap, dropped back and arched a long pass after Zack turns up the field wide open for a 65 yard touchdown play, 22-8.

With that touchdown, Dalton got out of sync. They tried a long pass which Zack intercepted and nobody could catch him to get our winning score 30 to 8. "That's what I'm talking about," Coach Sloan yelled in the locker room.

Coach Reed let us know that when we played together good things would happen. "None of those plays work without everybody doing their job. It's been a great effort in the second half tonight, guys."

It felt good when Quint came over and said good game to Zack and Me. Then as we finished getting dressed, I turned around and there were Stew and Bobby Snead standing there. A grin painted my face and Stew told Zack and me good game and introduced him to Bobby. "Bobby," Stew said. "I think I've got you somebody here that will give you a run for your money."

Bobby laughed. "Yeah, after watching Zack run through their whole defense I'll keep a hold on to my dollars."

"We've got to get back to campus, but we wanted to say great game guys," they both said as they left.

I shouted to them: "We'll see y'all Saturday. Zack's coming with me."

Beating Dalton was fun and an honor. Even though it was only junior high, a lot of supporters stayed to greet us as we came out to head home. Our cheerleaders were still there to congratulate us, too, but all that was really on our minds was that shake and burger. Those thoughts would change, of course, in the upcoming years.

The Owls played another in-state rival from the south in Tate University. It was a very tight game all the way through. The Generals from Tate matched up very well with Northeast Alabama. With 6 minutes to go in the game and the ball on their own 10 yard line the Owls were down 7 to 0. Play after play Stew led them all the way down to the 5 yard line. The highlight was a 30 yard pass to Bobby Snead on third and 15 to keep the drive alive. With 25 seconds left and 3rd down Stew called time out to talk with Coach Clark.

"Hell, Stew," the coach said. "I've gotten you this far can't you get it in from here?"

A smile came across Stew's face then and he shook his head.

I was standing there with the balls and Zack was behind me.

Coach Clark looked around. "What do you think," he asked.

I thought he was talking to me and I said, "We've been running the toss all game and Stew would be wide open for a throwback pass." I paused and nobody said anything. Coach Duncan says, "Tell Gross, the halfback, it's his time to shine and if you aren't in the clear the ball better make it to the bleachers."

They listened to me and, sure enough, the play worked, just like ours had on Thursday against Dalton. The Owls got a touchdown.

The celebration was short lived because Coach signaled for 2 and the win. Everybody was on their feet as Stew rolled to his right, was cut off and circled back left to find the tight end breaking his pattern off to make room for a catch. Owls won 8 to 7 and Quint ran over and was the first one to jump toward Stew. Their picture together made the *Marion Ledger* sports front page, with the headline "Brother O Brother, Still Perfect."

Zack told me this: "If I hadn't heard that myself, I would never have believed you."

In the after game interview, Casey Toms asked Coach Clark how he came up with the play. "Well," Coach Clark said. "Believe it or not, Stewart saw his younger brother, at QB, use that play just the other night with the same results. We have worked on the play before, in practice, but never in a game, till now."

"You are kidding me," Toms said.

Coach laughed. "No sir, I've got witnesses."

Coach Duncan came over to pat me on the back and said, "Boy you may have to sit with me in the press-box to call plays next week."

Zack and I listened to the players singing a chant again and enjoyed it all. We were about to walk out, when Coach Clark hollered, "Lil' Hayes hold on."

He came over to us and handed us each a game jersey. "Thanks, Coach," we said.

Stew was about to get in the shower and I showed him the jersey. I said, "I get to take mine with me."

Stew grinned, "Well, great call, Bob, I'm glad it worked."

"I bet you sure are," I said, grinning with him.

"What's with the jersey boys?" Dad asked as we walked out of the locker room where he and Mom and others were waiting for Stew.

Zack looked at Dad and said, "Coach Hayes you saw the same play Bob caught Thursday against Dalton? During the timeout Stew and Coach Clark were trying to come up with a play and Bob called for the throwback thinking they were asking him. So, we've got new jerseys."

Mom looked at me in amazement: "No wonder you're both smiling so much."

Then, Stew and Bobby walked out together shaking hands and accepting congratulations from all the folks standing around. Two young boys came up and asked if they would sign their programs and I looked at Dad. I said, "You'll have to widen the door at the house so Stew will be able to get his head through there now."

All was truly well with the Hayes family.

A week later the headline on the front page looked like this: "NE Alabama 10-0: Hayes Leads Owls to First Ever Undefeated Season."

It was great being able to witness the season like I did, from the summer on, being on the sideline doing my little part. The serious commitment everyone had was a treasure to behold. Watching the fan base grow and grow with each victory and listening to the cheers was truly exciting, especially with your older brother at quarterback

Commitment Is Crucial from All Involved

Christmas season was special this year with the Hayes family and for Stuart in general. Dad was enjoying watching all of us and being a proud papa. Mom enjoyed the cooking and having Stew bring friends with him to the house. Sharon's friends seemed to find their way over to visit whenever there were extra guys around. Quint and I liked being around the players and listening to their stories. It was also funny to watch them, sometimes. They really thought they were cool with the girls. Quint thought it was disgusting, but my views were starting to change, at least on that subject.

A couple of days before Christmas I was with Stewart in downtown Marion. It was nice and cold and you had to bundle up going from store to store. We were about to grab lunch at the West Marion Café, noted for their plate lunches and strawberry pie. About the same time up walked Gary Patterson, from Dalton. He had just played his last year at Georgia. Gary and Stew both shook hands and we went in and sat down together. "How are you doing, Bob? You still doing some coaching?" Gary asked.

The question kind of embarrassed me. "You answer that one, Stew." As we ate Stew told him about the Tate game and Gary said, "Well, now. I can believe it."

Gary looked around the café. "Stew," he said after awhile. "From all I read in the Ledger, I wish we had you this past year. We were just a few plays away from going to a bowl game."

I was ready to make a joke now. "Gary, don't say too much. Stew's cap doesn't fit him as it is."

"Would you boys like some strawberry pie?" the waitress asked, passing by. That may have been one of the stupidest questions ever, at least judging by the looks on our faces. We ordered pie all around.

Gary was still feeling serious, though. "Stew, I promise you this next year will be a tough one with more expectations. We went through that a couple of years ago but I know you can handle it."

Stew nodded. "What about you, Gary? Where are you headed next?"

"I've got it lined up to GA this next year. My knees can't handle it anymore. I couldn't accept any of the NFL offers. In fact, I didn't run any at practice for the last few games."

This kind of talk made me think of the future. But, just as I got to thinking, the pie arrived. Life often seemed to work that way in those days.

When all the well wishes were said, we both left with an extra piece of pie to go. We went to a couple of more stores and I realized the whole trip was about Stew trying to bump into Samantha Patterson.

"Well," I said. "At least I got to eat with Gary."

I heard from Stew that word got around from Samantha that she had wanted to meet Stew. But he wanted to try to be cool and "happen to run into her, knowing she was in town shopping." I thought that was ridiculous.

At NE Alabama Coach Duncan brought in a whole new indoor training regiment, the same one Coach Bryant utilized at Alabama. It was just damn hard on the players and it tested their commitment to play. Some years earlier it was said of the indoor workouts at Alabama that Ray Perkins had to step over a passed out Joe Namath on the steps to get into the workout area. But that was another lesson for us: just because you finished undefeated the previous year, doesn't mean you can let up. Stew had a quarterback from Florida State to transfer and, just as in all of his spring seasons before, he had to fight to keep his job. As in past years Stew worked and managed to keep his position.

Don't Let Your Players Get Complacent.
Competition Is a Vital Element

I, on the other hand, learned how it felt to be a blocking dummy. The returning players loved to welcome the incoming guys from the ninth grade to the team with serious contact. It felt good to withstand what they tried to dish out and it did help to really know the offense and have a clue what was coming at you.

That summer Zack and I would go over and workout with Stew and some of his teammates. Bobby Snead took a liking to Zack because they played the same position. He showed him the proper ways to field kicks, punts, and other techniques to utilize his speed. I learned from Rick Manning, the Owls all-conference punter, that I had really good form, but not enough ass to put into the punts just yet.

It Really Helps to Learn from Others

It was unique in our family that we had our Rebel games on Friday and then went off to watch Stew and the Owls on Saturday. There were a lot of times when we would leave at four or five in the morning to drive to Louisiana or Tennessee and be there for the away games.

Both the Rebels and the Owls were off to a 2 and 1 start. Stew was having a tough time with the four new starters on the offensive line. The fourth game took its toll and jammed his right shoulder, his throwing shoulder. Dad had him over to Doc West's office to treat his shoulder and back. One night I came in from a home game and the dance afterwards to find Stew in bed at our house. He would get up at six and meet Doc for care and then drive back to the athletic dorm for the rest of the day. The fun part was I would get to ride back with Stew and just hang out with the players watching TV all day.

It was a real educational process, listening to comments on whatever they were watching in the large TV room of the athletic dorm. I promise you, too, that most of the language was not what you'd hear in a classroom at school, which added to the entertainment value. Whether it was Tarzan, Lone Ranger or the Three Stooges, it was always funny. Being there, and earning our keep on the sidelines, we got to join the team for their pre-game meal. At that time it was usually steaks and potatoes. Nobody ever got sick during the game.

For a couple of games, Stew couldn't throw the ball more than 30 yards but he battled his butt off being a team captain. I felt bad watching him take some awful hits. At times, I had to help him up while getting the ball to the officials. My favorite line to use was this: "You having fun yet?"

At Stuart I was the third team quarterback and for the last three games, due to an injury, became the holder for kicks. All season long I had gotten to go downfield on three kick offs, late in the game, but I always paid attention to what was going on.

It was the last game of the season and our Rebel team was 7 and 2 playing a very strong, non-area game against Sexton High, who were 8 and 1. With four minutes to go in the game it was all tied at 14 apiece. We had the ball and were driving. With one minute left, Sammy Tatum broke free but was hit from behind and Sexton recovered a fumble at their 1 yard line. After a couple of quarterback sneaks and a give to the full back it was fourth down and 7 from their own 4 yard line. Their punter was not too good and was kicking out of the end zone with 36 seconds left.

Don't Waste Your Timeouts

During our last timeout, Zack was about to go and return the punt. I was next to the coach and I said, "Coach Sloan, if we fair catch, we can free kick."

"Do what?" Coach said.

I explained myself. I was always having to explain myself. "After a fair catch you can kick a field goal from that spot and they can't rush."

"Oh, yeah," Coach said. "I think I recall that now."

We hollered at Zack to fair catch no matter what. The Sexton punter got his kick out in a hurry and Zack made the grab at the 32 yard line. Coach told the official our intentions and sent out our kicker, Brett Robbins, with 27 seconds left. Nobody had a clue what is going on.

The Sexton players had to stand 10 yards away. Coach had senior quarterback Al Terry hold for this kick, instead of me, and he placed the tee down on the 32 yard line, left hash mark. Brett lined up, kicked and Rebels lead 17-14. It was the first free kick used in Alabama high school football. Brett squib kicked the kick off and Zack knocked down a Hail Mary pass as the clock hit zero.

Both sides of the packed stands were dumbfounded about what they had just seen. The Sexton faithful were booing and our Rebel fans were shocked but cheering. Papers all over the state mentioned the never before seen outcome. *Marion Ledger's* top writer, Casey Toms, said, "I really thought I had seen it all."

It Helps to Know the Rules

The Owls had their last home game the next day and Zack stayed over after our game with me because we had to get up early to join Dad at Paul's Diner for breakfast. As we took our seat at one of those blue booths, Mr. Red Parker came over to join us. He said, "I'm not going to beat around the bush—what the hell was that ending last night?"

Dad introduced Zack to Mr. Parker and I mentioned the free kick rule. "I saw it a few years earlier in Dad's rule book about scoring," I said.

Zack spoke up: "I just did what they told me but I saw the ball and really thought I had a chance to return it."

"BR did his job and it's history," I said.

The free kick was the buzz around the diner and it was even being talking about at the NE Alabama campus when we got there for the game. Coach Clark and Duncan asked us about the play and kick when we showed up. Coach Clark liked it. He said, "It's an ideal play to use at the right time, especially just before half to make the other team punt and take a shot. At the end of the game with very little time worked quite well last night."

This was Stew's final game and it was the first game in weeks that his shoulder felt good. Coach Clark opened the offense up and Stew responded by throwing 3 touchdowns. The Owls finished with a 7 and 3 record after a 42 to 14 win.

It was a cold Sunday morning in Stuart, Alabama a couple of weeks before Christmas. Dad was in the kitchen cooking breakfast, which he does a great job with, and Stew and I were about to match coins to see who loses and has to go outside to get the *Ledger*. Of course I lost. I put my jacket on and shouted, "I get the sports page first," as I ran out the door, headed for the end of the driveway.

I sat at the table with a cup of hot chocolate to my right. "Oh, oh crap," I said. I kept looking at the paper. "Stew," I said. "What is up with you? Here at Stuart, with your last game, Dad resigned and now at NE Alabama the headline reads that Coach Clark is leaving."

Everyone looked shocked.

I kept reading. "It says that he is going to Kentucky to be the assistant athletic director. All fingers point to Coach Duncan to move up to head coach for the Owls."

Stew nodded like everything made sense now. "I knew he was out of town last week and he had told me he was working on a few things and was going to let me know about them."

Dad weighed in then: "Coach played for "Bear" Bryant at Kentucky and they hope he can put some life back into their football program. I understand," Dad said. "It is a strong pull going back to your school and he was a heck of a player for the Wildcats."

Stew agreed with Dad. "I know he'd been having a little trouble with his knee during the year and wasn't as active in practice. It may have been set up that way to give Coach Ken a good opportunity to be head coach."

When the phone rang and Stew answered it. "Hey Coach," I heard him say, "You have pretty good timing. We were just reading about your move. Congratulations." After a few more little comments Stew handed the phone to Dad.

Dad said, "I'm glad the Kentucky position opened up." Then the next word or words was "Bull shit."

I looked at Stew and say "Must be something pretty serious for Dad to swear so early in the morning."

Dad ended the conversation by saying, "You too, and hope you'll have time to come for dinner before you go."

Dad hung up the phone then and saw two pairs of eyes staring at him. Make that three pairs as Quint came over to the table. "Breakfast close yet?" he asked.

"Okay, Dad," I said. "Tell us what's up."

"Coach Clark had told Red and me a couple of weeks ago about the Kentucky situation and to make things run smooth Coach Duncan will be named in a couple of days. Coach Bryant had a little hand in the mix to help both of them and I think it will work out great."

Dad's answer didn't satisfy me. "But what's with the B.S., Dad?"

"What B.S.?" Quint said.

Dad handed him some hot chocolate. "Just listen," he said. "Stew, with your strong junior year and a good last two games you were on the possible list to play in the Blue-Gray All-Star game in Montgomery, the one on Christmas Day. Coach said he was pulling out all stops and thought you were in." Dad looked around. We were all excited to hear what he would say next.

"Then," Dad went on, "he gets a call the other day. Coach Welch, from Texas A&M, agreed to be one of the coaches, but only if he could bring his own quarterback with him. The kid had gotten hurt during the season and was to be a good high draft possibility. The Blue-Gray guys wanted the high profile coach and it knocked you out."

Sometimes Things Just Don't Go Your Way

Stew surprised me by taking the news so well. "It would have been an honor and a chance, but at least I didn't lose anything or didn't know beforehand," he said.

"Let's eat," Sharon said as she walked into the kitchen and poured herself a cup of coffee. "What have I missed?"

"Just some B.S.," Quint said.

Two weeks later the presents had been opened and the football game was about to kick-off. One of the announcers was talking with the coach and Quint says, "Hope your team loses."

It was Coach Welch of Texas A&M at the Blue-Gray Game. "Would've, could've, but don't know about should've," said Stew. A couple hours later Christmas dinner was history and most everyone was napping throughout the house.

Talk about change. After our first post Christmas basketball practice I was about to leave and Coach Sloan called me into his office. "Bob I want to go over something with you. You have worked hard and made some good contributions as a tenth grader, especially that one very good call on the free kick. There is a family, the Byrd's, who have just moved to Stuart. They have a son, Pat, entering when school starts up. Pat played quarterback this past fall at Wilson High outside of Atlanta. His dad is one of the new managers at the mill and he wants to get settled in before class starts back."

I nodded, not sure where this was going.

Coach nodded back and went on talking. "They know quite a bit about football, his dad was a quarterback for Clemson, and liked what they saw here at Stuart. I wanted to let you in before anybody else, Bob. I know you've got a lot of thoughts dancing around in your head."

"Has Pat got a twin sister?" I asked, grinning,

"Crap, Bob, I'll make you think twin sister."

"Just trying to break some ice, Coach," I quipped and then I decided to get serious. "I'll give it all I've got and I want to be on Stuart's best team ever. I saw with the Owls how much fun and work that undefeated season was and it took the whole team. So, yes you can count on me and I won't shy away."

When I stood up and Coach Sloan shook my hand and thanked me for my trust. "Are they in town now?" I asked.

"No, they are finishing moving."

"Call me when they get here and I'll be glad to meet them." I said. I wasn't sure if I meant that or not, but knew Stew took his challenges head-on. It had worked out pretty well for him and I was going to try it, too.

Mom had a real good dinner on the table waiting when I got home. As we sat down Dad asked if Coach Sloan had found me.

I laughed. "I guess he found you first Dad."

"Yes," Dad said. "We talked a couple of days ago. You know that his job doing what's best for the Rebel program. I got myself in a fix years ago playing a kid that probably shouldn't have been starting and it cost us."

I understood. "I've been around enough to see that you've just gotta give it your best and I've heard you spell it out too many times, right, Dad? There's no I in team," I said.

Mom got to have her say then: "It shows a lot of character to put forth your best and be ready when called upon. You remember in little league when Coach Herb asked which was the most important position on the field?"

"Yes," I said without hesitation. "If one goes down, the next has to be ready to carry the team."

"No matter what happens," she said, "I like your attitude."

I laughed again. "Well, Mom, I don't see how I have a lot of choice, but we will see what happens."

A couple of days later, before practice started Coach Sloan asked if I could hang around a bit after practice. I had a big clue what the reason was, so I said, "No problem."

I had only talked with Pete and Zach about this. Pete was now a senior point guard and the only dog he had in this hunt was wanting me to do well. Zach just let me know that we would work together. He reminded me that we would be better for doing so.

I walked in to Coach Sloan's office and there was Mr. Byrd and Pat. After the introductions and handshakes, it became clear that Mr. Byrd had done his homework about the Stuart program. I thought it was good that he took the initiative and I knew it was awkward for Pat being the new guy.

Mr. Byrd said, "Bob, I looked at the other programs around Marion and I really liked the team and town concept here in Stuart. Your dad was a great coach, teacher, and leader. I've also liked how Coach Sloan has followed what your dad laid down."

I smiled. "Well, Mr. Byrd, if you're running for office, I guess you've got my vote."

Everybody laughed.

I went on. "I've been a Rebel since I was born and I'm just glad y'all aren't from the north."

Coach Sloan ignored my joke. "You two work together and we will have a solid base to work with for sure."

I said, "Sure, I'll get this over with in a hurry, Coach. You two talk a little bit more and I'll take Pat to get a shake."

"I'm in," Pat said. He smiled at me.

I turned to Mr. Byrd. "I'll just drop Pat off instead of coming back here. I've got to show him our one traffic light in town."

Try to Make the Best of the Situation

Pat Byrd was a down to earth guy coming from Wilson High in Freeman, Georgia, just north of Atlanta. It was a larger 3-A school. He told me about the town: "All around us was growing really fast and there just wasn't a great team concept at Wilson."

I nodded. "Well, don't get in a big hurry in Stuart, but with Marion across the bridge you get plenty to do around here."

We pull into the Rebel Drive-In and I asked Pat what flavor he wanted. We were looking at the board.

I said, "If you've got a weak stomach hold your ears."

"Why is that?" he asked.

I decided just to show him: "Hey, Miss Wright. How are you? Yes, Peanut Butter it'll be."

Pat laughed. "You are joking. I'll wait another time before I try that one. I better be safe and have a Chocolate Malt."

As we climb into my VW to leave, I pointed out that the office just past the Rebel is Doc West's. "Doc has been our team doctor since early in my dad's stint. He does a good job keeping everyone in good shape. His son Pete is our senior point guard on the basketball team and our family has been close since I was small."

"That's good. One of my uncles is a chiropractor back in Freeman."

"I hope you know where you moved to because I didn't ask your Dad."

"The house is on Holly Street close to a hill and church."

We drove around Stuart and I showed Pat the park with the city pool and baseball fields. I tried to tell Pat about our town. I tried to explain it all to him: so much was centered on our sports teams here and it was really cool to be appreciated. With my older brother being at NE Alabama for the last four years, during football most of my weekends were packed. I learned a lot, though, and had fun mingling with the players and coaches.

"Our house is right up here on the . . . . ., you missed it," Pat said.

"I know," I said. "But one of my best friends, Zack Morris, and the fastest guy on our team, lives right up here around the curve."

We pulled in and Zack came out to meet the new guy. After introductions we talked and Pat asked about classes. "You'll like it pretty well, I bet. We have a rotating schedule that doesn't let the same classes get as boring," Zack said.

"Even with basketball, Coach Sloan is always going over offense and plays during P.E. classes, so get ready," I said.

"Zack," Pat asked then. "Does Bob always get a peanut butter shake?"

Zach chuckled. "Well, every now and then he may slum for a grape."

"Grape?" Pat said in disgust.

"You'll get use to it and be able to tune him out," Zach said. "But if he comes into the house, tell your Mom to hide the peanut butter."

Pat was really laughing now. "By the way," he said. "You were the team with the free kick deal, right?"

I told him the truth: it had been a team effort. "I apprised Coach about the play, Zack made the fair catch, and Brett Robbins, who kicked the ball better than any kick I ever held for him. It was 42 yards but it would have been good from over 50."

We left and all went well. I dropped Pat off and told him to stop by basketball practice tomorrow, Saturday, and meet the guys. All but two play football. Of course, when I got home Zack called. I told him all about Pat. "His dad had played at Clemson and knows football. He has a September fifth birthday so his Dad held him back in the seventh grade which seemed to help with his size being a sophomore. He said it helped him in Georgia to be ready to play this past year."

Zach agreed that Pat seemed like he would fit in quite nicely. He didn't come across as an overbearing and know it all from the big city.

Spring practice went well. We helped each other out with formations and learning the offense. Pat was faster and could zip his throws well. I had to rely more on precision, touch, and knowledge. Our spring game went smoothly: we played two quarters, winning 14-0 over Collins. It turned out that we both led a touchdown drive.

There was a lot of excitement going into the Rebel season. We had a couple more guys move into Stuart from Marion and our workouts were going along well. The schedule was completed and for our second game we would travel to play South Lanier. The Wildcats had been one of the top teams, but they lost in the semi-finals of the State 3-A last year. With Stuart being 2-A, our Rebel team had a big task ahead on the road.

In the Alabama High School Association, only the top eight teams, in each of the four classes, got to participate in the play-offs which started just a few years earlier. It turned out that Coach Sloan was pushing us to be better and prove ourselves and he was making sure of that.

Have a Good Outlook for Your Team

A week before the season started, Coach Sloan called me into his office before heading home after practice. He said, "Bob you have worked hard, been consistent, and I like your effort. But," he said, "we are going to start with Pat and we need you to be ready and stay focused."

"Okay, Coach, you'll be able to count on me. One thing though. What is up with the South Lanier game?"

"Bob, we want to move forward and we've been pretty much at the top in our area. This may not be our year, but we will have a wealth of experience under our belts. There are going to be things I trust to you and Pat and this is one of them. Now, you listen, though—I still want your input."

I was glad about that. We shook hands and I hurried off; Zack was waiting for me, needing a ride home as usual.

"Pretty much what I had already known: Pat is going to be our starter," I told Zack in the car.

Zach made me feel better. "We're still going to need you, Bob. And you know you'll get your shots."

"Thanks, Zack," I said. I knew he was probably right.

We won our first game over North Concord 21-6. We woke up to get the *Marion Ledger* to see the scores from around the state and saw that South Lanier beat somebody 48-6. We were all excited and scared at the same time, something like playing the past city schools when Dad was coach.

The trip to play South Lanier got us on a greyhound type bus for a two hour ride. "Pat, don't get too used to this bus because we normally take those 'yellow dogs' parked in the back," I said.

"But," Zach added, "most of our away games don't take thirty minutes to get to so it is not that big of a problem."

Our Rebel team played hard, but was caught off guard with the Wildcat's passing game, and after falling behind 14-0 in the first quarter we hung in to lose 21-7. Our new defensive coach, Wes Roberts, let us know that we'll be ready next time.

Coach Sloan encouraged us, too. "Now you know what it is like to step up. We've got to keep doing that and working harder. I was proud y'all didn't give up and hung in when a lot of teams would fold. Let's get ready for Dalton," he said.

Most everybody filled Pat in on the importance of the Dalton game. "Yeah, Dad has already heard from his boss and others who live in Dalton," Pat said. Rebels won 20-3. The next morning, as usual, Zack and I rode into Marion since I am not going to watch Stew play. Our ritual usually started with a stop at Doc West to get worked on and "get the kinks out."

We got back into my VW, which used to be Stew's, and headed to town. "Let's see where we are with last night's game," Zack said.

Local radio station 1060 WMAR aired the replay of the game of the week. They always carried the Stuart and Dalton game. "Just in time," I said.

The announcer set up the play: "Rebels have the ball second and 7 at midfield, leading 7-0, just entering the second quarter. Byrd takes the snap and pitches to Morris sweeping right, he breaks a tackle, now he cuts to his left, picks up a block and he breaks clear and he is going to score from 50 yards away."

"You can smile, Zack," I said. "That was pretty good there."

The announcer continued: "Up 13-0 the Rebels line up for the P.A.T. with Pat Byrd to kick. Oh, bad snap but the holder, Bob Hayes, gets it down and the kick is good for a 14-0 lead. Usually they don't get their name mentioned, being the snapper and holder, unless something goes bad but Hayes kept his eyes on a two hopper and got it down for Pat Byrd to make the kick."

I laughed. "I didn't even realize it, but I'll take it."

We Rebels rolled on until the next to last game against Tarver, a pretty good 3-A school in nearby Lee County. They had an all-state end, Leroy Garrett, that broke two returns for touchdowns and Pat had a last second field-goal, from 49 yards, hit the up-right and we lost, at home, 22-21. The "at home" part made it much worse.

Another good year, Concord County Champions, but we muddied up the big picture with an 8 and 2 record.

At lunch Sunday, everyone was there—for a change. Stew was working for a bank in Birmingham and doing a little scouting for Coach Duncan of NE Alabama. Sharon and her best friend, Beth, were sharing an apartment. After two years of junior college she was at the East Marion Bank loan department and teaching lifeguard classes at the Y, when needed.

I said, "Dad, what did you see us do, or better yet, not do this past year?"

"Well, Son, Coach Sloan kept everything pretty basic and I can see that four or five new guys in there. But y'all were close in the two losses. Then it was Coach Wes's first year to be a coordinator with the defense."

Stew chimed in then: "Wes was a good nose-guard at Tate and actually a decent guy I respected when we played them. Even when we beat them bad, his senior year, we talked a minute after the game."

After lunch it was time to play a few games of h-o-r-s-e in the backyard before Stew had to leave. He still beat me but it was close. I've got to work on my hook shot to beat Stew. Here I was talking about trying to beat a guy, who happened to be my older brother, at a game where he once made 100 straight free throws to win a contest. Just like all Rebels, from Stuart, I always kept trying and giving it our best.

Basketball season was progressing and we were holding our own in most all of the games. I really wanted more playing time and I thought I needed it to feel more comfortable on the court. If you feel comfortable, you can play without trying not to mess up. I learned a good lesson one Friday night playing a top team from north of Concord County. The Baxter High Lions were all about basketball the way Stuart was about football. They came to town and our gym was packed, mainly to see the Lions, since they had finished third in the State the previous year.

My butt was getting a little sore from sitting and we were up by 3 with two minutes left in the game. Ryan Cullop, a senior guard, fouled out. Coach Reed turned to me and said, "Okay, Bob, here's your chance. They are going to be fouling you since you're coming off the bench, but you can do it."

We were trying to slow it down a bit and, as the ball swung to my side, I was slapped two or three times, to the line I go. I stepped up and made the first two free throws. We hustled back and the scene repeats a couple of more times. They were full court pressing. I faked to midcourt and Tom Humphrey caught my nod and I took off toward the goal, catching his lob pass and making the lay-up. I got fouled and added the free throw with the lay-up for a 3 point play. Baxter missed a couple of shots and we held on to upset one of the top 2-A basketball teams. It was a thrill to get the hugs, handshakes, and pats on the back. It meant a lot that Zack and Pat were the first two from our stands to congratulate me. I have to admit that some of the hugs from the cheerleaders were right up there as well.

Never mind that Ryan Cullop had scored 18 points and guarded an all-state player holding him to 10. It was what happened in the last two minutes that got all the attention. The Saturday morning *Marion Ledger's* top sports headline: "Rebels upset Baxter." The second line read, "Hayes steps up, scores 11 points in the last 2 minutes."

It Pays to Be Ready to Play

After the Baxter game, football was always on our radar at Stuart. Playing sports got us a pass and we didn't have to dress for regular P.E. classes. After every season, Dad always reviewed the game films and looked for traits and plays we did and didn't do well. It helped to have the thought "what if." For example, what if we were playing for a championship and I had to go in to lead the team?

I walked in and talked to Coach Sloan, mentioning my intention of reviewing the games. His comment was simply, "Let me know what you find." My film sessions started and right off the bat I noticed how most all of our pass plays came off of play action. I also had a thought, maybe a little selfish, but a pretty good plan, as well. If I were to hold on kicks and also do some of the placement punting, then what could we do to throw something different at a foe with special teams?

I was just starting the tape of a game and Coach Roberts walked by the film area and asked who I had on. "The Dalton game," I said.

He said, "By the way Bob, great game the other night with Baxter, that was something special."

"Thanks, Coach," I said.

"Coach, I haven't asked you since you've been here, but what do you remember the most in your last game with the Owls?"

"Well, we thought we had a great chance but Stew showed his mettle and led one heck of a drive that we couldn't do anything to stop."

I started thinking. "Let me ask you this," I said. "Did you guys watch for the "waterbucket" play that we did against UT-W?"

"It was my job to watch the center every time, and the huddle."

"Coach Sloan had asked me about the play. I've been watching these games and I wonder, what do you think if we lined up our huddle to the side for all of our kick attempts? Then, if a team gets lazy, because we do it every time, we'll fire it at them." I waited to hear what he would think about my idea.

Coach Roberts nodded. "I like that idea, Bob, and the other teams will have to respect it as well. Keep working and by the way and tell Stew to stop by next time he's home."

Always Look for Positive Changes

A few days went by and Zack sat down and started watching the games with me. "Look here, Zack," I said. "After Pat fakes the handoff on 26 Pass, you just stop at the line and the play moves outside."

Zach nodded. "Yeah, I hardly ever get hit after the fake."

"Look at it again. After the fake you turn to your left, to see if somebody breaks through from the backside, then instead of just sitting there, you should turn back toward the quarterback and drift toward the opposite side. If the downfield isn't open, judging from the ten plays I've seen, you'll be off to the races."

Zach smiled. "I see what you are talking about more or less like a screen."

"Okay," I said, "let's just keep this one between you and I and if we get a chance we'll do it."

"What catches your eye on some of the plays, Bob?" Zach asked.

"Mainly watching the play, not just following the ball to see how everyone reacts. Stew had a saying I would hear from time to time, 'would've, could've, and should've.' I always think about that when I watch plays." I looked at Zach and went on talking. "Plus Dad would review the games after the season for ideas like this. I learned after the Baxter game there are a few of us that have to be ready to step up if somebody goes down."

Try to Visualize the "What If"

I was reviewing the Tarver game when Coach Sloan joined me. He said, "Bob, I see this is about to get ugly here in a few plays."

He was right. It did get ugly as Leroy Garrett broke a couple of tackles and dashed down the sideline for a touchdown on a punt return. I said, "After he picks up the bouncing ball, we get out of our lanes and he is off to the races. Coach, against a return guy like Garrett you may want to have Zach and Freddy to back the coverage up."

Coach Sloan nodded: "That's good thinking, Bob. Also, Coach Roberts mentioned the line up on kicks and I like it. I think we ought to work that in the summer."

This encouragement got me going. "Coach," I said, "with special teams, we didn't utilize much with them the whole year. Having Pat and myself, hopefully gives us some room to throw a pass or two on some of these teams that rush everybody."

"What else have you noticed that stands out?" Coach Sloan asked.

"We're pretty straight forward on first down plays. We had very few passes on first down. My Dad did that a lot."

The coach looked a little surprised. "Bob, we've got everybody back on the line and we'll be able to do more this year, I promise."

I was worried then. "You asked me, Coach."

"I trust you also, Bob."

That comment made me feel better and, at the very least, noticed.

Pat Byrd fit in quite well in Stuart and he was very welcome in our neighborhood also. The welcome part had to do with one of our neighbors, Kathy Townsend. Kathy made a lot of progress: she'd grown from the tomboy who made the little league team to a cheerleader for the Rebels. Quint and Matt Townsend kept Pat in check most of the time and stayed on his case quite a bit. Not having a brother at home made picking and playing tricks a pleasure for both Pat and Matt. I was glad to let Pat deal with those two sneaks that you couldn't trust. They both knew Pat wouldn't retaliate the way I would, but I encouraged him one hundred percent.

Spring training was underway and, sure enough, Coach Sloan had us running more options as well as a straight passing game with more experience and trust in our offense. After the first week of practice everything was moving quite well. But that was about to change. On Saturday, Pat was at the Townsend's and Kathy was beating him at hoops. Then he tried to dunk a shot, slipped and "crack"—Pat broke his right hand.

Practice on Monday took on a new meaning with a cast on Pat's hand. The doctor said it would heal up fine as long as he was careful. The new meaning came from a question I overheard in the locker room. Coach Sloan asked Pat if he could throw left handed. I took that a little personal that Coach trusted my thinking more than my field performance.

The new meaning was "I'll show you." After drills I got into the huddle to start a series of plays. "Look guys, we are going to do this as a team and everybody do your job. I'm not going to let y' all down. All hands in and on three team." Everyone sticks their hands on top of each other's and I count down, 1-2-3 and TEAM!

We ran plays against our younger guys without tackling. The scrimmage was tomorrow and two weeks after that we would play Collins in our spring game. We had some of our regular defensive starters against our offense. The Rebel offense marched down the field gaining big chunks on play after play. After a break we did situations where Coach Sloan gives us the down and distance to set up the play.

"Okay, Bob, first and 10," Coach yelled. "Left 11 option," he yelled again as Zack gained 10 before losing his balance. "Second and 6," came another order as Tony Carter, our big fullback caught a pass in the flat for a big gain. We played together and it made my job a lot easier with the first unit.

As our game approached, I spent time reviewing last year's game with Collins and made notes of what we usually did on the first down. I wanted to make sure we didn't repeat that. On our first play, just like in practice, Left 11 option gained 14 yards as I kept the ball. Next play Tony caught the ball in the right flat after faking to Zack to gained 8 yards. We followed that with 26 pass and with another fake hand-off to Zack, our TE Chris Cooper hauled in my throw for 15 yards.

"Is it my turn yet," Zack asked me in the huddle. A new little twist we put in was a 26 trap that lets Zack cut back and he did so down to the 10 yard line. We lined up in a power formation in which I faked to Zack running behind Tony and dumped it over the line to a wide open Chris for our first score. Pat came out with his hand still in a cast and kicked the extra point.

Into the second quarter we got the ball back, leading 14-0. We were at our 40 yard line and in the huddle I told the left side of the line to block down and said, "Let's go with 26 pass." I patted Zack on the helmet. After I faked they were really moving to cover and Zack was all alone back to my left. I gave a little pump toward Chris and lobbed it about 7 yards over to Zack and he was off to the races for an uncontested score. Pat came in for his third kick and we blanked Collins 21-0 playing two quarters.

As I got to the sideline, Coach Sloan said, "Hold on, Bob. Now where in the play book am I going to find that pass play?"

I said, "I thought it may be better to show you."

"I'm not fond of surprises Bob." Coach Sloan crossed his arms over his chest.

Here I was, explaining myself again. "When I was reviewing the game films that play was open about every time."

"Next time let me know first."

Everybody did their job and we had a lot to look forward to. I earned accolades for leading the Rebels, in Pat's absence, and was named the player of the game. After the game Dad shook my hand, which was a little indication of maturity, and congratulated me. He said, "That's how you earn respect son."

"How did you like the dump off to Zack on 26 pass?" I asked him.

"Pretty good because I coached that play for 18 years and never looked at it like that." Dad looked at me. And after seeing you and Coach Sloan on the sideline I don't think he had either."

Be Ready When the Time Comes

The summer was progressing and I found a construction job doing regular labor working on a new high school in the next county. After meeting my boss on the site, the first chore was digging out a walkway with our shovels. "You kinda look familiar," I said to a guy holding up his shovel.

"Leroy Garrett," he said.

"Leroy too many of us at Stuart only know you from behind after chasing you all night."

Leroy laughed. "I sorta liked that game myself."

Leroy turned out to be a genuinely good guy. He also had a good looking sister who was on their cheerleading squad. We talked a lot of football and as the last day on the job came up, it was shaking hands and "I'll see you in about two months." We exchanged good lucks and said we hoped we were both undefeated when we met again.

Meanwhile at Stuart, our booster club, led by Doc West, had revamped our locker room. We were not allowed in for a whole week. Coach Sloan called us together the day before our first official practice to make sure we had all our equipment. "Okay young men," he said. "We have a challenge ahead of us. Coach Roberts and I want the best out of you thirty-five here. I've never done this before in my coaching career but you will see as you walk in. Now file in and take a seat at your locker."

As we walked in the door to turn left into the locker room the line slows down and each head looks up. Hanging from the rafter was a sign with 3 lines under Stuart Rebels:

1. WIN
2. COUNTY CHAMPIONS
3. STATE CHAMPIONS

"Starting tomorrow this is what we are here to do, heads are nodding around the room, and I want everything you've got and we are going to go all out. You give us that effort and we can do it in one practice a day."

That brought out a big yell.

"So you don't think I'm pulling a fast one some of you on special teams will have to put forth a little more time."

"Coach they don't mind at all," says Dave Allen a starting senior tackle, who was not on special teams.

"Get your stuff situated. We'll be in helmets and shoulder pads at three tomorrow."

Have a Goal but Know When You are Ready for it

Practice started out great and was fast paced. It was special that with Pat Byrd, Tony Carter, Chris Cooper, and Zack Morris, we were watched by college scouts daily. Chris really liked baseball more than football but at Stuart there wasn't a ton of emphasis placed on the game.

Everybody was at full speed and, after a week and a half, we had our first live scrimmage. I lined up to run the offense against our first team defense. In the huddle I told the guys, "We ain't going to make this easy for them, so listen up." First play was 26 pass and Tyler running a go pattern. Our defense was expecting the run, like we mainly do, but the ball landed in Tyler's hands for a touchdown after he got behind the coverage with ease.

In the end we didn't have enough tricks up our sleeve to totally get the best of them, but Coach liked everyone's effort. And then he ran our butts off.

After that spring game, I realized that getting a chance to produce on the field was a positive step. I had been told before, "What you do can speak louder than what you say," so Pat and I conversed a lot more with plays. He trusted me even more and knew what to look for with certain formations.

We were having a cookout the night before our first game, thanks to our booster club. Pat, Zack, and I were putting away some burgers and Pat said, "This is why we choose Stuart and thanks guys." This was too good when the Mom's had homemade ice cream and cakes for us. "Quit looking, Bob," Chris said. "Nobody had the gall to make any peanut butter ice cream."

We got past our first game with a 24-0 blanking of a normally tough Taylorsville High. School started on Tuesday, after Labor Day, and regular routines began. Zack and I had taken a couple of extra classes in the past and with our rotating schedule we were open on Friday mornings the first two periods. Well, the second class we were Coach Sloan's teacher's aides which meant free period, especially on Fridays. But rules were rules and we had to be at homeroom, in person, at eight am for roll call to be able to play that night. After that ten minute ordeal we would go by Doc West's office for a treatment and over to eat breakfast at Paul's Diner. We would then come back for our one class, skip lunch because the team would go to the Sizzler Steak House at 3:30 for pre-game meal, and then watch a game film or just go over Coach Sloan's game plan. Pat joined us for that part. Then it was time for the pep rally which was usually entertaining because a couple of players would always have to get up there with Coach and say a few words in front of the school and fans. Most of the time those few words would get botched up big time. Then we had about thirty free minutes to get stuff together, make sure the girl you may have a date with after the game was still going to go. Of course, you had to make sure Coach didn't see that planning session. After that, it was on to eat.

Next we played a first time foe in Richton and on our second series Pat scrambled and overthrew a pass that was returned for a touchdown. We moved down to score and then went ahead on an interception by Ray Epperson. Into the second quarter Pat ran an option and came down awkward on the ball and had to leave the game. I ran 11 Option and Zack ran it to the 10. I got to make the next call and tried the same play to the right, 18 Option, and I walked in for the score.

We then went full steam and after Pat came back in the third quarter to set up a couple of touchdown drives, I finished the game running for 2 and throwing for 2 touchdowns, completing all 7 passes I threw. The last one got me a few words from Coach Sloan. In the fourth quarter we were up 52-12 and we are at the 30 going for another score. Chris Cooper, our tight end, is begging me to throw him a pass. "Bob, everybody has scored but me, just once, we won't be here next year to play these guys." I called 22 pass and Coop was open and got his first touchdown of the year. Coming off the field I didn't even give Coach a chance to ask. I just said, "Coop almost was crying to catch a touchdown and we gotta have him happy, Coach."

Coach Sloan shook his head. "No more passes, Bob. Got it?"

After another long touchdown run by our third team halfback we won 64-19.

In the locker room after the game Coach Duncan, of NE Alabama, walked over to tell Zack and me good game. "Lil' Hayes, that was a good showing tonight and, Zack, you made a couple of runs look too easy."

I said, "Thanks, Coach." I paused a second. "One thing, though, did you like any of the passes I threw?" I just knew he was going to compliment one of the touchdown passes.

"You threw a 12 yard out pass that I really liked."

This answer showed me that he was more interested in the process and not just the outcome.

The Proper Process Will Produce More Results

It felt good to contribute and gain the confidence of others. Especially if Pat goes down with an injury, I knew we had a couple of players to step up and be ready if called on. Our next week was big, playing Dalton, but Coach kept it low key this year. We had South Lanier coming to town the following week and he didn't want us to get too high. During the game, our defense was dominating and Pat did a good job of ball control and grinding out first downs. We put Dalton away 17-0.

The Thursday before games was just a walk through to make sure of our line up with special teams and certain situations. This week we practiced a couple of plays off special teams to make sure we had them down pat.

South Lanier came to Stuart and this year we were no longer awed by their larger team and higher ranking. We took our first drive down the field and, after a couple of first downs, we were going for a fourth and 3. Zack's feet slipped out from under him and we gave the ball back. Pat came over and asked me if I saw anything and I mentioned that they forgot about Zack after the fake on 22 pass. "Gotcha," Pat said.

The next series on second down comes 26 pass and Pat held on, drifted another couple of steps, and lofted it to Zack who took off untouched for a 60 yard touchdown. I went out to place the tee for the extra point and, as we line up toward the side, South Lanier didn't budge. I extended my arm and fist which signals center Paul Daniels, nicknamed Jack (of course), to snap the ball over to Zack for an easy 2 point play to go up 8-0.

South Lanier had an all-state quarterback in Matt Gunderson. I watched the next series and saw something, after a couple of plays, I remember seeing before. On a third and one, South Lanier broke the huddle and I looked at Pat, saying, "They're going to throw."

Gunderson fakes to their fullback and lofted a scoring pass to their tight end. "How'd you know that, Bob?" Pat asked.

"The fullback's stance," I said.

Our kick-off return team huddled up and I got Coach Roberts and "Big" Tony Carter, our middle line backer and fullback, together. I said, "Coach, I saw this years ago when Curt West played here at Stuart. Their fullback is doing the same thing. When he gets in a 3 point stance, they are going to pass. When he gets in a 4 point, he is the lead blocker for a run."

Coach looked at Tony and instructed him to hold his fist up in the air when the fullback gets in a 3-point stance to indicate pass.

Pat drove us down the field with a good mix of plays and, with them keying on Zack, he bootleged one for a 20 yard score. When our defense hit the field, their fullback was right on the money to indicate pass or run, 3 and out they go. We stalled and settled for a 35 yard field goal to go up 18-7. As South Lanier got the ball, Ray Epperson intercepted a Gunderson overthrow at midfield. With the clock winding down before the half, Pat tried to hit Coop with a corner throw that sailed wide. I was about to go out and hold for a 43 yard field goal and Coach Sloan called for me to make the call to fake and throw left or right. South overloaded to their right and I call "right."

"Jack" Daniels snapped it back and Pat made his move to kick. I pulled up and rolled right and Zack was heading toward the goal line all by his lonesome. I just lofted one and he corralled it in for an easy score—with a kick by Pat, this time, and we went in 25-7.

We came out with some short play action passes and controlled the ball well. Coop caught one over the middle for a score and we were up 32-7. I got to take over for Pat and drove the Rebels down, where the keep on an option was wide open, and I stumbled into the end-zone to make it 39-7. Midway through the fourth quarter Gunderson was about to take the snap and Tony had his fist up in the air. I walked by Coach Roberts and said, "I think it is safe that they are going to throw every play now."

"Good call, Bob. That's why they just have 7 on the board."

"Sorry, Coach," I said, as a tipped ball falls their way and the final score ends 39-14.

In Monday's paper the Stuart Rebels were ranked, for the first time, as #8 in the State.

Revenge week # 2 was next as we got ready to play Tarver High and tried to contain Leroy Garrett. It worked out that we were both 4-0 just like Leroy and I had hoped for when we shook hands on our last day of summer work together. I knew that going to their stadium would be a big challenge. In practice I reminded Pat how notorious the officials in Lee

County are. I said, "Let's keep everybody's emotions in check. It's always got to be 'yes, sir' and 'no, sir' to the officials."

Coach Sloan reminded us of the big goal ahead and told us not to get caught up in the hype of the rankings and articles. Luckily at that time the papers only talked with the coaches in high school. On Thursday we worked on some different alignments to contain Leroy.

On Friday morning, Zack and I were entertaining our game day ritual at Paul's Diner, when Mr. Red stopped by our booth. He reminded us to stay calm and not to get ahead of ourselves. He said, "I'm sure your Dad keeps you two in check."

After a few minutes, we thanked Mr. Parker and to our delight he took care of our check. Zack looked at me and whispered, "Cool. That's the fifth week in a row somebody has picked up the check."

Tarver players were already on the field as our first group jogged out to get loose. I stopped by and shake hands with Leroy and we wished each other well. We agreed to see each at midfield after the game. At the half we were trailing 17-14. We sat down and Coach asked Pat and I what we thought. "They're moving very quick with our first moves Coach," Pat said.

"Our traps with both Zack and Freddy, wing-back, should keep them off guard," I added. "Then Pat should have a lot of room for our open passing game."

Our half-time plan worked like a charm. I hung a couple of punts that Leroy couldn't return and we defeated Tarver 27-14. At midfield we shook hands and wished each other luck. He said, "Y'all keep it up Bob. It was good the way you guys came back on us."

I said, "Sorry 'bout not giving you a chance with my punts, but if I did Coach would have had my butt."

Leroy smiled and we parted to different sides of the field.

The Monday *Marion Ledger* shows the Stuart Rebels are ranked 4th in the State class 2-A after beating two top big teams in back to back weeks.

At practice that day, Coach Sloan had some words for us. "Men, Collins may well be the toughest game on our schedule. I'm not trying to blow smoke up your butts. Just because of the past three weeks, playing big opponents, we still have to take care of business one game at a time."

I knew he was right.

Our ritual stayed the same and, true to form, our breakfast ticket gets paid for. A fun part started to happen with our home games. We sat and watched fans get to the stadium almost two hours early, just to get a seat. Doc West got everybody "popped up" before going out and we maintained an even keel.

Pat and I were starting our throwing and Quint hung by us since he enjoyed game-day manager status. He asked, "Why do you two always throw on this side of the field, away from our stands?"

I said, "We have to check out the other team's cheerleaders first before we get serious."

"Sounds like a plan, I guess," Quint said.

Then Pat spoke up. "My Dad asked me that and I just said you were superstitious." We both smiled. We then started our jogging and throwing15 yarders to each other, meaning it was time to get serious.

We handled our next three games, all by at least 35 points. Pat played well and left room for me to score as well. Into the week of our next to last game, the front page headline spelled it out: "Stuart ranked #1 in State 2-A"

Up came our chance against our other county rival, North Concord. At breakfast on Friday morning, Mr. Ryan, Chevrolet dealer and sponsor for our games, stopped by our booth to wish us luck. As he grabbed our ticket he mentioned that we have to pay him back if we lose. This was the first game we look like we are trying not to lose instead of playing to win. We moved the ball well but got a couple of bad breaks as they returned a fumble 90 yards for a touchdown. After Freddy caught a pass he slipped, the ball pops up, and was returned 50 yards for a score. Tied at 14 we were at midfield and up came a fourth down. On the sideline I said, "Coach, they've been sending everybody on punts."

Coach nodded.

I went in to punt and called for a pass left to Coop. It worked like a charm and we were at the 20. Pat got us down to the five on second down and, while turning the corner, got tripped and then kicked in the head. He thought he was back at Wilson in Atlanta. We called time and Coach and I decided to run our roll-out pass we use for 2-point plays. I jogged into the huddle and I figuredwe needed to loosen up. I said, "Okay, guys let's put this in because I don't have the money to pay for breakfast."

"What the hell?" Jack Daniels said.

There was no time to explain now. "Let's just do it," I said.

Usually Zack was open in the flat but the linebacker jumped his pattern. Deep right corner was covered and I see our split-end, Tal Hopson, coming across the middle, from the right side, so I slung it between two linebackers. He hung onto it for the touchdown. Big Tony got the hand-off on the option for the 2 point play and we win 22-14.

As I got back to the sideline, I saw that Doc West had gotten Pat back to his senses. "Great relief, Bob," Pat said. "You'll have to show me how Hop is the one to wind up catching flood pass."

I laughed. "I've got to look at the film first to be able to know myself." As the clock hit :00, our fans came on the field as we head to our busses. Mr. Ryan shook my hand and let me know that was close. He said, "I was hoping I wasn't about to get my money back."

"Me too," I said.

"Me three," Zack said, walking up.

Concord County Champs for the third straight year but nobody on the Rebels team was happy with just that.

We handled St. Martin High 29-9 to finish the regular season ranked #1, 10 and 0. This was uncharted territory for Stuart heading to the play-offs for the first time ever. There had been some really good Rebel teams but this was a first.

At this point in time the top eight teams were in the play-offs. Being #1 the Stuart Rebel were slated to host Canton, from the mid-north part of the state in the first round. Canton had a solid and well coached team. Our routines stayed the same. Coach Sloan did his best to keep us on an even keel, but the even keel got a challenge. Since no team from our county had made it to the play-offs the excitement was really building. Our normal little Thursday walk through even had a different tone.

Coach Sloan held us in the locker room and advised us to play smart and play hard. He said, "Today when we go out, first we will do our pre-game warm-up as a team."

Little did we know what was about to transpire. As we went out the door to the stadium there was a victory line all the way to the field and our stands were about filled, to just add fuel to the fire. It was amazing and it was proof how special something like this can be. Our band was playing and our fans "yelled" the whole time.

Friday morning Zack and I stopped by Doc West's office for a treatment and he was more excited than we were. Doc had been on the sidelines for about 25 years and he couldn't quit talking. I said, "Doc, I think you need to lie on the table and we'll find a way to do some type of an adjustment on you."

We slid into a booth at Paul's Diner and Ms. Winchester came over to take our order, as she had most weeks. I got the pancake breakfast and Zack looked up and said, "Big Country breakfast."

Ms. Winchester looked up in surprise and I went ahead and said it: "Zack are you damn stupid?"

"What?" he asked.

"You've had the pancake breakfast for 10 weeks in a row and you ain't about to change now."

"I'm with you, Bob," Ms. Winchester said.

Zach got the pancakes.

As we were about to finish Mr. Paul himself joined us. He asked how Dad and the family were doing and noticed that Dad was getting a little later on coming in.

I said, "He's earned it, I guess."

Mr. Paul said, "Bob, he is super proud of you, Zack, and the whole team. It's been a pleasure having you two in here every week. Good luck tonight." He picked up our ticket and shook our hands. We walked out to a few more "good luck guys" as we nodded and I don't think our feet hit the floor while we were walking.

We were able to only get one film on Canton and Pat and I watched it a good five or six times together. You don't have a lot of weaknesses when you get this far. After about the third time we had stopped the projector and I said, "Wait a second."

Pat said, "What, Bob?"

"We need to look at our play chart from the last few games and see what we haven't done."

"Good idea, as always."

"They move to the ball well so I'll be on the lookout to see what they do after the first 26 pass and you fake to Zack. Then, some pump fakes may be in order."

The Sizzler was good as always and we enjoyed our routine of watching our fans come to the stadium which started to fill up fast. It was getting quite cold and Pat looked at me and said, "Let's go out for about five minutes before the rest since it has never been this cool."

Know How to Prepare for the Conditions

We started to loosen up and I said, "Pat, make sure you let me know a play ahead of time that you may get dinged so I can warm my helmet up."

We both chuckled and looked around us. I think we were having the same thought: "This IS pretty neat."

We were able to drive down and Tal Hopson made a good catch to get us into field goal position. They moved to cover our huddle and Pat made good from 34 yards out. As he came over I informed him to dump off to Zack on 26 pass. We hold and after a few runs Pat set up the pass and Zack strode away for 48 yards and a touchdown.

We continue to grind out first downs and we got a little lax with a lead but win 27-20. Step 1 accomplished.

Week 2 of the play-offs was going to be different because it was the week of Thanksgiving. We Rebels would be hosting the # 4 ranked Aggies of Clayton County, located between Birmingham and Montgomery. They were big, fast, and dangerous.

On Wednesday, after practice, Coach called Pat and me into his office. He said, "We are going to score any way we can and get them out of their base offense. You both stay ready and let's not take any chances."

On Thanksgiving morning we had our walk through practice at 9 am so everybody could chow down at lunch and watch the annual Detroit Lions and Dallas Cowboys home games that afternoon.

We covered our formations and then Coach Sloan called for the offense. He said, "Bob take Freddy's spot at wing-back. Pat run slot left—21 sweep and Zack pitch to Bob on a reverse. Coop from the right TE cheat out a couple of spots and run a deep post. Their safety loves to come up and you should be in daylight."

I said, "Coach, you sure you don't want me to try and out run their team?"

He shook his head and everybody else laughs. We ran the play a few times to get our pitches and timing down, completing the pass each time.

Prepare for Your Specific Plays

Coach called us up and let us know that on Friday at eleven am the offense was to be at Mrs. Patterson's house, cheerleader sponsor and girl's

PE teacher, to watch a couple of games on TV together. The defense would be at Coach Roberts' house.

"Pat, Coach said Mrs. Patterson's house not Mrs. Townsend's house," Big Tony said to bring more laughs.

As we walked off the field Zack asked me about going to Paul's Diner for breakfast and by Doc West office. I called Paul's yesterday and knew that they would be open. Ms. Winchester had said she would have come in herself if they hadn't been. "Should I ask Pat to join us?" I said.

Zach said, "If you are going to make me stick with pancakes, to be sure and not take any chances, then he's out." We both laughed.

Our day fell in line as planned and we watched the Nebraska vs. Oklahoma game which was intense, in-between dozing off. We made our trek to the Sizzler and back to the field-house.

We started to hit the field to begin warm-ups and Coach Roberts gave the call for no yelling and jumping around. He wanted us to save it for when we come out for the game.

Pat and I went out and the weather was a lot better than the week before and everything was going according to plan as we headed back into the locker room before the game. I walked in and Coach Sloan said, "Put this on."

It is a new jersey, #44.

"Quint," he said. "Put on Bob's #11."

Zack took the opening kick-off about 20 yards and was plastered by #75, but luckily hangs on. We gained a first down and Pat punted the ball away. After we held Coach called 28 sweep and then lay-out pass. After the sweep play Freddy, wingback, stays two steps from the sideline. Pat took the snap, dropped straight back, and lofted it to a wide open running Freddy for a 60 yard touchdown. As I went out to hold Coach said, "Kick it no matter where they line up." As we lined up they didn't cover our huddle and Pat's kick was good for a 7-0 lead.

Big Tony made a good play to tip a pass up in the air and safety Ray Epperson made a diving catch for the interception. Pat drove the team down and scored on 11 option, but also had the breath knocked out of him. I had to go in to run our extra point play, wearing #44, and Zack took the hand-off in for a 15-0 lead.

Coach Roberts was throwing a lot of slants and blitzes which were working real well. We made a little progress to get into field goal range. I set the tee at the 30 yard line in the middle of the field. The Aggies didn't cover our huddle and I gave "Jack" Daniels the signal to snap it to Zack and he swung it around our blockers and down the sideline for a touchdown. We had them out of sync because we were up 22-0. After we got the ball back, and did not make the first down, I punt it out at the 10. After a first down they tried a pass over the middle and this time our outside linebacker, Trey Knight, dropped back toward the middle and intercepted it at the 45. Coach Sloan looked at me and said, 'Grab your helmet." I went, instead of Freddy, and the reverse pass was the call. I got the ball from Zack, plant and hit Coop in stride, wide open, for another score to make it 29 to 0.

When Coach told Pat and me we were going to try and score any way possible he was not joking. In the first half we scored on a lay-out pass, fake field goal "waterbucket" play, and a halfback reverse pass for 3 scores.

Clayton County manage a couple of scores and we got conservative to win 29-20. It was now on to the Championship game. Coach let us know it was a total team game. We would find out soon who and where we play. He advised us not to leave just yet; we were waiting on the call from the other semifinal game. Right after he said that Quint let Coach know his phone had just rung.

"OK, listen up. I'll have the final details tomorrow but I know we are traveling next week to play Moss Point, down on the Florida line somewhere. Think of what you have done so far, your teammates and don't go out and do anything stupid."

We sat and Zack said, "How 'bout Passquale's Pizza?"

I said, "I'm good with that, and what about you, Pat? You can bring my neighbor with you."

"Will do," Pat said.

We started to leave and my dad was in Coach Sloan's office talking and I had to stick my head in because I was on my way to eat and had no money. "Great game, Bob," Dad said. "Way to be there when called on."

I said, "Coach, can you believe how dumb they were to not cover us on kicks and they didn't pick up my number on the extra point play either."

Coach smiled.

I looked at my dad. "You got a 10 spot, Dad? I asked.

He handed me the money. "Be careful," he said.

Zack and I walked out and hoards of Rebel fans were still there to greet us. We went down the lines shaking hands and talked to Lynn and Joyce, two of our majorettes. They take us up on meeting for Pizza. Zack looked at me and said, "We can't let Pat have the only girl eating with us."

I said, "I've only got $15 with me, so don't go making extra plans tonight, maybe Lynn will take me up on tomorrow night."

She and Cooper had been on the outs and we talked all the time. We had left it kind of mutual being together, I informed Zack.

Zach said, "I know Joyce has been trying to get you and Lynn together."

On Saturday, I cringed as Quint and I walked into the Rebel Drive-In to get lunch. Coach Reed was standing there and he shook my hand and I said, "Sorry, Coach."

"I don't guess another week will kill us since we've gotten this far," he said. The unique aspect of the Rebel basketball team was that all of the players on the team, except two, Cliff Yancey and Joe Howell, play football. That meant only two had been practicing basketball. I said, "At least we have shot some hoops in the backyard, Coach."

Coach said, "We'll cross that bridge next week."

It was almost impossible to find any type of state map in all of Concord County. They'd all gotten snatched up Saturday morning, to find how to get to Moss Point High. It was located two miles from the Florida state line, about 325 miles away from Stuart.

Coach Sloan and Coach Roberts worked tirelessly during the weekend to secure our game plan. Moss Point had more speed than any other team we'd seen. For an added bonus they had two potential All-Americans, players named Bull and Lightning. At least we were to have officials from somewhere else in the state.

Since we got to prepare and practice our routines were similar. The rest of the school and Town were going nuts working out details to go. After a seven am pep rally on Thursday morning, we boarded a Greyhound bus southbound with our "goal" sign in the front seat. You may have guessed it but Zack and I managed to sit together and he brought up a disturbing thought. "What are we going to do about breakfast on Friday?" he asked.

"I thought about that for you Zack and I filled in Coach Sloan that wherever the team eats for breakfast on Friday, they better have pancakes," I said.

After a lunch stop we got down to Moss Point and we prepared for our normal Thursday walk through. Before we put on our sweats and jersey's Coach Roberts advised us to hold on as he pulled out older purple jerseys and had everyone to wear one, except you did not wear your same number. We normally wore our "old gold" and we would in Friday's game but not today. Just in case somebody had been looking, which they probably would.

We did our normal playing around. We had our drop-kick competition going on and I hit one from 42 yards to take the lead. Pat missed to the left on both chances, allowing me to win our drop-kick title.

On the other end of the field the team bunt-kick contest was getting a lot of support. It was a version of that little game you played on the desktop at school with a paper ball folded like a pyramid. You scored a touchdown when any part of the ball touches the line, played 10 yards apart. "Big Tony" was in the finals with safety Ray Epperson. Now Ray was in a dilemma: should he really try to and win and risk getting his ass kicked by Tony, as he his threatening to do, or does he secure a place in his good graces?

Coach Roberts stopped by to see the final match. Ray said, "Coach if I win, can I stay in your room tonight instead of next door with an adjoining room to 'Big Tony?'"

That comment brought some laughs.

"Big Tony" missed a couple of chances from close range and then Ray bopped a kick toward the line that spun and stopped dead on for the win. Ray didn't know if he should start running, but Quint was called over by Tony, behind Ray's back, and grabbed a cup of water. He held Ray's hand up like in a boxing ring and then doused Ray's head with the water. "The thrill of victory Ray," said "Big Tony," grinning from ear to ear.

I bet the biggest question on the minds of the folks looking out from the fences and stands was "Is this the #1 ranked Team in the state?"

Friday morning we walked a few hundred yards to a restaurant close to our team hotel, at the Spring Lake Inn, about 15 minutes from Moss Point, in the state of Florida.

I had a plan to ease Zack's mind about our breakfast superstition. At the hotel I secured a piece of poster board and a magic marker. I spelled out, "PAUL'S DINER" which was tacked up in the restaurant as we feasted on our pancake breakfast.

After breakfast we had a few position meetings and Coach Sloan advised Pat and me to be alert because they had a reputation of playing a little beyond the limits. Actually Coach said, "Hell, they play just downright dirty a lot of times." He looked at me. "Bob, be ready and keep your helmet in your hands this time so you don't have to run and get it."

At about one in the afternoon, Doc West pulled into the hotel with my Dad as his co-pilot, and Mom and Mrs. West in the back seats. Because of the warm sunshine, Doc West pulled out a portable treatment table and set it up by the pool. Word was circulating that he had arrived and the migration starts as players come to get worked on.

By the pool, I talked to dad who was hanging out near Dr. West. "Good trip down Dad?" I asked.

Dad said, "It has been good and I am probably more anxious than you guys are."

I felt the weight of my obligations then. "We won't leave anything in the tank I promise you that," I said.

Dad went over to speak to the coaches then. The doors to most rooms were open and I told Zack that Doc was set up by the pool. Zach said, "I've got to finish watching Jeopardy."

"You ain't smart enough for that show Zack," "Big Tony" said as he walked out of his room. Everybody seemed to be relaxed and at ease with themselves.

The unique aspect, as the season progressed to this point, was the contribution from Doc West. He had been around Stuart as long as I could remember and had always been there whether he had a son playing or not. With this Rebel team we had been able to have the same starting line-up for each game. I decided that, if I ever got into coaching, my team would always have a chiropractor on staff.

An hour and a half before kickoff the Rebel stands were full. It was reported by the *Marion Ledger* that there were 13 chartered buses, not including band buses, and hundreds of others who had made the raid on state maps around town so they could drive themselves.

Two ol' wise fans from Stuart, Jack Roberts and Charles Fortenberry were standing along the fence talking and looking over the place. A guy, about their age, from Moss Point struck up a football conversation with them. He said, "I hear you've got a pretty good team, up there close to Marion."

Jack said, "We do. Those boys are pretty well balanced."

The man said, "You guys ever wager on your Rebel's?"

Jack looked at Charles and said, "Well now, we have once or twice."

"We have won both our play-off games by at least 30 points. What would you say if I even gave you 7 points?" the man asked.

Jack looked back at Charles a couple of times and Charles said, "Yep, I'm in."

Jack looked back at the man from Moss Point and said, "I'll take five hundred dollars on that."

"Five hundred dollars!" the man shouted. "I was just talking about twenty or thirty bucks."

"Well," Jack said. "That ain't worth my time looking you up for no thirty dollars." The man from Moss Point strode off scratching his head.

We boarded the bus with our gear on from the hotel. You could hear a pin drop on the ride to Moss Point. Our bus pulled up near the back of our locker room. First things first, as our sign got carried into the door. "Let's roll," Pat said.

"Right behind ya," I said. We tapped the sign, as everyone would do, as always, going out the door, and made our way down about fifteen steps and then turned the corner together to jog onto the field.

The Rebel faithful, hit their feet, the band struck up "Dixie," and the roar was the loudest we had ever heard. Just the emotion generated by being the first two out, and our fans being there for quite some time, was something I will never forget. "Our side tonight," I yelled at Pat because of the cheering. We started to throw and I felt the tears roll down my cheeks. Quint came over and I advised him to remember what this sounds like because it could truly be a once in a lifetime experience.

You Have to Have the Emotion—You Can't Fake it

The Stuart Rebels received and drove down to 18 and were stalled. I went out to place the tee, wearing my normal #11, and Moss Point covered our huddle. I felt time was running down and looked at Pat and said, "Let's take the five and not waste a time out."

The Official marked off a delay of game penalty and we calmly set up. I was down on my knee and their coach was not just yelling at me he was dog cussing me. My mom would've kicked his butt. I'd never had a coach to yell, much less cuss. "Jack" Daniels' snap was true as was Pat's kick. I slowly picked up the tee and looked at the coach and hold my arms up to signal good. Rebels lead Moss Point 3-0.

That was as good as our offense would get for most of the half. The speed of Moss Point was real and they clicked off a couple of touchdowns to lead 14-3 into the second quarter. With three minutes left in the half, Moss Point was driving and "Big Tony" jumped to deflect a ball that Ray Epperson made another diving interception at our 19.

"Bob take off," yelled Coach Sloan. Chris Cooper got free, everybody handled their blocks, the exchanges with Pat to Zack to me were smooth, and Coop hauled my throw into his arms and raced toward the goal line. They had a player nicknamed "Lightning" and we saw why as he knocked Coop out of bounds at the 2 yard line for a 79 yard gain. The next play "Big Tony" broke through 2 tacklers for a touchdown. Our try for 2 was good and we got into halftime down only 14-11 and momentum on our side.

In the locker room everybody stayed poised while Coaches Sloan and Roberts secure our second half strategy. "Can you believe how much that Coach is cussing at us," Ray said.

"I've got a plan," Wes Baker one of our cornerbacks said.

"Linemen, we've got to have larger splits up front. Pat, I believe they are set up for some traps. So if I don't get the call in focus on 53 and 26 traps," Coach Sloan said.

"Coach, their safety is flying up to make hits so the dump pass to Coop looks like it is there for the taking," I said.

We huddled up and file out with everyone getting to tap the sign one more time. Our plan worked to a T. We moved the ball like we did on the first drive and took the lead on a 23 yard trap play by Freddy, to lead 18-14. At the start of the fourth quarter Wes Baker saw his plan unfold in front of him. Moss Point ran a sweep to their own sideline and "Big Tony" was dragging the runner down and Wes drew a bead on their Coach, dove over Tony and nailed a perfect hit on the Coach. While Wes was getting up he delivers the "stop your cussing" message.

It was the fourth down at midfield and Moss Point dropped to punt. The punter kicked the ball and it went straight up and then bounced backward for -4 yards. The Rebel faithful let out a true yell and Pat drove us down and hit Coop on a dump pass from 15 yards out. We missed the two point play but led 24-14.

Knowing they had to throw, Coach Sloan designed a coverage for "Lightning." He put Pat and Zack in to help triple cover the guy. Everybody else covered their man and Moss Point was stymied. We got the ball back and it was the loudest countdown from 10 to 1 we had ever heard. 24-14 and Alabama State 2-A champions from Stuart.

The sea of Rebel fans was a sight to behold. So many hugs, a few good kisses, tears, and smiles everywhere as the third goal on our board had been reached. "Another great throw Bob," sounded a familiar voice behind me, as Dad reached to hug me.

"Dad, this one is gonna cost you a twenty." He laughed and reached into his pocket. He gave me the bill and I stuffed it into my sock. Mr. Jack and Mr. Charles could have been, at least, twenty dollars richer, if they had found the guy.

***Championships Live Forever
and They Are Worth the Effort***

PART III

In Stuart the streets, sidewalks, and walkways got a break. Everybody, not just the players, were walking on cloud nine; their feet barely touched ground. We tried to keep our routines intact. Zack and I made our Friday morning breakfast trip to Paul's Diner. As we walked in Ms. Winchester gave us both a hug and congratulated us. "Go ahead, Zack. It's fine to order the big country breakfast now," I said and we all laughed.

Mr. Paul stopped by and said he was putting up a Stuart team photo. He told us had made the trip down for the game and before he left, took care of our check. I had to admit that it felt great to shake so many hands and get the kind of compliments we got.

Our basketball team was slow to get moving having only Cliff and Joe, who didn't play football. In mid-January, we Rebels put it together to win the Concord County Championship over Collins. The Stuart fans were great and loved seeing us bring home another championship. This was special because, after football, nobody thought much about our basketball chances.

As basketball season was about to close, with only a week left in the season, I had a different thought at our Thursday evening family dinner. "Dad, Zack and I were discussing this because we got to looking back. Do you know that since the ninth grade I haven't had a free week during the school year since the eighth grade? There has always been some type of practice, maybe except for the last few days of the year after baseball."

"Mom, you will just have to find something for Bob to do," Quint said. He was just about to start junior high football spring training.

I got an answer for the free time I thought I was about to have for a few weeks. On Monday Coach Sloan called me to his office. He looked serious and he said, "I just got off the phone with Coach Duncan and he would like you, if you have the interest, to come over and practice a couple of weeks at NE Alabama. They've finished their indoor workouts and he would be able to get a better look, since you had Pat playing here."

I didn't miss a beat. "I'll be there tomorrow."

Coach Sloan smiled. "Knowing you, Bob, I told Coach Ken you would. It'll give you a chance to do some things and you know their offense. Trust me, come scrimmage, things will move a little faster so be ready."

Well, getting my arm ready to start baseball would have to wait a couple of weeks. I told Zack and Pat after school on Monday what I was about to do. I knew that the next couple of weeks would be a big step up. I got over to the Owl field-house a little early to get my equipment. I was looking through the shoulder pads reserved for quarterbacks and found a pair with the name of S. Hayes, #14, written inside. Talk about following in my brother's footsteps—not many get to follow with the same pair of pads. I knew a few of the older guys that were freshmen when Stew was a senior and they made me feel welcome and not like a total fish out of water.

I had a couple of days of throwing and handing off in drills which was the same sort of thing I had done at Stuart. On Thursday the second half of practice was a scrimmage. About midway through Coach Ponder, the quarterback coach, said, "Lil' Hayes, get in here." I ran three plays and all went pretty smooth with no mistakes. The next call was our fake 25 and roll left to hit the full back in the flat. After I called the play, I figured the first team defense kinda knew our plays and I needed to be careful. I took the snap, faked and as I rolled left I saw the linebacker making a move toward the fullback. The split end was running a post so I lofted it to him and he caught it and ran for a touchdown.

As I jogged off the field, Coach Duncan was standing there with his arms crossed. He looked at me and said, "'Lil' Hayes that was the worst damn, piss-poor pass I have ever seen."

My face fell suddenly. I had been grinning. "Well, Coach," I said, "what about him scoring?"

He shrugged. "You were just lucky, maybe a good read but, hell, you've got to get your shoulders turned square and not just float a wounded duck out there."

Coach Proper Procedures and Technique

A short time later we moved down to run goal-line offense and, better yet, goal-line defense with the first team defense in there. Coach Sloan was right: the pace and the players both moved a little faster. On our option, in high school, I had been used to making the inside fake and having a few steps to decide to turn it up or pitch. The call was option right and after the fake I took maybe two steps and wham! I knew it was daylight but all I saw was darkness. Pulling me up off the ground was Richard Roundtree, "Tree," an All-Conference defensive end. He said good pitch, but I was busy trying to figure out where I was at. Luckily the next two plays were hand-offs and I went in the right direction. But, you see, that type of hit had never happened to me before.

On Saturday morning, I showed up for our 10 am practice and scrimmage to go along with a high school coach's clinic. I was getting dressed and about to take the field with the other quarterbacks when Coach Ponder came by. He said, "Bob, today go back in, change clothes, and just watch. We've got quite a few high school coaches here today."

My practice with the team was kind of a gray area, at that time, so back in I went to put my jeans on. I got in four additional practices and Coach Duncan said he would get back with me in a few weeks. The last thing he said was, "Son, I really appreciate all your effort."

I knew my situation and understood what I was facing. Football-wise it was great to be a part of a championship team. I remember telling Coach Sloan that I wanted to be part of the best team in Stuart history and so far that was the case. Our 2-A team was pretty stout. Pat Byrd, quarterback, signed with his home state Georgia Bulldogs. "Big Tony" Carter, fullback and linebacker, signed with Arkansas. Then, my best friend, Zack Morris signed with Auburn. Chris Cooper, our tight end, would sign to play baseball for Marion Junior College.

The start of baseball practice at Stuart had a different ring to it. This year two teachers, that coached some basketball for our junior high, were taking over the baseball program. This was usually the duty of the assistant football coach and didn't hold a lot of promise. Head Coach Ingram and Coach Rollins both graduated from Stuart. They had both had played basketball and baseball.

Practice had been going well. All of us on the team, except for three players, had played football. Pat, Zack, and I were the three pitchers and I played third base while the other two played center field when not pitching.

We got to opening game, playing at North Central, and it was a cool spring day. We got off the bus and I went over and asked Tripp, trainer and score-keeper, where I was batting in the line-up. He said, "Bob, you're not batting or in the line-up."

"What the crap?" I said. I ran over to Coach Ingram and pulled him to the side and asked why I wasn't at third base.

"Bob," he said, "Just relax. It's the first game. You're just relieving today. It's to let you warm-up more on the side."

I made my case to just bring me in from third but watching the game from the side was what I did.

As the game progressed we were tied at four a piece and Coach told me to start warming up. Going to the bottom of the seventh, after we had a long inning, I took over for Zack on the mound.

There was no score in the seventh, but in the eighth, we scored a run to go up 5-4. After a couple of errors, North Central had bases loaded and two outs. Their shortstop, who also was a good basketball player that signed to play at Tillman, was up to bat. I'd gotten a 2-2 count on him and I figured he may not hit it too deep. All of a sudden I remembered throwing a blooper pitch to a Thomas kid when I was 10 years old. So, I lofted a slow arching pitch that the batter couldn't hold back and popped out to Cooper at second base. We Rebels win 5-4 and our catcher, Billy Gray, came out and said, "You better be glad that worked." Billy couldn't believe the story about throwing that pitch some eight years earlier.

On the bus ride back Billy, one of the players that didn't play football, was sitting next to Zack and me talking about our game since we both pitched and he caught. "Billy, you've got a lot to learn about where Bob gets some of his ideas." Zach said. "And the weirdest part is, he's usually right."

In the paper the next day Bob Hayes was noted as the winning pitcher. It was another coaching lesson—sticking to a game plan, encouraging the players to accept it, and following through.

Sometimes Players Hate it when the Coach Is Right

That baseball season was fun and we got beat by Dalton, of all teams, to make it to the State play-offs in baseball. The schedule and games felt a lot like little league: we'd play baseball and after game the game we'd get a shake at the Rebel Drive-In.

On Tuesday Coach Sloan called me down to his office. I walked in to find Coach Duncan talking with him. He rose and shook my hand and apologized for not getting to me sooner. He said, "I saw you pitch back at that North Central game. I tell you I just shook my head when you threw that pitch to get the last out."

I laughed and told him the old story.

"Okay, Bob," he said after awhile, "this is what I've got. I think you've got some talent, wished you had more speed and I like, no, I love your knowledge of the game. As you saw a few weeks ago, Ralph Maddox will be a junior and you will be fourth or fifth on the depth chart, which is already pretty solid. There is a good chance you will be our scout team quarterback, which means red-shirted and I promise you it's no walk in the park. But I've seen what you can contribute to a program and I think you can handle the chore."

"Coach Duncan," I said, "I've always loved being around and being a part of the team. I grew up an Owl, with Stew there, and I'll do my part to help our team."

He reached out and shook my hand and even gave me my old pat on the head. "I was telling Coach Sloan about this yesterday and he checked with your classes and grades which should allow you to receive some grant money for tuition and we have a book plan to help also. I've worked it out for you to be on the athletic meal ticket." He laughed. "Hell, you earned that as a ball boy the first year I was coaching here."

I thanked him. I was very honored.

He went on. "Bob, you'll be getting the practice and summer workout info in a few weeks. Glad to have you and I know I can count on you a lot more than most."

I walked back toward the classrooms talking with Zack and "Big Tony" as Mrs. Jernigan was about to start Civics class. Zack, who was usually a little shy, stands up and said, "Mrs. Jernigan I've got an announcement. Just 15 minutes ago, Bob Hayes signed to become part of the NE Alabama Owls."

Everybody started clapping and I turned four shades of red. That was a total shock from Zack. Instead of our normal lunchroom food, a car full of us headed to the West Marion Café for lunch and strawberry pie. Lucky for us Dad was there having lunch. I got a handshake, a hug, and, wouldn't you know it, a free lunch, too.

Just Keep Working as Hard as You Can

I got home and Mom had some snacks sitting on the counter, but the hugs came first today. "Where would you like to have dinner tonight? Mom asked.

I thought for a second. "Doesn't Paul's have their rib-eye special on Tuesday?"

She thought so. She said, "I'll call your Dad and we'll just meet him at 6. Save him a trip."

"I may just meet you and Quint. I'd like to pick up Lynn on my way," I said.

Dinner was great, but it came with more big news. Lynn told us that she had accepted a scholarship to study finance at Birmingham Southern College. She had some relatives in the banking business, so it was a no-brainer.

"You sure helped me through that accounting class," I reminded her.

Now that we knew where we were both heading for college, all of that anxiety was over. We made our way back to her house and I walked her up to the front door. We were making small talk and I happened to turn my head and in doing so our faces were only inches apart. It seemed like the only thing to do then: we kissed. Afterwards, our eyes popped open. "It's about time," Lynn said.

I laughed. "No kidding," I said. "You don't know how many times I've wanted to do this. But the timing has never been right. You and Cooper have been off and on. It's not like this is the big city. I don't want to have anybody mad at me, like Coop." I thought for a second. "Or you," I said.

That was a great evening.

We tried to keep in touch, of course, but it became like a lot of plans: time faded it away. It was just that Lynn had always been special. I loved how casual she was. Even as a majorette, she was casual. She'd always been a stunner, but hadn't ever taken herself too seriously.

Summer was hot, as always, in Stuart. The time zipped by in a hurry with work in a lumber yard stacking boards and running and throwing in the late afternoon. All in preparation for day one of practice when I would have to run a mile and then 10 and 60 yard sprints

On day one at NE Alabama I was running my sprints and this six foot five, two hundred and forty-five pound guy went zipping by me. Speed wasn't my strong suit but this big guy was just too awesome. After we were done, I walked over to introduce myself. "I'm Bob Hayes," I said, sticking out my right hand.

"Hey," he said, Calvin Radford," and the largest hand I had ever seen appeared before me. Calvin was all-everything at a small, black high school in north Georgia, but primarily a defensive end. I knew enough about my situation as scout team quarterback to know that this guy was gonna be getting a lot of chances hitting me in practice. "Calvin, you got a favorite beverage you're partial to?"

"Schlitz is pretty good, if you're asking for honesty."

I thought to myself, well, I did sign on to get an education.

"Tree," Richard Roundtree, walked by and shook my hand and said, "Glad to have you back Lil' Hayes." Then he looked at Calvin and said, "Is this here the Radford kid we signed?"

I wondered about calling the biggest person I've ever seen 'kid' as I look back at Tree, but I didn't say anything. I just introduced the two. It turns out they are from different ends of Georgia. "We will see what he's got before long," Tree said.

"I just hope it is not at my expense," I said as we all shared a laugh.

So, the rest of the afternoon, now that running was over, went on like this: shaking hands and meeting the other players, finding out where everyone was from and recognizing those I'd played against in high school. The outdoor food for the first night barbeque was really good, and it included my first taste of barbequed goat, but you could tell that the freshmen were more worried about the seven am meeting and practice the next day.

I walked into the team meeting room at 6:45. A hand grabs the back of my T-shirt and Ralph Maddox, quarterback, said, "Lil' Hayes, come on we're on the front row."

At five 'til, Coach Duncan walked in and there were some wide-eyed freshmen in the room, half scared to death. Two freshmen walked in and Coach greeted them this way: "Boys, what time is it?"

"6:55, Coach," they said.

"Lesson #1, Coach Tony, our conditioning coach who's standing over here, will give you two a lesson in Coach Duncan time after practice," he said.

The older ones give a few cat calls.

The first couple of days in helmets, shoulder pads and shorts consisted of drills and running play after play. Precision was one of the main themes that you focused on—not just to do it, but to do it the right way. You can see this in the way we started practice: five centers and five quarterbacks went out on the field first to take snaps, for seven minutes, with drop-backs for hand-offs and passes.

Did I mention that it was hot in the deep-South on the first of August? I began to notice that after practice and a meeting most took off back to their room for a nap and air conditioning. But I also noticed that a lot of the older guys didn't drag around quite as much for the afternoon practice and I didn't see them after lunch. "Okay 'Mad-Dog' (Ralph Maddox)," I said, "where in the heck are some of you guys getting off to after lunch?"

"All right, Hayes," he said. "You're in tomorrow."

"In where?" I asked.

"Mad-Dog" grinned. "You'll see for yourself."

The next day after lunch, I stuck with "Mad-Dog" and into the back seat I climbed. We drove about three miles out to a park called "Lithonia Springs." There was a small amount of play-ground equipment, a couple of picnic tables under some Oak trees and I also saw a small stream off to the side. There were a few of the senior players sitting in the creek and Kent Stamps, a center, saw me and called, "Lil' Hayes come on and hop right in."

Well, it was a toasty ninety-eight degrees in the shade and that made me think it was time to keep up with the big boys. I walked over, saw the sandy bottom and hopped right in like I was told. "Son-of a-, it's cold," I shouted and they all got their chuckles.

"Just wait till you sit down," Stamps said. Sit I did as my eyes rolled back into my head. But, it was amazing how much better you felt after soaking in that cold water. They told me it helped rejuvenate the muscles. "My brother never told me about this park during his days."

"It was here but it was grown over. It was only a couple of years ago that they cleaned it up," Bob Coleman said, senior line backer. A couple of them asked about Stew and I filled them in and they all told me that he was a good player, but an ever better leader. "He looked out for everybody and wasn't stuck on himself," Tree said as he was walking up behind us, getting ready to cool off.

After the first week of practice I had lost eight to ten pounds and we were just about to start full pads. Dr. Weaver, team doctor from Marion, stopped me as I weighed walking out of the training room. "Hey, Bob, how you liking it?' he asked.

I said, "Pretty well but you just can't prepare enough."

He smiled at me. "Bob," he said, "do you drink beer?"

I shrugged. "Not much really."

"Well," he said, "looking at your weight chart it wouldn't hurt you to have a couple after practice."

Calvin was walking behind me. I thought about how full pads started tomorrow. "Calvin, you thirsty?" I asked.

"Hayes, what kind of dumb question is that?" he said and laughed.

"Well, hop in," I said. "We'll make a pit stop before dinner, on me."

We started to climb into my Chevy Vega and one of my roommates, Dave Yates, said, "Hey, I heard and I'm in."

We made the five mile drive to Buster's Quick Shop which was fifty yards past the city limits of Pace. I soon learned that they had some of the coldest beverages you could find and I purchased a six pack of cold Schlitz for Calvin and myself. Dave got himself a few Miller's and we took our time heading back to dinner. "Heck," I said, "I'm just following doctor's orders," and we all three did a mock toast.

Practice went according to plan and quite a few discovered that football was not really for them. I even got a few good words regarding my throwing against the first team secondary. It was easier with no rush coming at you, I promise.

As we got into the start of the season I was running the other team's plays. One of the younger assistants held up a play diagram and we ran the play. We were still trying to show that we fit in even going against our first team defense. After our second game we came up short playing in South Louisiana. The bad part was our defensive line didn't get a sack of the quarterback the whole game. Come Tuesday they would work on that really well.

Here was what really well looked like. After warm-ups, quarterbacks were always first out for seven minutes taking snaps, Defensive line coach and coordinator, Tate Reeves, called for the defensive line, the third team offensive line and Hayes. Down to the corner of the practice field we went. "As I told you in the meeting the object is to get off of your man, get him the hell out of the way and sack the quarterback. Hayes you take the snap, drop back and you can move from tackle to tackle."

I was thinking, not stupid enough to say it out loud, "Thanks, Coach. At least, I won't be a total sitting duck."

We lined up over the ball. I got under the center, barked out "blue" which was our first sound and do a seven step drop. Tree was the first to get back as I stepped to my left and he wrapped his right arm around my chest and slings me down. There was an art to getting hit as a quarterback. Stew had told me when you feel the pressure, or see it, to hold onto to ball and go with the hit. He said if you try to fight the hit the ball can come loose quite easily.

Also Tree had told me, one day while sitting in the creek, "Hayes, you're going to be taking some hits, but in practice we ain't gonna cheap shot you." Somehow that made me feel better; at least, a little bit.

Learn Good Fundamentals for All Types of Situations

Coach grabbed Calvin by the face mask and yelled: "Dammit, Cal, stay low, quit standing up, slap the side of the tackle's helmet and hit the damn quarterback."

This time Calvin blew by and I was able to turn a bit to not take the blunt of the hit. "Bullshit, guys," Coach Reeves said. "Don't feel sorry for his ass. Hit him like you would in a game."

At least I saw our head trainer, Coach Skip Hall, shaking his head in disgust after that comment. There were a couple of thoughts that went through my head at the bottom of the pile: I wished that Mom had introduced me to golf. I held up good except on hits from Mo' Wainright, a transfer from Florida.

About every time, though, a buckle, a snap, finger-nail or something would catch me and those little things hurt the worst. I knew that this was unintentional. It turned out that on the next to last play Mo' hit me, I slipped and he landed on top with my shoulder hitting the ground first. I managed to make the next play and Coach Reeves blew his whistle for the period to end. "You okay, Hayes?" he asked.

"Yes, sir. I'm good."

He said, "You showed a lot, Hayes. Now go over and see Coach Hall."

I did what he told me to, thinking to myself: "Welcome to College Football."

At least I didn't have to run sprints as I made my way to shower and then the training room for three ice packs on my shoulder and arm. Each of the first team line stopped by to check on me and I assured them we all have a job to do. "Lil' Hayes we'll have you a couple of cold ones here shortly," Tree said.

"I didn't hear that," said Coach Skip.

You Have to Do Your Duty. Sometimes that Requires Taking the Bitter with the Bitter

Luckily we had an away game and I was able to go back home for the weekend and see Doc West. After a few treatments he was able to help my neck and shoulder get better. I was glad to see that we had four quarterback sacks, and Mo' returned one fumble for a touchdown. I read this in the *Marion Ledger* while eating Dad's home-cooked breakfast.

We faded that year to finish 6 and 4, losing a couple of games in the last minute of play. My school work went well and it was time for the Christmas break. It was good to see some of the guys back home and Pat, Zack, and I got together for lunch at the West Marion Diner. We swapped stories of our first fall of football.

On Christmas Eve, the Hayes family was having a light dinner with friends stopping by. Doc West and his family were over as well, including Curt and Pete. Of course the main conversation amongst the guys, sitting in the den together like a junior high party, was football. I listened intently and for the first time I noticed that Quint had a little to say about football and he had a good year on the Rebel Junior High team.

I was asked by Doc West how the season went and I was surprised by my reply. "Well," I said. "You saw how that one week went, but it was different just being on the practice squad and no real game to prepare for. We scrimmaged some on Monday's, along with the ones that didn't play in the games, but the spark and intensity isn't there." I thought for a second about what I'd said. "Now, it would get intense trying to not get your head knocked off but I missed the preparation part the most."

I looked over at my dad. "Dad, after saying that, I really feel coaching may be in my future."

I saw a smile come across his face and he said, "Well, I've seen you have more input than any kid over the years. You flat made some good calls for me and at NE Alabama."

"I'm gonna give it my all when we get back and see what happens."

With another holiday season gone, I was looking for a couple of classes take during the upcoming semester. I needed an active PE class and my pencil happened to lodge in the dance class section of my catalog. Modern Dance was an active class that I could use that 3 hour credits and might actually get more benefit with footwork that would help more than a basketball or a tennis class. I took a chance and signed up for the course.

Getting back on campus we had our first team meeting. Coach Duncan was not pleased with our 6 and 4 record over the past year. In a week we were going to start indoors. Coach told us that he was reverting back to his days at Alabama and Coach Bryant's indoor regimen. Knowing that reputation, you could hear quite a few "oh shits" around the room.

"You're going to become better players. All of us are going to work harder. I saw an Owl team a few years ago finish undefeated and they worked their butts off to do so. If that is not what you want to achieve then good luck with your education."

The next day we had a scheduled time to get our clothes for workouts and time for our groups. Among the quarterbacks there was a new name and face. It belonged to Mitch Fontenot, a transfer from LSU. His name fit and when he introduced himself to the rest of us his lingo was all Cajun. As we were getting our stuff, Steve Staten, last year's back-up, spoke first. "What are we getting into?" he said to "Mad-Dog."

I jumped in to the conversation. "I know "Bear" Bryant had a knack for working some asses off. He was famous for his Junction Boys when he was at Texas A&M," I said.

"Coach didn't quite mention this indoor stuff befo I done come on up here, you know," Mitch answered and we all looked at each other, trying to figure out what he had just said.

We finished talking with each other by asking what went on during the holidays. We were all curious with what Mitch was going to share with us. "We just hung out by Gator Bayou, sucked on some mud-bugs and threw back a few Jax beers. It was either that or shucking a few oysters."

We'd heard word that Mitch could throw a football through a carwash without getting it wet, but it just may have been the wrong carwash too. It was just unique listening to his lingo.

The basement of the athletic dorm had been made over. My partial scholarship had me at Brewer Hall, across the street from Ayers Hall. There was no longer a TV room, game room, or ping-pong tables. Those relics gave way to a mat room, a stationary double blocking dummy, and an open room. Another aspect you noticed walking in was quite a few plastic lined garbage cans. I was sure the reason for those would present itself.

At 3:30 on Monday afternoon it was time for group B, which was made up of quarterbacks and receivers, along with the specialty players. The first words we heard came from Mitch asking why there were so many garbage cans. First up for us quarterbacks was jumping rope for fifteen minutes. Then we got to go over to the mats and do grass drills. This was high intensity running in place and when the coach hollered "down" or blew the whistle you would hit the mat like a belly buster and pop back up to continue running in place. The running in place on the soft mats was a lot harder than you'd imagine. After about fifteen minutes, Mitch was bent over one of those garbage cans puking his guts up.

"Is that those mud-bugs or the oysters, Mitch," "Mad-Dog" said and he started laughing. Then we had the privilege of getting in a four point stance and hitting one dummy, backing up with your feet moving, and then hitting the other dummy. The painful aspect of this was your knees hitting the carpeted surface which burned the heck out of you.

The next week of indoors had new challenge to it. The rest of the team got to put on a helmet with boxing gloves to pound at each other. The quarterbacks got to get on the mats and hog wrestle. In the middle of the circle you would face each other, on all fours, and try to push the other out of the circle. Staten and I faced off and I put up a good struggle but finally got out muscled. I then watched "Mad-Dog" just blow Mitch straight back before he knew what happened. At least Mitch wasn't paying as much homage to those garbage cans. The next time we hog-wrestled, it was me, all of 5'10" and 175 versus "Mad-Dog" at 6'3" and 225. We were getting ready and "Mad-Dog" said, "Just don't let the wall hit your head behind you."

"Well," I said, "bring your big ass on."

Coach Ponder blew the whistle, I put up a slight resistance and I let him push me back real fast. Close to the circle I peeled around and let his momentum carry his butt right on out. The rest of the guys clapped for me and gave "Mad-Dog" a hard time. "Lil' Hayes you're the only one in here that would come up with that move."

"Yeah," I said. "Trouble is it'll only work once."

After a few weeks I was handling the indoors pretty well except for one day. Stew happened to come by to see Coach Duncan. He was in the basement talking and watching when it was our turn to hit the mats. The young, Coach Norris, was trying to show Stew how many grass drills I could do. It was pretty miserable. Stew stuck around to have dinner with me and I warned him not to show back up at that time again.

He said, "Well, at least I didn't have to watch you throw up."

I laughed. "I bet you're going to tell me how you used to stretch out over there on a couch and watch TV when you lived here instead of this."

The part I was having difficulty with was the modern dance class. Ms. Sobiesk had us doing dance procedures and I was hurting in places I never knew I had. The different positions and stances were using totally different muscles than those used by football and workouts. I had even given thought to dropping the class, but I needed the hours and I liked the time slot. I have to admit there were some nice classmates also: 6 guys and 18 girls in the class.

It was a little difficult talking to Ms. Sobiesk. She was from Switzerland and, to be honest with you, very attractive. She did like how I was using her class become more agile in football. Ms. Sobiesk had worked with some of the football players when she was at Duke and came to NE 'Alabama to become head of the dance department. Just like with indoors, with dance you started to adjust and improve.

We survived the indoor workouts and the quarterbacks and receivers were going out to work on some new patterns along with throwing and catching. During lunch I had a note on our message board: Coach Duncan called me to his office. The meeting would shine a light on my future career path—of course, I didn't know it at the time.

At the time, I just tried to think if I had done anything wrong or gotten caught being out of line. So far as I knew, that wasn't the case. I did go out with the Dean's daughter, but that evening had gone well. At least I thought so.

I walked in to Coach's office. We shook hands and he asked me to sit down. "Lil' Hayes how did you like the indoors?" I said.

"Coach," I said, "I can't quite give you a good answer face to face." Coach got a chuckle out of that one. "But," I said, "If you were looking to test some character and commitment, then I think you succeeded very well."

"Bob, I have been watching things and I have something I want to present to you. I was proud of your efforts during the season with our scout team. I know you had a couple of tough days and you showed a lot of character. With Mitch coming in from LSU, and he has hung in better than we thought, it doesn't help your standing too well." Coach paused to see how I was taking this.

I nodded at him. I waited to hear what he would say next.

He said, "Now then, I've got a couple of extra scholarships to work with and I want to propose something to you."

I was getting pretty nervous. I said, "Let's have it, Coach. I'm not 100% sure as yet."

"We don't get to have as big of a staff at this level. I'm not going to kid you I talked to your Dad last night to get his take."

I didn't really like the idea of being the last to know: "Tell me first before I ask what his thoughts were."

"Okay," he said. "I would like for you to become, what I've termed, a Coaches' Assistant since you are still in undergrad classes. You would throw to our receivers in practice, help with holding for kickers and come fall help with plays for our scout team and be able to keep the play charts at games. Coach Sloan had told me you were real good with special teams and I want to call on you for help with that as well. It would allow us to become more efficient and be better prepared. This way I can put you on full scholarship."

After a few moments of silence I spoke up. "Okay, Coach," I said. "I have two quick questions. First one, why the hell didn't you think of this before indoors started? Second, what did Dad have to say?"

Those two questions brought a smile to Coach Duncan's face. "Okay, Bob," he said. "Do you really want me to answer?"

I laughed. "You better believe it."

"Okay," Coach said again. He was laughing, too. "One, we weren't sure Mitch would make it and two, your dad thought it is a good idea. He thought you would be a great fit."

"Coach I mentioned to Dad and Stew, during the holidays, that coaching might be in my future. During the season I missed the game preps and watching film to get ready for games."

"That is one other aspect you will be able to help out with. Film is not one of Ralph's strong points and I'm not sure yet what Mitch's strong points will be. I do know that you'll be an asset in that area. And besides I already know you've earned their trust," Coach said.

"Coach, once an Owl, always an Owl. And I think this help me a lot more with my future. I appreciate you looking out for me in that aspect."

"Bob, I'm mostly looking out for myself—I think you'll really help our program. We have some improving to do and I appreciate your integrity. After spring we are going to put you in Coach Ponder's office."

We shook hands and I told Coach I had to get to dance class.

"Hayes," he said "that is the first time I've heard that out of a player in my office."

"Well," I said to Coach. "Have you ever met Ms. Sobiesk?"

Coach shook his head.

"I tell you, it would be worth your effort." I went out the door smiling.

Be Open to Ideas and Suggestions and Don't Let Ego Get in the Way

I made it out to our last session of throwing before the start of outdoor spring practice, in pads, come Monday. We warmed up as usual but I went over to throw with the receivers and Coach Bailey. He said, "Bob, I think you made a good decision and glad to have you working with me."

"Coach, watching you throw I can see why."

"Don't start any crap this soon Hayes," he said, smiling.

I stayed back instead of doing reps while throwing patterns. When we were done Coach Ponder, offensive coordinator, called everybody up. "We've got one little change," he said. "Hayes is going to become a student assistant working with our offense and kicking game. He'll be doing the throwing in practice to you receivers and he'll help in other areas later on."

Coach Ponder looked at me. I figured I ought to say something. "Guys," I said, "when I came here I wanted to earn a scholarship and try and help our Owls win. The scholarship part came today. I told Coach Duncan I wished he had this idea before the start of indoors, but I guess I will have a lot better appreciation for doing it. I promise you this, though: if any of you have to do any extra running, it won't be coming from me."

They all laughed and gave me a hand.

After practice Coach Hall, the trainer, was not in his office so I used his phone, since it had a State watts line where long distance was no charge. I talked with Mom and she mentioned that Stew would be home Saturday and Dad said he would grill out. I said, "I may bring one of the guys so have an extra steak ready." I told her to tell my dad we'd talk Saturday.

Some of us guys went out to Tal's Shed, which was the only place to hear a band and try to meet and mingle. It was located in Pace, or right on the city limits across from Buster's Quick Shop, our favorite beverage station. I had been talking to Mitch and almost forgot about going home the next day, Saturday, to eat. "Mitch, you got anything going tomorrow?"

"Not I be thankin' of," he said with that Cajun lingo.

"You up for going over to a little cook out and have a good steak?"

"What you be talking 'bout Hayes, I'm in for that. Any stray women round yo area?" he asked.

"Well, I'll just pick you up about two. Bring some extra clothes and we'll stay over and go out in Marion tomorrow night." I decided not to answer the part about the women. We tipped bottles and listened to a few more songs.

On our way to Stuart I filled Mitch in on my background to NE Alabama and how Stew was a quarterback during the undefeated season, and how Dad had been the high school coach for eighteen years.

Mitch said, "I see you have been round that since you be knee high."

"Heck Mitch," I said. "I can remember listening to LSU games on my little radio since the Tigers mainly played at night."

"Yeah game day down in Baton Rouge was some kind of special. Heck even not playing you signed a ton of programs, balls and everything."

We came into Stuart and I told Mitch not to blink or he would miss it: "Up ahead is our only traffic light." I pulled into the Rebel Drive-In. I looked at Mitch and asked him what flavor of shake he'd like.

"What's your call, Hayes?" he asked.

I told him peanut butter, of course.

"Make it two," Mitch said.

I was surprised. "Mitch," I said, "I know you ain't right because you're the only one to go with that."

Mitch said, "Hayes, I haven't seen you make too many bad choices." He paused for a second and pretended to think hard. "Well, maybe with that Brenda girl last night."

"You missed the boat, Mitch," I said. "You should see her roommate, Jessica. Now Jessica is the one I was trying to get the low down on. I have a class with Brenda."

Mitch looked impressed. He even liked the shake. It was perfect. On to the house we went.

As we passed Rebel High School I told Mitch how special it was being a part of the State Championship team.

"Yeah, I bet," Mitch said. "We got beat in the finals my senior year on a damn Hail-Mary pass, the last play of the game."

I shook my head. "Now that sounds disgusting."

When we got home, we did all the introductions. Mitch tried to explain a little bit about Cajun culture and Quint really took a liking to his lingo. Stew pulled in and joins us in the back yard. I introduced the two and tell Mitch, "You remember that day we were paired on the mats and did all those dang grass drills? Well, it is Stew's fault for being in there and Coach Norris thought it was funny to be showing out in front of him."

"Stew, don't be turning your back on me or I done find me somethin' to throw at you. I puked for five minutes after that."

"You're safe, Stew," I said. "If he throws it, there's a good chance it won't get close to you."

"Your ass Bob," Mitch replied and everybody chuckled.

"Mitch, what kind of offense did you run in high school?" Dad asked.

"A little bit of everything but we threw the heck out of the football and I got to move around a lot, which I liked. When I got to LSU they wanted a more straight back and over the top motion."

"Dad," I said," I was thinking that Mitch may be way more productive and comfortable with the throwing motion he used in high school."

"That's probably true," Dad said. "Sometimes changing a player's motion can do more harm than good."

"That's what I been feelin' myself," Mitch said.

"We've got a little time," Dad said. "Quint, go get your game ball."

Mitch and I started throwing a few, to warm up a little bit. Now understand that when you throw with Mitch, he keeps you on your toes because not everyone will come right to you. My dad was watching us. He said, "Mitch, show me what motion you used in high school."

Mitch dropped down a bit on his motion, not quite side-armed, but everyone started hitting me right in my hands and with more zip to boot.

My mom was watching, too, and she said, "He over-strides throwing the other way too much."

I grinned. "Mitch, Dad ain't the only coach in this family."

Mitch said, "Mama Hayes, if you do the cookin' like you coach and I know I'm in for a treat."

"Quint, go deep," I said.

Mitch lofted one with an easy and natural motion that fell right in Quint's arms. Mitch said, "That there felt as smooth as a gator's belly."

Dad laughed. "There's a comparison I've never heard before." Then Dad turned to me: "Now, Bob, you may have some explaining to do to Coach Ponder."

"I'm on it," I said.

"Enough coaching, now," Mom said. "Let's eat."

We let Mitch talk about his fishing and hunting gators from time to time. Mom brought out a big dish of strawberry pudding. Mitch put a few helpings in his bowl and said, "Coach Mama, this be the best strawberry dish I ever done had. We've got a lot of 'berries over in Ponchatoula but this is the best dessert I've eaten."

"Mitch, you just got out of doing the dishes," Stew said and everybody chuckled.

In the car going back to Pace the next day, I told Mitch to warm up regular, like he has been. I told him that I'd talk to Coach Ponder and then let him know when to change.

Mitch thanked me and said, "Hayes, that was the best food I've had since I been up here and the jawin' around was good too. Great family you've got there."

I had to agree with that.

On Monday at lunch I caught a break: Coach Duncan and Coach Ponder were eating together. I took my time walking by, trying to catch their eye, and when they said hello to me I told them I had a question. "Sure Hayes," Coach Duncan said, "have a seat."

I sat down and said, "I may have an answer to a question I bet you both have had."

"What question is that?" Coach Ponder asked, raising an eyebrow.

"You both know that Mitch was one of the top three Louisiana players of the year coming out of high school. He went home with me this past weekend and we talked with Dad and Stew for awhile. He said they changed his motion up when he got to LSU and it led to a lot of frustration. We threw some for Dad and Stew and realized that when he drops his release point down a bit, you'll see why he was so highly touted."

"We were told he was too small school and was intimidated. You know how he seems a little jittery," Coach Duncan said.

"Trust me Coach, that's just his nervous energy. If, after warm-ups, you let him do his thing, I believe you will see the quarterback you were looking to get."

"Mitch has made it this far, Hayes, so we'll see this afternoon," Coach Ponder said.

I got changed for practice and walked out with Mitch. "You got a break," I told him. "I talked with both Coach Ponder and Duncan at lunch and after warm-ups you should go back to your fun high school days of throwing like Saturday."

"Hayes, that be some fiddlin' to my ears. You too good man."

I smiled. "Well, whatever you just said I'll take your word it's something good. Just relax and do your thing."

After warm-ups, we broke off and did our individual drill. I threw to the receivers. Coach Bailey was able to stand out with them and see better the way they catch and tuck the ball in. We were about to go to team passing drills and Coach Bailey called the receivers together. That's when I threw in a comment: "Okay, guys, when Mitch is up I promise you be ready for some fast balls."

Coach Ponder called for the backs and receivers to huddle up and I looked at Coach Bailey and said, "Watch Mitch. You're gonna see something special."

The third play Mitch took the snap as the receivers were all going to run curl patterns. Mitch dropped back and gave a pump fake left, turned his feet to the right and uncorked one for the inside receiver, Pat Perry—otherwise known as "P.P." He put his hands up. Everyone turned to look when they heard a loud bam. The sound came when the ball zipped through his hands, hit his helmet, and bounced about twenty feet high. It knocked "PP" flat. "PP" shook his head a bit, jogged back to the huddle, and looked over at me and said, "You weren't joking, were you?"

That got everybody's attention and the rest of the drill Mitch was right on the money. You could hear the ball whistle on some of his throws.

One of the hardest throws for a quarterback to make is a deep out. With "PP's" speed the coaches put in a double out and Mitch flung out a frozen rope that "PP" caught this time, right on the money. He even got the ball out fast enough that the receivers had time to turn up field instead of just going out. Mitch did a good job of hiding his enthusiasm, not wanting to appear too cocky.

I walked by Coach Ponder. He looked at me and shook his head. I quietly said, "Told you so."

What Works for One May Not Work for the Other

As spring training came to a close Mitch had moved right there with Ralph Maddox for starting quarterback. Coach Duncan didn't want to show his hand this early but told the coaches that if we had a game right now Mitch would be the call. "Lil' Hayes," he said, "you were right on the mark with Mitch. Now I can see why he had the stats he did in high school."

Coach Ponder said the way Mitch could throw the ball would give us a lot more options.

"Hayes, one of your jobs is not to let Mitch get too cocky and to keep him out of trouble," Coach Duncan said.

The summer was going pretty well. Just like in the days when Stew was staying in Pace at NE Alabama, we had a good contingent of players doing the same under Coach Duncan. I had made a trip down to Mitch's home in Mound Bayou which sat close to Ville Platte, Louisiana. He even took me on a gator hunt; we got four on the trip, but none real big. I also got my first taste of boiled crawfish, etouffee, and gumbo.

We were getting our things together. I reached for my tennis shoes out of the closet and a rubber football caught my eye. I had to drop my shoes and use both hands to hoist it up. It was a regular size weighted rubber football. "I use to throw that thing around quite a bit," Mitch said. "When those dudes at LSU turned me around and tinkered with my throwing I had forgotten about it."

I said, "Well, it is going up to NE Alabama with us. Dad used to be real good using some natural methods of working out. They always seemed to work well and I believe this weighted ball will fit right in."

Since the close of spring practice Coach Ponder had been wide-eyed and open to expanding the offense to make use of Mitch's throwing ability. I appreciated the trust he put with me by asking questions about what I thought of certain plays with different routes to them, since I had a desk in the corner of his office. It made me feel like I was watching the films with Dad back in Stuart.

The start of practice was about to commence and I had to show Mitch, before hand, the secret of Lithonia Springs.

He said, "Hayes, you be doin' a bang up job of makin' me feel at home."

"Mitch," I said, "don't you go getting a big head because that's one of my jobs. Heck throwing that rubber ball of yours I'm chunking the ball better than I ever have."

Routines started to take shape and that attitude among the coaching staff became a lot more up-beat, what with the indoor workouts, spring practice, and Mitch's ability. We were having a game-type scrimmage and I was charting the plays and showing our two freshmen quarterbacks what to look for. During our halftime break I saw Mr. Casey Toms, *Marion Ledger* sports reporter, watching from the sidelines. I stopped by and talked with him for a few minutes and we asked about each other's families. He asked, "Bob, is this Fontenot kid the real deal?"

I nodded. "He is learning the offense well and he's got a cannon for an arm."

"You just made my day with that comment," Casey said, smiling.

I was a little confused. "What did I say that was so special?"

"Cannon for an arm," he said, and chuckled.

"If all goes well the first game you may have just helped to launch 'The Cajun Cannon.'" He laughed at his own joke. "Bob, after practice I'd like to talk with you and Mitch, if you don't mind. I like the direction Coach Duncan is working with you, following your Dad."

"That's some big shoes there, Mr. Toms," I said. I wasn't really sure I knew why he wanted to talk, but I decided to trust him. "We'll talk to you in a bit. Help yourself to the water." It was just a 96 degree afternoon.

Our talk with Mr. Toms went well. I said I liked my path toward coaching and being with the team.

Mitch gave a good response at the end of his questions. "Mr. Toms, Hayes here, has opened a big door for me and says I can trust you. Plus, he's had me over to Marion and Stuart a few times. I'll be glad to talk with you or your assistant after every game, but just don't go takin' no cheap ones at me. That way I know I can be up front with y'all."

Know What to Say so You Won't be Taken the Wrong Way

The week before the opening game with Tillman, our defensive coordinator, Coach Washburn, gave me the notebook and a list of plays for our scout team to run against the defense. The fourth play was a trap that caught one of our linebackers moving the wrong way and it went for a good gain. Good play, I thought. A few more got Coach Washburn's orders to "run it again." The old thought of would've, could've, and should've hit me. The plays that gave our defense trouble were pretty good plays or they wouldn't be such a pain in the butt. So, I put an asterisk in the bottom right corner of the play sheet for two reasons. One, if they give us trouble, there was a good chance we would be seeing them in a game. Two, I would just make me a copy of those plays to keep for myself. Then I would have a notebook full of each team's best plays to hold for myself, hopefully for future use.

Know When an Opportunity Presents Itself

After running the opponent's plays for three days, I gave him a copy of their best plays and when they like to run them. He appreciated that. I figured it would give him a better idea of which defense to call. I also noted that on the three films I watched of Tillman, four out of five times following a turnover the second play was a bit different, like a half back pass or a reverse. Most coaches liked to go for a play on the first.

The afternoon turned out great for the Owls. Defensive end Calvin Radford had 4 sacks. Linebacker Will Addison, on the second play following an Owl fumble, faked a blitz, and dropped back outside to intercept a screen pass and score a touchdown. But the largest boom was the "Cajun Cannon." Mitch was "smooth as a gators belly" and threw for 285 yards and 2 touchdowns. His accuracy ate up the clock with ball control and NE Alabama won 31-3.

Our routines fell in line and, with classes, there was not a lot of spare time. Mitch and I watched the film together every Monday night. I pointed out the small things on proper reads, positioning, and technique. One important aspect I wanted Mitch to appreciate came by way of my little league coach, Herb Gladden. I know if I threw the ball outside that I was coming across my body. It was essential to know what feels uncomfortable when you were learning how to perform. If you did this, you could keep from repeating the same mistakes.

Self Help Techniques Save a lot of Future Mistakes

I also looked at our receivers with their proper receiving duties and routes for them and the quarterbacks to be on the same page.

The season was going really good and we were hosting West Memphis. Before the game, I saw a familiar face walking into the Coaches office: Coach Dale Clark, Assistant Director at Kentucky, who was Stews' head coach at NE Alabama. "Lil' Hayes it's good to see you, Son," Coach Clark said. "Coach Duncan tells me you've been doing a super job and Mitch is playing great."

I thanked him. "How's everything in the Bluegrass State?"

"Well," he said. "Football-wise it's not as good as I wanted it to be at this point, but I think we have made some progress. I may have to get you up to Lexington to help before long Bob."

I laughed. "Just give me a call Coach and take it easy on Alabama next week."

The season went well and the Owls ended up 8 and 2. Mitch put together a great year was named All-Conference Quarterback. After the last game, Mom and Dad were talking with us, making plans for an after season grill out. "Coach Mama," Mitch said, "just make that strawberry pudding again and I ain't gonna be ashamed for asking."

Mom laughed.

All went well with the cookout and one of the special touches came when Mom presented Mitch with a scrapbook of all his articles from the *Marion Ledger*. Mitch was clearly touched: "Y'all just be too good of Folk, especially you, Coach Mama." The subject never came up before, but with tears in his eyes he gave Mom a hug and said it had been eleven years since his own mother had died in an accident and he was appreciative of all she had done.

It turned out that the lady at his house in Louisiana was his aunt, which made more sense now. Mitch recovered from his tears and started joking again: "Sharon, all you got to do is get me fixed up with that red head at your bank Bob's been braggin' 'bout and all will be well."

Sometimes You Never Know a Person's Situation

In mid-January, we had our big weekend for recruits to come visit. Coach Ponder was laying it on the staff that we needed a couple of receivers and hopefully two kids from a junior college in South Mississippi. Coach let me talk to them a bit and I thought I may have something for them.

"What have you got Hayes?" Coach Ponder asked.

"Just trust me," I said.

The two receivers turned out to be twins, Jake and Jesse Jaynes. They were smallish in size at 5' 10," but they could run and catch. After dinner I showed them the athletic dorm and took them to meet Mitch. We had it planned that after the intro and small talk, Mitch would say that Jennifer was waiting on him. After he left I would say, "Guys let me show you this." THIS being the scrapbook Mom had made. Then I would say, "Twins, you will have the chance to be receivers for the best quarterback in the South. LSU made a couple of mistakes and everything fell into place up here. Heck, he is from Mound Bayou, Louisiana and goes right by your junior College on his way home. Also guys, the ratio of girls to guys at NE Alabama is 3 to 1."

Sunday afternoon at the 5 pm coaches meeting there was a big board with the recruits on it. Coach Ponder said, "Hayes, just what in hell did you tell the Jaynes twins?"

I was surprised. I said, "I told them they get to play with Mitch, on a winning team, which they weren't able to do in junior college, and the girl to guy ratio is 3 to 1. I also showed them a scrapbook my Mom made for Mitch throughout the season."

Coach Ponder and Coach Bailey's eyes both lit up.

"That's our boy, Hayes," Coach Ponder said.

"Okay, Coaches, I want to get some of your input before we start indoors," Coach Duncan asked. "Hayes, you went through it last year. What do you think?"

"I think we have time to add a few more specialty exercises and maybe one or two sessions."

"What specialty?" the coach asked.

"Last year, I know I went from just getting fingertips over the basketball rim to being able to dunk a volleyball. The quarterbacks were jumping rope plus I took a modern dance class. It was a little humbling at first but I hurt in muscles I never knew I had. Another part is that, one day, you could have Ms. Sobiesk lead a workout. She told me she did it for players at Duke and I promise most of you won't miss the session if you have seen who I'm talking about." I paused and laughed. "Heck, half our team will have eye strain."

"Hayes, that seems like a good idea. What's the other specialty?"

"I know in working with Mitch, throwing his weighted football, it takes a toll on your hands catching it. Coach Bailey has been adamant with our receivers using their hands catching the ball. Well, for about 10 minutes each receiver needs to play and work with molding clay to strengthen their fingers. I happened to have picked up some play-dough during the holidays and thought molding clay would be stronger." I looked around, hoping they wouldn't think I was crazy. "My dad was always looking for natural ways to get better and stronger for his players. I know Mitch isn't going to get weaker."

Coach Duncan looked at Coach Ponder and Bailey and they both said, "It makes sense, Hayes."

As indoors started, the backs and receivers got to play with molding clay for 10 minutes before workouts. Coach Ponder called me to our office and I went with him to meet Ms. Sobiesk. After the introductions, just Diane and Steve here, she said it was good to see me again. It was easy to say likewise. She turned to get her schedule book and I looked at Coach Ponder and said, "Coach, you can shut your jaw now."

When Ms. Sobiesk turned back, she said, "Coach Steve, it will be a little different but I'll work their asses off and I believe you and the rest of the staff will like the outcome."

As we walked out, Coach Ponder said, "Hayes, this may well be the best suggestion I've ever heard of, after meeting Diane. I didn't know we even had a dance department."

Be Open to New Ideas

During spring training the low percentage of dropped passes made it evident that working with clay was a good thing. The coaches liked the over-all quickness we seemed to be having with just a couple of simple ideas regarding our activities. I promised you there was never an objection about Ms. Sobiesk's workouts or her attire. Hugh Hefner missed out on her.

I sent the Jayne twins our specialty workouts, like rope jumping, 15 minutes playing with clay, and some dance and kick steps courtesy of Ms. Sobiesk. In my letter back they asked if I had mistakenly sent them a recess activity sheet. I thought I had better call them and confirm the reason behind these strange workouts. At Southeast Junior College, they had to finish their classes to be eligible for fall semester. Growing up twenty miles from Louisiana, Jake and Jesse were the only two that could understand Mitch all the time. I'd been close to him for a year and a half and I still had trouble at times.

Getting ready for the season Casey Toms wrote that "Mitch Fontenot, 'Cajun Cannon,' is the best quarterback in all of Alabama including Auburn and the Crimson Tide. Whatever went wrong in Baton Rouge with this young man 'sho nuff' got corrected when he got to Pace and NE Alabama." Preseason ticket sales were the best ever for the Owls.

Everybody had worked hard and Mitch was throwing better than ever. With a little change in the schedule the Owls opened at Montgomery University (MU), a big team from the South Conference that always has some good athletes. If you weren't prepared, they could be a dangerous team.

The game started and we, the Owls, received and went 3 and out. MU did a good job of bringing extra help with their safeties. They had a tough time blocking Calvin Radford and he got his first sack on the third play. Our next possession went like the first with 3 and out. Mitch came over and got the headset from Coach Bailey to talk with Coach Ponder in the press box because he was the one that calls the plays down and I write them on my chart standing next to Coach Bailey.

After the third series I looked at Coach Bailey and said, "Are they supposed to be this good?"

I had a feeling something was wrong. I ask Joe-Joe, one of our managers to go up and tell my dad to come to the fence behind our bench. We started to wear Preston Carter, our punter, out with 4 straight punts. After the last punt, Dad was at the fence and I ran over to talk to him. "Dad, they ain't this damn good," I said. "Take your binoculars and watch their coaches in the press box when Coach Ponder calls a play. I remember in high school a team was able to pick up our walkie-talkie signals and knew what we were calling. Their safeties are making too many plays. If you see them waiting on Coach Ponder then give me a thumbs up."

Dad nodded. "You may be on it, Bob," he said.

After the second play and an incomplete to Jake Jaynes, I looked over and Dad gave me a thumbs up. Then there was a draw for 3 yards and Preston boomed a good punt. I called Mitch over and said, "Listen they have tweaked the headsets. They can hear what Coach Ponder is calling because we end our pass plays with the word 'pass.' Coach Ponder may go ape but he is going to have to trust us. We can't tell him over the head-set."

Mitch's eyes were so wide. He was too stunned to speak.

Coach Duncan was in agreement and we told Mitch on the second play to fake the handoff, and let Jesse go deep, pass 26-Z Go. Mitch was going on the field and Coach Bailey told Coach Ponder that the Head Man said run it at them this series.

On second down, Mitch stepped back to hand off to our tail back, Justin Grant, and pulled the ball out. As their safeties flew up, Jesse was all by himself, leaving Mitch to loft one into his arms for a touchdown. MU's coaches weren't sure if we just got lucky or if they heard something wrong. We came back with a sweep and Justin stopped and threw a pass back to a wide open Mitch for a 40 yard score right before the half.

In the locker-room we told Coach Ponder the deal and he said he had the feeling something was wrong, too. At the start of the second half he stayed on the sideline and called plays next to Coach Bailey and myself.

Coach Duncan was pissed, as might be expected. "We are going to toast their ass this next half and have fun!" he said. All of the Owls were in agreement, especially Preston who about got worn out punting.

Coach Duncan's having fun came to the tune of scoring 35 second half points, including a final touchdown on a pass play with a minute left in the game. We won 49-0. When Coach Duncan went out to shake hands at midfield after the game, he stopped and pointed his finger at the MU coach. He said, "Thanks to your damn headsets, you deserve every one of those points."

Mitch loved to be able to start the year throwing 5 touchdown passes and breaking Stew's record of 4.

A unique thing happened in the second game. Mitch was back to pass, tucked the ball under his arm, and took off running—he didn't want to risk a bad throw. When he got tackled, he landed on the football and in the process bit down on his tongue. Blood went everywhere and it took a couple of stitches to close the cut. After that it was amazing because everybody could understand what he was saying. His Cajun accent was slowed down. Don't worry, though; it only lasted a couple of weeks.

The year went well. We lost a close one to an out of state larger school, Arkansas State, but scored 27 points in the process. The Owls finished 9 and 1 and had the best record of any college team in the state of Alabama. The Cajun Cannon was making a lot of noise throughout the state. It turned out that Mitch Fontenot got invited the play in the famed Senior Bowl held in Mobile, AL while Calvin Radford played in the East-West All Star game in the San Francisco area. After all was said and done Mitch would become a star quarterback for the Hamilton Tiger-Cats of the Canadian Football League and Calvin would get drafted by the Detroit Lions. He became their sack leader.

The NCAA was lowering their scholarship limit with major colleges and teams like Alabama, Texas, and Penn State, who were notorious for signing a lot of players just to keep them from going elsewhere. Alabama had a mediocre year or worse according to some, finishing 7 and 4. There looked to be some changes coming in Tuscaloosa.

The week after Christmas, I was back home in Stuart. I had picked up Quint and headed into Marion. Right before we left, there was a call for me. That struck me as a little odd since I was staying on campus at NE 'Alabama.

As I talked on the phone, Quint was impatiently waiting. All he must of heard was, "How about an hour at the West Marion Café? Okay, meet you there."

"Meet who and where?" Quint asked after I hung up the phone.

"Coach Duncan was about to be in town and he is going to join us for lunch."

"Cool," Quint said. "What do you think he wants?"

"I guess you'll get to find out with me. I bet it's probably recruiting related."

Quint and I got a table and the waitress came over for our drink order. I said, "Well, we're expecting another so just bring 3 sweet teas and make sure you don't run out of pies."

We talked about the past seasons we'd both had. Quint had gotten to play a little in some mop-up rolls for Coach Sloan and the Rebels. "Bob," he said. "It has been fun having Mitch around. He never gets boring. I wonder what he is about to have for lunch down in Mound Bayou?"

I was sitting facing the door. When Coach Duncan walked in, I waved him over. We all shook hands and Coach picked a little at Quint. We looked at the menu and all had to go with special #1: country fried steak with white gravy, mashed potatoes, fried okra, and field peas. Where I was seated I couldn't see the back of the restaurant, so it was Quint who first spotted Lynn. He said, "Bob, didn't that girl getting up go to Stuart when you did?"

I turned to look and, sure enough, there was Lynn Elliott with her mother, about to leave. "Excuse me a minute, Coach," I said.

I walked over and tapped Lynn on the shoulder. We shared a hug and I greeted her mom as well. At that moment I really regretted the fact that we'd never dated too much in high school. She had always been so special, mostly during our senior year, and we were always real friendly with each other. There were never any hard feelings, but our timing just didn't match well, especially being at a small school.

We talked for a minute then. She was majoring in business and banking at Birmingham Southern College. She told me that she was probably going to be moving to Lexington, Kentucky within the next year, to work for a bank her uncle ran.

"Lynn, I know you won't say this," Mrs. Elliott said. She turned to me, "Bob, just last week Lynn won the Miss BSC beauty contest and will be in the running for Miss Alabama in May."

I grinned. "I'm not a bit surprised. I tried to talk you into our high school pageant and you wouldn't," I said. "I've always known you had real talent."

Lynn beamed at me. Her face turned pink.

I brought them over to meet Coach and Quint.

Before she left she said, "Just call me at home when you get a chance," and then I watched her walk out the door.

"Hayes, if you need to leave, after looking at the young lady, I understand," Coach said.

I shook my head. "We dated a few times toward the end of high school, but it was nothing too serious."

Coach Duncan shook his head. "Well," he said, "you may have made a bad decision there."

I thought to myself that he was probably right.

Quint changed the subject for us. "Okay, Coach," he said. "What's up?"

"Bob," he said, "I have been in Tuscaloosa the past couple of days. Coach Bryant called and we were discussing a few things. Primarily, Coach wants to abandon the wishbone and is in need of an offensive coordinator. It will be a big jump in pay from NE Alabama and I think it will also pave the way for better options later on as well."

"Well, congratulations, Coach. From what I've heard so far that sounds like a very good opportunity. You could go to, say, Arkansas State that beat us and if that didn't work out you may be back to square one."

"This is my whole point of meeting with you, Bob. I've liked your insight. I like how you've pull a lot from your dad. You have experience beyond your years."

Quint laughed. "Careful, Coach Duncan. You don't want to give Bob too much praise."

"Well, I've never given praise to two ball boys helping us to win games like I have with you two," the coach said, and Quint had to smile at that. Coach Duncan went on. "While meeting with Coach Bryant, and the situation there, I would like for you to become a graduate assistant and work with our quarterbacks. What you were able to help Mitch do was fantastic. You would start in two weeks."

I was very surprised. I looked at Quint and his eyes were as big as the blue saucers on the table, so I believed it sounded good.

Coach Duncan said, "Coach Bryant is tired of reading how we had the best quarterback in the state and I mentioned you were the one to help him along. Plus, he knows your dad and has talked with Stew a couple of times."

The waitress came by. I said, "Yes, ma'am, three pieces of the strawberry pie."

I said, "Coach, some things have to come first, like ordering the pie."

That comment made everyone laugh.

I went on. "I can't think of a better situation to up my resume, Coach. So, count me in. You looked out for me before and I appreciate it again."

"Bob you have earned this chance. There are a lot that would take a pay cut to do what you are being offered."

I nodded and let him know I understood.

"I trust you not to let this out, just your family," Coach Duncan said. "You, too, Quint. Just until it gets announced on Tuesday."

This was Friday so I didn't think it would be a problem. "Should I wait till then to move stuff out of my dorm apartment"?

"Since nobody is there I don't see anything it will hurt and I've got you the same set up at Bryant Hall being a GA."

"In that case," I said, "Quint may make a few dollars to help me to put my stuff in a van and take it on to Tuscaloosa."

As we started to leave Coach said, "If I were you, Bob, I'd be calling the young lady that left awhile ago. You just put in the work like you have the past couple of years and it won't be any different than what you've been doing. Plus, you won't have to worry about scout team duties."

We shook hands and Coach gave me his card and new numbers where I could reach him if I needed anything. We walked back to the car and Quint said, "I can't believe what I just saw and heard. Recruiting my butt."

"I wasn't expecting it either. I heard a bit about a change but not the whole package."

"Brother, I'm proud as heck for you, this is big time, and yes, I'll help you move your stuff to Tuscaloosa. And heck, Lynn looked awesome."

Hard and Good Work Can Create Opportunities

"Are you going to let me tell, Dad?" Quint asked.

"Well, he is not usually up to too much on Friday afternoon so let's just stop by his office since we are close by."

We walked in and Mr. Red Parker was standing in the doorway talking with Dad. "Look what the dogs done drug up," Mr. Parker said.

We shook hands and took a seat as Mr. Parker left.

"Let me guess, West Marion Café, and how many pieces of pie?" Dad asked.

"We had lunch with Coach Duncan," Quint said, almost shouting.

"Did anything become of the meeting?"

"Yeah, I'd say so. Bob ran into Lynn Elliott again. She was there with her Mom."

Dad laughed and shook his head.

Quint went on. "The other part is Coach is going back to Alabama as offensive coordinator and Bob is going to be his GA."

That comment brought Dad to his feet. He said, "I had heard there was a good possibility Coach Bryant might be going in a different direction with his offense. Dammitt, Bob, I'm proud as heck for you."

Quint kept talking. "We're moving his stuff over next week from the dorm at NE Alabama. Coach said we need to keep it just in the family till Tuesday after the press conference."

"Bob, I know it was an uphill battle with you playing, but you have more than made up for that in your coaching work.""

Mitch helped a lot in that department, Dad."

"Son, that is one of the secrets is finding what works and getting everybody, say somebody like Mitch, on the same page. Then good things can happen."

In high school I had called Lynn Elliott to go out to Paul's Diner when I signed and we even had our first real kiss. Maybe seeing her today was a good omen. I made the call and Mrs. Elliott answered the phone. "Hey, Bob," she said. "It was good to see you today, but you just missed Lynn. She had to go back to Birmingham for some type of function, but she left her number for you to call her there."

Maybe it wasn't a total lost cause.

Mom pulled into the drive and I had to tell Quint to slow down.

"Okay, Quint," she said. "What's up? You aren't always this eager to help me get bags out of the car."

"Mom," Quint said. "You will have to keep a secret till Tuesday."

"Okay, Quint, what's the secret?"

"Your son, Bob, has got himself a new job."

"Now where in the world would this job be?" Mom asked. She was already smiling.

Quint said, "Try the University of Alabama. We're moving his stuff over on Tuesday."

Mom was surprised. "When did this happen, Quint?"

"We had lunch with Coach Duncan today and he asked Bob to make the change with him going as Offensive coordinator. Bob will be a GA with the QB's."

"Bob, you have worked so hard to earn this chance." She gave me a hug and a huge smile.

It was a breath of fresh air to see Quint excited about something regarding me. At breakfast that Sunday morning I told Quint we would go by and get my office material, take that down Monday afternoon, and see what I would need in the apartment waiting on me at the dorm.

Quint said, "I thought everything was great being on the sideline with Stew playing, but with you being at Alabama, that's going to be really special."

I got a little worried then. "Quint," I said, "don't get too excited too fast."

Coach Bryant's press conference turned out to be on Monday morning and we were on our way to the Alabama campus. We stopped in Birmingham for a barbeque at the famous Deep South Café. A TV inside had one of the local stations giving highlights of the press conference from Tuscaloosa. Everything that happened with Coach Bryant was big news in the state. They chronicled the success of the last two seasons Coach Duncan had at NE Alabama with quarterback Mitch Fontenot. Then the reporter said that he was even bringing his young GA Bob Hayes, from Stuart, with him. With that Quint spilled his sweet tea—luckily it was almost empty.

Just after lunch we pulled in to the Alabama campus and I spotted Coach Duncan's car. We walked into the coaches' offices. The name on her desk said Jane Fowler and she was very nice and pleasant. "Ms. Fowler, I'm Bob Hayes," I said, extending my hand.

"Not any more, young man. Now you're Coach Hayes."

I smiled. "It's nice to meet you," I said. "This is my younger brother, Quint."

"That's a cute name you've got."

"Thanks ma'am." my little brother's face turned a little red.

"Is Coach Duncan back in?"

"He should be back real soon. Walk back here and I'll show you to your office."

"Office?" Quint said. "It used to be desk." That comment got a smile from Ms. Fowler.

I said, "I've just got a few things with me, ma'am."

"Coach Hayes," Ms. Fowler said, "just make yourself at home and if you need any supplies or have questions just let me know."

"Thanks, Ms Fowler."

She smiled at me. "Jane will do just fine."

We walked out to the car and each of us brought a box into my new office. We started to unload the contents. "Quint," I said, "go out and bring the other box in."

"Gotcha, Coach Hayes," he said with a big smile.

On his way back in, Quint turned the corner and was walking to my office when a door opened. A tall gentleman asked Quint, "Is your last name Hayes?"

"Yes sir," he replied.

"I know I am getting older but you dang GA's keep getting younger and younger."

Quint almost dropped the box to look up and see Coach Bryant talking to him. "Uh, Coach Bryant," he said nervously. "I'm Bob's younger brother, Quint. He's right next door."

Coach Bryant was chuckling as they both walked. He extended his hand to introduce himself.

I laughed and said, "Like I don't know who you are, Coach Bryant."

"Bob," he said. "Welcome to our staff. Coach Duncan has told me some good things about you and we need some help around here."

"You will get my best Coach."

"That is what I am counting on," he said. "How has your Dad been doing these days?"

"Trying to stay busy, I think. He still keeps his eyes and ears open to stay in touch with other coaches."

Coach Bryant walked out and Coach Duncan walked in. "There you guys are. Finding everything okay?"

"Yes. We're going to go back and do my apartment stuff Tuesday or Wednesday before Quint has to start back to school."

"Sounds good, Bob. Bryant Hall is just down the street and Jane has got the keys to apartment A where you'll be. Also, she has a couple of files on two key recruits I want you to look at. See what you can come up with—the sort of thing you did with the Jaynes twins."

I said I would look at the files and he thanked me.

"Our first meeting will be Wednesday at 7 am," he said as he turned to go.

Apartment A at Bryant Hall featured a living room, kitchen, bathroom, and large bedroom. "I see my bed," Quint said pointing to the couch.

I said, "We'll see when the time comes."

We stopped back at the coaching office and I got the files from Jane and I let her know we'd be back in a couple of days.

In the car, I talked with Quint. "What did you think Lil' brother?"

"I almost wet my pants when Coach Bryant walked out and asked me my name."

I laughed. "Quint, I guess I have been around coaches longer than you with Dad retiring when Stew was a senior in high School. I feel pretty comfortable, even though this is pretty tall cotton." I reminded Quint about dinner in Birmingham on our way back home.

"Great by me, he said."

We pulled up about the same time at the Social Grill, a great local place in the downtown area. It had a quaint charm to it with a lot of family photos and local paintings. We walked in and got a booth and looked over the large chalk board at the specials.

Stew started talking immediately. "Bob, you did yourself proud today from what I saw on the news. Coach Duncan had mentioned to me he thought he was leaving NE Alabama, but I didn't know you were on the same ride. I'm proud of you, Bob."

"Thanks, Stew." I thought for a second. "It's funny that a lot of this started because of you and getting to be a ball boy."

"Well, we've all been around this awhile—it's our life. I talked to Mom and she said you've got quite a few calls to return when you get home."

"Welcome to the big time," Quint said.

"Look guys I'm just a GA here, and I admit the arena is a lot larger, but that's all. We'll just have to see what happens from here."

Dinner was real good and their banana pudding was the best I'd had, besides Mom's. I told my brothers to hold on and I went over and pushed a dime into the pay phone. I was really excited when she answered. "I finally get to speak with you, Lynn. How are you?"

"I see you're quite busy. My boss had a TV on at the bank, since he is a big 'Bama fan. I did a double take when I heard your name." There was a pause. "I'm proud for you," she said after a moment.

"Thanks. That's actually what we were talking about when I saw you and your Mom at the diner last week." I told her that Quint was with me having been to Tuscaloosa. I told her about our dinner with Stew at the Social Grill. I told her we were heading back to Stuart.

She said, "I have a feeling you will be busy getting acquainted but it would be good to see you soon."

"Yes," I said. "That would be real good." I thought for a second. "I'm moving my stuff in a day to an apartment at the athletic dorm and we start meetings this week." I remembered something. "Now, what is this moving to Kentucky deal you mentioned the other day?"

"Well, you know, my uncle at the bank in Lexington has a position available. It's a pretty good opportunity."

"Now you sound like the one getting into the big time." I smiled. "In a couple of days, on our way back through, I'll call when we leave Tuscaloosa and meet you for a bite to eat."

"I suppose I'll take you up on that. It'll be great to see you again."

I agreed. I knew I would look forward to see Lynn all week.

Since he had been respectful to all of us, I give Mr. Toms a call at the *Marion Ledger*. Of course his first question was had I met Coach Bryant. I related the story of Quint bringing the box in and meeting Coach before I did. I told Toms how I had been fortunate enough to have been around Coach Duncan since Stew was to be a junior for NE 'Alabama and he had liked some of my work. I said, "Coming out of high school I told Coach Duncan I would do my best to help the Owls win and I plan to do the same for Alabama and Coach Bryant."

Casey Toms continued to ask me questions about my career and my beliefs about coaching. I said, "Mr. Toms it is about the players" when he asked the most important aspect with coaching I have seen this far. "We try to get them in the best position to succeed whether it is in the classroom or on field and it allows them to grasp their effort and use it later in life."

Coaching is about the Players

We talked a bit more and I told Mr. Toms to call on me at any time. He was also glad to cover the progress Mitch had made and was scheduled to talk with him before the Senior Bowl.

Quint and I got my belongings loaded into a small U-haul truck and we headed to Tuscaloosa from Pace. "Okay, Quint," I said. "Let's get started."

"Wait," Quint said. "I thought we were already started."

"No," I said. "Look in the file and tell me about the first recruit there."

Quint read me details about Colt Turner, a wide receiver, from Greenville, South Carolina. According to the report, he was the fastest high school runner in the state and just out ran everybody. "It says here that teams would kick everything out of bounds to not give him a chance to return any kicks." Quint said.

"Does the file have anything about any connections with Alabama?" I asked.

"He had an uncle that played but hurt his knee his second year and went back to South Carolina."

"That is what I need to know. And the second file, Quint?"

"Says here that Ed Hollingsworth is a quarterback from Canton High."

"Dang," I said. "We beat them in the first round of the playoffs at Stuart. That is up close to Tennessee and I know the kid comes from a solid program. That will be a good target."

We got my stuff unloaded and situated in Apartment A of Bryant Hall on the campus of the University of Alabama. That does have a pretty good ring to it. We walked off to the coaches' office and as we walked in we said, "Hell-o Ms. Fowler."

Ms. Fowler smiled at us and shook her head. "Jane will do just fine, Coach Hayes."

"That will take a lot of getting use to for me, Ms. Fowler," Quint said.

I had a few messages and one asked me to bring a sports coat to the meeting on Wednesday morning. I just do as I'm told and don't question authority.

Before leaving I made my call to Lynn Elliott in Birmingham. We decided were going to meet at Baxter's, a good seafood restaurant on the highway that will be easy to stop in. Driving toward Birmingham, I had the feeling Stew probably had at the drive-in when I popped up from the back seat. Having Quint as my shadow limited the conversation I would have with Lynn.

The three of us had dinner and the trout almandine was really good. I told Lynn that I didn't have a clue about my schedule, what with recruits coming in and being at a new place and all. Our timing was always a bit off, even back in high school, at least in terms of going out together. We had some great conversations but only just a few dates and most were with other people around. Lynn was supposed to move to Kentucky in 2 weeks and her schedule was packed getting ready to move. I walked her to her car and said, "Maybe we will play the Wildcats in the next year or two." We said we would try to stay in touch but that can only go so far. After she handed me a piece of paper with her Kentucky information on it, I finally decided I didn't care who was watching. I embraced Lynn and gave her a very warm good-bye kiss. "Lynn that will have to do for a while," I told her, "but it was better than some card to remember you by."

"I agree," she said "And you should have done it more than just once or twice a long time ago."

I nodded. Suddenly I felt very sad about the past. I looked at her and she looked at me, and after a moment she smiled, very slowly. Then off in our separate ways we went, ... again.

As I get in the truck all I could say to Quint was would've, could've and should've. "Brother, you sure showed me how to say bye to a girl."

I laughed knowing it would be a long good-bye.

Mom had a big lunch prepared on Sunday. It was fun listening to all the advice from everyone. Dad just kept saying, "Keep being yourself. That's worked good so far." He stopped and thought for a second. When he spoke again, he spoke very seriously. "Bob," he said, "you've been around the game for a while. All the games out back here help mold the knowledge you have. Keep coaching the game and not just a position. The little things we talk about are all part of the position and the game."

Mom broke in with dessert. "I figure we should be done with the talk," she said.

That reminded me of something. "Mom, I do have to order one of your pound cakes to take with me."

"No problem," she said.

On Monday, after having breakfast with Dad at Paul's Diner and shaking a lot of hands, I stopped to talk with Coach Sloan for a bit. Then I went to Tuscaloosa. I got settled in and met with Coach Albright who was in charge of Bryant Hall. We had dinner together on Monday night and exchanged a few stories. I arrived early on Wednesday morning—I knew that Coach Duncan time was a bit early and I wasn't taking any chances with Coach Bryant. Of course, his was about ten minutes early.

In the meeting, after all the introductions, it became clear that we were expected to be a lot better than 7 and 4. We were going to be working on a new offense and we discussed all the details to go with that. As the meeting ended Coach Bryant stated that a couple of big pieces to the puzzle were landing the Hollingsworth and Turner kids. After he said that he added, "Coach Duncan, you and Coach Hayes meet me in the lobby in fifteen minutes."

We met in the lobby and made our way to a large black Lincoln Town Car. I slid into the back seat with Coach Bryant and Coach Duncan up front. I leaned forward and asked Coach Duncan, "How long of a drive do we have?"

"About 7 minutes," he says with a grin.

Coach Bryant said, "Son, you're not still at NE Alabama, anymore. You're not afraid of flying, are you?"

"I will let you know shortly, Coach Bryant," I said. "There's a first time for everything."

This made the coaches laugh.

I got out of the car at the municipal airport and looked at a private plane with words *The University of Alabama* written on the side. 'Welcome to the big time,' I said to myself.

Once we were on the plane, our first stop will be Greenville, SC. "Bob I wanted to bring you along because Coach Duncan says you related to the kids real well and I want to see for myself."

We landed and had a meeting with Colt and his family. Once the introductions were made, Mrs. Turner walked over to the table and sits down. I followed her and struck up a conversation. "Mrs. Turner, I read that your brother Rex played a couple of years before a knee injury got him."

Mrs. Turner nodded. "Yes," she said, "it really changed his plans."

"I imagine so," I said. "Well, I thought about that and the first thing I checked on for Colt was how solid, knowledgeable, and available the tutors are. And I wanted to tell you about the scheduled study times for the players."

Mrs. Turner smiled. "That's good to know Coach Hayes. Mainly what I hear is all football this and football that."

I nodded. "But you saw what can happen, with your brother, and we want to make sure every player has the opportunity to get his education and have a chance to prosper when all the cheering fades away."

Mrs. Turner nodded again. "Yes, she said." "That is what I want for my son."

"We'll help make him into a better player than he's ever thought of being, but first and foremost we will get him that education."

Coach Bryant stepped in. He said, "Mrs. Turner, I agree 100% with what I heard Coach Hayes say. If you ever have any concerns I'm available. My whole staff is available. Just a call away."

Mrs. Turner thanked him and they started talking about her favorite activities. I sat down with Colt and let him know what I explained to his mother. I said, "I grew up with my mother being a coach at the house and she didn't let anything get passed she didn't agree with."

Colt laughed. "That sounds familiar," he said.

I nodded and decided to get down to business. "Colt," I said, "one of my jobs is to work with the quarterbacks and receivers. It is going to be a blast getting out of the wishbone and giving you an opportunity to perform." Then I related the story of throwing a touchdown pass in practice and getting cussed out. I ended the story by saying, "The process is what reaps rewards and doing it the right way. I will be showing you small things you will have never thought of to make you a better player."

"Like what," Colt said. He seemed pretty skeptical.

"Well," I said. "You every play with play-dough?"

He made a face. "I don't think so and I might not want to get caught doing so. At least not around some of my friends here."

"Well, you may want to start. It really helps to strengthen your fingers and hands."

"Coach," he said, "you got me with that one."

"Now, Colt here is what I have learned growing up with the game and what you will get with Coach Bryant. All of you players coming out here have the will to win, no doubt about it. The secret, and Coach's strength, is having the will to PREPARE to win. That is why Coach Bryant has been so successful."

You Have to Have the Will to Prepare to Win

We said our goodbyes and went to get into the car. Coach Bryant was getting a hug from Mrs. Turner. I said, "That's not a bad sign I don't think."

As we drove off I get my order from Coach Bryant. "Bob," he said, "you will be the one to keep in contact with Mrs. Turner. Good job, everyone."

Back, then, to the plane and to Canton, Alabama. We were off to meet with the Hollingsworth's. The twin engine Cessna screeched to a halt on a small runway outside of Canton, Alabama. A car took us by their house which was a smallish two bedroom about a mile from the school. This meeting was similar to our meeting with the Turner's. I talked with Ed and reminded him that I was a quarterback at Stuart. He said, "I was there at the play-off game with my older brother being an end and safety. You guys had a complete team."

"Ed," I went on, "Coach Sloan, at Stuart, is kinda similar to Coach Bryant. He has the organization down pat and you know what to expect with practice and especially in a game. Ed, you are going to have fun showing off a new offense at quarterback, but I have a different question for you."

"What's that?" Ed asked.

"Well, I wonder did you take Alabama history in the seventh or eighth grade?"

Ed looked puzzled. "The seventh, I'm pretty sure. Why?"

I reached into my coat pocket and pulled out a folded road map of the state. I said, "We know you have been to Knoxville a couple of times and have visited Tuscaloosa. See here, this outline is the state of Alabama. Tuscaloosa, down here, is "THE UNIVERSITY OF ALABAMA" not the University of Tuscaloosa. The best I can see is that Canton is inside the State of Alabama and always will be. It ain't goin' no-where."

When I said this, Ed chuckled. I laughed, too, and then went on: "You'll have the opportunity to represent every car tag you see at your school and all over Canton that displays 'The Heart of Dixie.' It's on every one."

As we boarded the plane Coach Bryant asked me what I had shown the Hollingsworth kid. "Coach, just a map to remind him he lives in Alabama and not Tennessee. Also our university is the one for the whole state and not just Tuscaloosa. I thought it would be something he could use to explain his decision to his buddies. So he could prove that it's not about promises."

"Coach Duncan," Coach Bryant said, "your young one proved his mettle today and I am proud of both of you. I have a feeling we're headed in the right direction."

We got back to campus with our goal accomplished, maybe even a little ahead of time. The two prominent commitments, Hollingsworth and Turner, helped to pave the way for others when they get to see who else is coming to Alabama. After that, you use the signees as building blocks for the future of the football program

At the office, Coach Bryant asked me to hold on a second. He came back out and then we were on our way to J.T.'S—his wife had already had dinner. J.T'S was a local restaurant owned by a former player that had great steaks and was open early to accommodate Coach Bryant on his way to the office. As we pulled in I looked at Coach Duncan and declared that this place reminded me a lot of Paul's Diner, back in Marion. Coach Bryant agreed and assured me they'll take good care of us. He said, "Bob, when you come in just sign the ticket and J.T. will take it from there."

"I can take orders quite well, Coach."

We sat at a corner table, which was Coach Bryant's regular place—it's always reserved for him. Just like at Paul's Diner, there are a lot of the sports photos and banners on the wall, but in J.T.'S it's an all Alabama collection. We ordered and J.T. Slade, himself, walked out and sat down with us. Coach Bryant did the introductions and J.T. said, "Nice to meet you, Coach Bob, and welcome back, Coach Duncan."

"Any new coffee machines, JT?" Coach Duncan asked.

Coach Bryant shakes his head as the other two begin to laugh. "Okay, what is this story," I said.

Coach Duncan said, "Bob, when I was first here I was an early bird, like yourself, and I would get to the offices quite early. I still hardly ever would beat Coach Bryant. JT had just opened his restaurant and word got around pretty quick that Coach liked the place. So, JT has his guy from Old South Coffee to come over and put one of the new automatic coffee makers in Coach's office. All you had to do was hit the button for the eye to warm up, put in a filter, open the pack of coffee, and hit the start button for it to do its deal." Coach Duncan paused then and looked around the table.

"The first day it worked like a charm and Coach had his pot of fresh coffee right there," he went on. "The second day he starts it up, and I am down the hall, and there is the loudest cursing going on you have ever heard. I run down the hall and coffee is everywhere. I get a couple of towels and sop it up." Everyone laughed.

"On the third day it is a repeat of the second and the cursing starts and there is damn coffee everywhere again. It gets cleaned up and I know I better get JT on the phone. I go to my office and explain the ordeal and JT says ask Coach how many times he is hitting the start button?" Coach Duncan stopped talking and looked at Coach Bryant. They both chuckled. "Well," Coach Duncan said, "it turns out that on the spill days, the coffee wouldn't start fast enough for Coach Bryant and, like most geniuses, he hit the button a couple of more times and, presto, it begins. BUT, being automatic, the thing starts the cycle again and there is no room in the pot for the next round. That is where the lake of coffee would get started."

Coach Duncan finished the story: "At first, I wanted hold out on the info, but I decided to tell Coach. He learned to just hit that sucker one time. A lot of us kinda knew that but were afraid to tell him it was his own fault." Everybody got another big laugh just picturing that happening again.

The talk started to be about everything but football and it was a great way to end a busy day. It sure beat riding in a car all day. As we left, I reminded Coach Duncan I would meet him at eight the next morning.

I walked in at seven and said good morning to Ms. Fowler—catching myself and then saying Jane instead. This brought a smile to her face.

A great thing about our office was that some of the local restaurants and bakeries would send over a box of donuts and pastries each day. My favorites came from Shipley's, the ones that Danny O'Keith sent over. Being a few blocks away, it was usually my early morning stop. I would chat with Danny and talk with a few of the other local guys.

I walked into Coach Duncan's office at eight a.m. and Coach Robbins, the receivers coach, was there as well. I wanted to get a take on what they were expecting with our position players, receivers and quarterbacks, and I wanted to be able to plan and went over the molding clay work and rope jumping we had the receivers do and Coach Robbins was all for it.

Then I asked, "By the way what has been one of your better Coach Bryant stories relating to a player?"

"Well, it has to do with the handling of a player and an issue," Coach Robbins said. "A few years ago we were playing Baylor and we were up twenty points at half. Coach Bryant always points out that the first five minutes of the second half are the most crucial. Well, Chris Giles, our young returner, blasts the kick-off up the gut and is about to score. At the five yard line he starts to hold the ball up and his knee hits it and the ball bounces out of the end zone for a touchback. Giles comes to the sideline with tears in his eyes and all Coach Bryant says to him, at that time, was, 'Son, just hold on for five more yards. There were 10 other guys blocking their butts off to get you open. You don't reward them by showing off the ball.'"

The First Five Minutes of the Second half are the Most Crucial

Coach Robbins continued the story: "In the press conference, after the game, although we won by 35, the first question was, were we going to bench Chris Giles for his mistake. Well, Coach Bryant said, 'No, I have to take the blame there. We haven't worked with Chris enough on our return game and we've just got to get him to hold on to that ball for 5 more yards. He'll know what to do from now on.'" Coach Robbins paused and looked at all of us. "That was it. No further questions were asked about it. Coach never blames any of his players."

"Thanks, Coach Robbins," I said. "That is what I want to know."

Don't Blame Your Players

After our meeting I asked Jane what I needed to do to get the last three offensive game films. She smiled and made a call to Frank Wise, film coordinator, and told me they will be in the film room in five minutes. It took a while to adjust to all these little things that were handled by someone else and help to benefit the program and staff.

I started to look at the last film, being the Sun Bowl game, to get an idea of the techniques the returning receivers and quarterbacks utilize with the offense. I ran a few plays back and forth and jotted down a few notes. I had made it through the Auburn game film and I was hitting the light switch to change games, when I noticed that Coach Bryant was standing there. He just about scared me to death.

"Coach Bob," he said "I noticed you've been in here for a good bit. What are you looking for?"

"Coach Bryant," I answered, "I'm looking at the passing game out of the wishbone and how the receivers utilized a style of possession catches."

"Meaning?" Coach Bryant asked.

"They are not looking to move forward with the ball as much and, so, not using their hands to make a lot of catches. It also makes them a little easier to cover, but a lot of the patterns depend on play action. Then you have the timing issues when you have gone to a couple of straight passes."

"I like that assumption, Bob. You're going to help get us on track."

I had a couple of classes left to finish my Masters degree. The instructors just figured I would learn more from Coach Bryant than from anything they could shove at me. My last couple of classes were of the survey variety and I wrote out coaching plans and filled in my version. Believe it or not I started thinking along the lines of would've, could've, and should've, but this time with me calling the shots. As a result, a whole different sense came into focus. I was working under the greatest winner of all time, but I knew that, in order to develop, I had to increase my own awareness as well.

Indoors was going well and nobody had died. The receivers and quarterbacks had added jumping rope to their routines. We were just a few weeks from starting our outside drills, like we did at NE Alabama, when I brought up a new subject in our offense meeting. "Coach Duncan," I said, "when I was reviewing a few of the game films, I noticed that the offense sometimes tried to pass in the red zone and got stymied and looked stuck. I know you remember the Tate game when Stew reversed his field and completed the 2 point pass for the win." I looked at Coach Duncan and he nodded and told me to keep talking.

"Now then, I know you like to narrow it down to a handful of calls when we get into that situation. We need to go over those plays. We can call it our "egg package" because the plays are going to get scrambled, and the players will have a clue where to run to in that case. It is the same when we practice 'fire' on botched snaps with holders and kicks," I said.

Know All of the Aspects of Your Plays

After I finished speaking, silence filled the room. Finally, to my relief, Coach Robbins spoke up: "Coach Duncan, that makes more sense than of lot of plays I have ever drawn up. All it takes is a good linebacker or another, which we face all the time, that can disrupt a play and we can be screwed."

Coach Bryant was standing inside the door. He seemed to pop up everywhere. He said, "Coaches, you bet your butts we will be working on that."

After the meeting Coach Duncan calls me into his office. "Bob, I like the way you see more than just x's and o's. I know you are younger but do not be afraid to speak up like you did in there. Coach has liked what you have been doing, too." He paused then and looked at me closely. "How has the family been doing back in Stuart?"

"Well, honestly," I said, "I haven't heard a lot and just talked to the folks a little off and on. I take it all is going well. Quint looks like he will be the starter going into his junior year, at least the way their spring practice is going. I may get him down here this weekend for the Auburn basketball game."

The players were receptive to our changes except for one part with our quarterbacks and receivers. Word had gotten around about them using the clay for their hands and jumping rope for agility. The big guys had started calling them the "sissies." Senior to be quarterback and last year's starter, Jeff Austin, said, "I can handle the flack because since we've started this, Coach Hayes, I can now palm a basketball and dunk it, both of which I couldn't do before."

"'JA' if he can get you throwing to the right colored jersey, we'll all be in better shape," Grant Sims, the starting wide out, said. And everybody chuckled.

Have Measuring Sticks to Gauge Your Progress

Coach Duncan addressed the group and said that there will be more pressure on them to perform outside the wishbone pattern. "We've been working with some different wrinkles on your patterns and we're going to get with the program."

The receivers left to go with Coach Robbins and we talked with the four quarterbacks. Coach Duncan said, "Guys, we're going to be a lot more specific than you have been coached in the past. We're going to be telling you what we want you to do and how to do it the right way. You're going to know what you should be doing."

Coach Duncan called on me. "Quarterbacks," I said, "when you make an errant throw, we want you to learn why you did it. Do yourself a favor and don't make excuses: they will get you in trouble. Just like Bobby Joe does deer hunting, we're going to aim small and miss small. I guarantee you: we will cut down on mistakes."

It Helps to be Precise

We had a couple of weeks of specialty work outside with just quarterbacks and receivers, to work on new patterns as well as passing and catching. Jeff Austin, quarterback, can't believe how much more velocity he has on his throws. "'JA' that's why we've been working on those little things, to prepare you to get better. I learned a good lesson from my high school coach: you can focus and get better and not waste time. We didn't even do two-a-days."

"What kind of record did you have your last year," JA said.

"Let's see, now, we went, something like, 13-0 and 2-A state champions."

"I'll change the subject, now, Coach Hayes."

We started running patterns and working on the quarterbacks' footwork. "JA" got under center and Coach Duncan was watching intently as "JA" took the snap and dropped back. "Again," Coach Duncan said.

I said, "'JA" you know the snap count. Now get your feet moving a half step ahead and you won't get tripped up by the center or guards, got it?" I turned to the other three, to let them know that we didn't expect them to make the same mistake the one ahead of them made. "Paying attention to what is going on is how you improve.

There are no dumb questions, guys," I said.

Learn to Watch and Apply

We ran a seven yard in pattern with the outside receiver (X) breaking just behind the inside receiver (Z) going straight up the field. "JA" dropped back and completed the ball to Grant Sims. I looked at Coach Duncan and he pointed at me.

I said, "Let's get this precise bit off on the right foot. What was wrong, 'JA'? What was wrong with that, Grant?"

They both shrugged their shoulders, not sure what to say.

"'JA' and all the quarterbacks, you've got to put that pass just in front of his number. His number is 81, so you hit him on the one. I promise you half of the defense backs in this league would bat that one down. Out front is where it has to be, so throw the ball to where he is going."

Then I turned to Grant. "Now, Grant, why in heck have we been working for a month strengthening our hands? We want to use them to catch the ball with, not your arms. Here is how it should look. 'JA' throws just in front of the lead number, you use your hands to catch and tuck the ball in under your left arm and by doing so you can still run." I looked at Grant and he was nodding. I kept going. "Why tuck it under the left? 95 % of the time you will get hit from the right side and you don't want to put the ball where it can get knocked out. Plus, you lose two or three steps when you pause to catch it with your arms. Now this is what you do in a passing offense."

4 P's: Proper Procedures Produces Profits

We continued to work on throws and perform them the proper way. Bobby Joe was throwing a deep fade and zipped it too far outside. "Okay, Bobby Joe, watch this."

We repeated the play and I lofted the ball to the receiver to his outside and put an arc to it. I looked at Bobby Joe. "Now then," I said, "our guy only needs a half-a-step on his man to make this catch and if you are off a bit he can get into position to correct his route, throw it too flat and it can be batted down."

The rest of the two weeks went according to plan. Coach Bryant was happy with the way we were teaching them, teaching them the way to do things right. His philosophy was always to teach the players the right way.

Coach Duncan, Coach Robbins, and I have been working on our egg package. The next to the last day before full contact started, Coach Bryant wanted to see what we had. We had the receivers and quarterbacks up to explain that if we run a roll right, and we are on the 10 yard line, the safeties don't have too far to back up. I said, "Guys, we have a four-second timer in our head. If 'JA' is rolling right and a couple of DB's jump your route, then instead of running out of bounds or stopping, at four seconds we are going to reverse back to the left. 'JA' or our quarterback is going to spin right and start going back to his left. Quarterbacks, this is one of the reasons we work so much on getting your shoulders square to make this throw. The tight end, whom is running a drag at the back of the end-zone, now becomes the #1 target. The fullback, who had been blocking down to the right will turn to help and if uncovered will go to the short flat and the outside defensive end has to go for the quarterback or the fullback. We now know where the heck we are running to in a very critical situation and that is a huge advantage. If you decide to run make a pump fake like you are going to throw over the guy."

We ran the play the first time and "JA" made his right turn and completed the pass to the tight end back at the back of the end zone. "'JA,'" I said, "that won't cut it, throw the ball head high. That was our tight end should have a height advantage."

We ran a few more and the object in doing so was learning not to panic in game situations. Then if the play can't be found up to the bleachers goes the pass and don't force it.

Coach Bryant called me over to where he was standing alone observing. He said, "Coach Bob, I like your insight to the game. I've been around the game awhile and we have never done anything like this. You keep it up and it'll be hard for me to keep you around here and that's a good thing. Plus the kids are seeing benefits with their preparations and they are taking to it."

Our spring practices went well and I was looking forward to the Spring Game, ready to showcase what we had been working on with the new offense. Coach Bryant had other ideas. He came up with the most boring game plan possible in regards to offense. He announced during our offense meeting, "Coaches this is not the place to show our hand. If we run up a bunch of points who have we beaten?" He waited for someone to answer, but no one did. "I would rather save our offense for Southern Cal come September fourth."

In the big picture, I agree.

My dad and brothers make it to Tuscaloosa for the A-Day Spring game. Since Mom had to be somewhere with Sharon, at least a pound cake and pudding came with them, as well as with a big batch of oatmeal cookies. We were in my office and Coach Bryant stuck his head in and greeted everyone. He also grabbed a couple of the cookies. He told my dad that he thought I might get sick on him when we flew on the recruiting visit, but actually I hung in there pretty well.

Coach Bryant asked my dad to step into his office with him for a minute and there was no telling what they were discussing. As Coach

Duncan's office cleared, we stepped in and there were greetings all around. He said, "Stew, this younger brother of yours is doing coaching the way you did quarterbacking for me, which is damn good."

"Coach Duncan," Quint said, I warned you about bragging too much on Bob."

"Lil' Hayes, I heard you had a good spring and Coach Sloan says you'll be starting come season time."

I said, "Coach I look to get Quint down here for a quarterback camp or two and make sure he doesn't slack off this summer. I'm sure Mom and Dad would welcome the break." Coach and Stew laughed.

All went well with no players getting hurt, which was always a bonus. The next week we had an over-all team meeting. Coach Bryant announces that four players have worked very hard and have earned themselves a scholarship. This announcement was special and as he called their names they got a well deserved round of applause from the rest of their teammates.

Coach Bryant then called Coach Duncan up front and said he has another change to make. "Team, Coach here has been the Offensive Coordinator and quarterbacks coach. He brought Coach Hayes in to be his GA and Bob has now gotten his Master's degree. We have been pleased with the effort he has put forth, and as of today, he is now our quarterback coach under Coach Duncan."

I have to say, that caught me by surprise. Coach calls me up front as the players applaud. I said, "I appreciate all of your work ethic and striving to get better. We'll be going over some individual stuff in the next week. Guys, you know we have 142 days until we go out west and kick some Southern Cal butt. We'll be ready." That brought some yells and whoops.

After the meeting I went in to talk with Coach Duncan. I said, "Coach isn't this a little quick?"

Coach Duncan said, "If I didn't think you could handle it we wouldn't be having this discussion."

Good point, I thought.

"Bob, you have been doing everything already. The quarterbacks have really liked what you've been showing them. They appreciate the methods you use. Coach Bryant agrees and that's exactly what he talked to your Dad about Saturday."

"Coach, it's no wonder my dad finds out so much stuff before me."

Coach Duncan laughed. "Bob, you'll just have a little more clout and I'll tell you now you will need to be working on putting down your drills for our quarterbacks camps this summer."

"No problem with that," I said.

"Also, Bob, your Mom's cookies helped to seal the deal with Coach Bryant."

As my eyes grew wide, Coach Duncan started laughing.

Finally he said, "Also, after Coach Bryant's press conference in the morning get ready for a few phone calls."

I was on the phone talking to my Dad. "How in heck do you get your information, like talking to Coach Bryant when you were down here?"

"Bob, it goes back to trust, honesty and sometimes a little luck. I had a player some years ago that had all the tools to play the game. Coach Bryant came to talk with me at Stuart and I gave him an honest evaluation. Coach Bryant asked the player about football and he told him he loved the game. When he asked him about school, he said, 'Coach I don't much care for them there books.' After that he started talking with me about other players in our area. You will learn that sometimes the coaches are too eager for a kid to sign big instead of, say, at NE Alabama and you get too much bull."

He kept talking: "Bob keep in touch with your friends and I mean coaching friends because you may need a big favor some day. That's the way coaching jobs can come and go. In a matter of a year I have seen whole staffs let go and everybody is back to square one."

"Okay, Dad," I said when we were finished talking, "Sounds good to me. Thanks again. Tell Mom I'll be up in two weeks. I'll stay at the house, unless you've rented out my room, because I'm supposed to do a little talk at the athletic banquet at Stuart. Make sure you and Mom plan to attend and tell Doc West I'll be by to see him."

"Dammit Bob," he said. "Anything else you want me to do for you?"

"Yeah, remind Mom she had better make Coach Bryant a batch of oatmeal cookies so I don't get in his doghouse."

Dad had to chuckle at that one.

"I'll see to that order for you."

Don't Forget Where you Came from and Remember Your Friends

At six am the next morning, I walked into Shipley's and Danny O'Keith had me a hot apple fritter waiting. I poured myself a cup of fresh hot coffee and said hello to everyone. "Congratulations, Coach Hayes," Danny said.

"Also long as you are Danny Donut, I'm still Bob to you."

"You got it," he said.

"Danny, come season I might have something for you to help me with. I may meet with my quarterbacks early on Thursdays and it would be good to stop in and get them a snack. It may help to wake them up."

Danny laughed. "Just let me know and it'll be ready."

I walked out with a couple of hot cinnamon twists for Ms. Jane—those are her favorites.

I had told Jane to put Mr. Toms call through to me any time I wasn't in a meeting. When she put his call through, I took it right away. "Sometimes situations present themselves and I was able to be at the right place at the right time," I explained.

He asked another question: "What do you have to say when people talk about your inexperience?"

I said, "Mr. Toms, you have seen me around the game since midget league. What they will get is a fresh outlook backed by real good lessons from real good people and coaches. I trust Doc West. You know, he's your Chiropractor too. I trust him very much and he has always been there for me and has good advice."

We talk a while longer and I give him the same option that Mitch Fontenot did when he was at NE Alabama, the one about not taking any cheap-shots. After he asked, I told him I would be back at Stuart in a couple of weeks.

Coach Duncan had told me I would get a few calls. Ticket requests started coming in for certain games and I didn't know if I would get tickets myself. I'm glad I was single, at least in that regard.

Coach Duncan was right. I did get a couple of interesting calls. One was from Gary Patterson. He was the star player from Dalton and last time I saw him, Stew and I had lunch with him in Marion. He was now the defensive coach at UT-Winston. He said, "Bob, I saw the article in today's State paper, up here, and I'm not surprised you are at Alabama this soon in your career."

He went on to say this: "I'm glad you are not still at NE Alabama. I wouldn't want to have to face you."

I laughed. "Thanks a lot, Gary. I read you've been doing a super job. Just don't try showing them how to do things too much yourself. You'll hurt those kids."

We talked a bit longer and ask about families and stuff back home. I put his information in my rolodex file, just to hold on to.

The other interesting call came from Bobby Snead, former wide out at NE Alabama with Stew. We talked a bit and he told me that, when I'd brought Zack Morris over, and we worked out, he really liked the instructing and teaching. He was coaching offense and special teams at a Division II school in Mississippi and he had just played for a championship, but came up short. I put his information in my rolodex file, too.

After talking with Dad, I thought highly of keeping up with those I could trust in the coaching business. I resolved to make it a point to keep up with them—you never know when you may need a friend.

Be Careful about Burning Bridges

Part IV

Our meetings continued and Coach Robbins, receiver's coach, and I listed the drills we want our players to work on the most. We then did our individual assessment of throws and catches and any route changes we might need to make.

We, Alabama, hosted a camp for three full days. During that time, we helped the high school players with proper technique, specific drills, passing, and catching. Our quarterbacks on campus helped as well as past players, some were now playing in the NFL, which gave the event a very high profile. We also got to see some seniors to be and added info to their recruiting file.

Quint came down to stay and attended the camp and I did my best to not single him out. The camp went well and the question and answer times were enjoyable. I was told the college and pro players were asked to speak with the campers and that was one of the main reasons they attend: to have the opportunity to be around these older guys and to learn some specifics. A lot of times proper technique was not taught to the kids and with just a little instruction their talent level could rise dramatically.

I took an old page from Dad and Doc West's book and turned the talks into more of a question and answer session. Most of the kids seemed to learn a little more when they heard specific answers, especially from players they had been watching on TV. Plus, I felt it brought things to a little more personal level.

Ask What Questions They Have and You Can Give a Specific Response

Coach Duncan liked the sessions and the players did as well. They found it easier to do in a question and answer format because they weren't always sure what to talk about. For the quarterbacks, I got to end it by stressing education and the desire to prepare to play better. Quint told me that he understood how much more work he had to do to get better. He said, "Bob, I was feeling pretty good about myself coming down here. Now I know how much more I have got to put into my game."

"Well, little brother," I said. "I've got an even better lesson for you in the morning. We are going to work out with a few of the players you have been seeing during camp."

"That may be too cool," Quint said and I could tell he was a little nervous.

We got dressed to go to JT's for one of his choice T-Bone steaks and "JA" and Bobby Joe, our top two quarterbacks, walked into the lobby. I asked them to join us for dinner. Quint got his ears full and "JA" picked at him a bit since his little brother wasn't there. Of course, Quint loved every minute of it. But in addition to the teasing, "JA" also gave him a piece of advice: "I know it is hard taking instructions from an older brother but Coach Hayes has helped us a lot. I'm not saying it because he is picking up our dinner tab either." We laughed a bit and, when JT himself stopped by to shake hands, we tried to leave Quint behind to clean up.

Our workout was going well and Trent Anderson, who played for Tampa Bay, and I was discussing the longer throw. "I see too many guys that don't follow through enough and that is where you get the 'dropping it off the table' arc," Trent said. "Otherwise the ball will hang or come out a little too flat." He went over to Quint and showed him a couple of times. I was proud to see my little brother pick it up pretty well.

After lunch, Quint was about to drive back to Stuart, the longest trip he had driven solo. "Bob," he said, "the camp was great, but the chance to meet Trent, JA, Bobby Joe, and the rest was too good. I now see a little of what it was like for you hanging around with Stew when he was playing." He laughed and said, "Being a little brother does have some good points."

I smiled at him. "Just keep your head screwed on straight and you'll be good. You see now how much extra you have to put into it."

Quint nodded.

"Call when you get home," I said. "If I'm not in my office, just leave a message with Jane."

The rest of the week I was finishing up my files on some of the high school kids we had in for our camp. There was a knock on my office door and a familiar voice asked for Lil' Hayes. "Coach Clark, it's great to see you," I said as I stood to shake hands.

"I was in town to talk with Coach Bryant and I wanted to congratulate you in person. It just took me a little longer to get down this way, but, Son, I'm proud of you."

I was very glad to see him. "How is everything at Kentucky?" I asked.

"I wish it was a lot better. From what I have heard about your work, I may have to bring you up before too long."

"Thanks, Coach Clark. You know, it makes it a lot easier working under Coach Bryant. A lot of people do well under him."

"You keep working hard Bob and you'll get your share of opportunities."

"If so, Coach, I'll be asking you for advice. I guess making it to the NCAA Final Four keeps everyone happy up there. But, knowing you, a bowl game is what you are shooting for."

Coach Clark smiled. "You bet, and don't be surprised if I come calling on you."

"I'll believe it when I see it Coach."

We bid each other farewell and once again I recognized what Dad had told me: it was always beneficial to keep up with your friends, especially the ones in good places.

We awaited the arrival of our incoming freshmen to campus for the start of practice. We had three quarterbacks coming in, two we signed and one we invited to walk-on. When they showed up for the first meeting it was almost funny watching the looks on the young men's faces. Coach Bryant talked to them first and let them know they were here to be a part of a national championship team.

We started workouts and don't forget: it got really hot in Tuscaloosa, Alabama also. The main thing freshmen didn't seem to realize was that there are so many with equal or better talent. Most were used to being the fastest, toughest or biggest on their team and here that was suddenly not the case. This change could frustrate the best of players, at least until they could up their game and learn the finer details.

Our two, or my two, prize recruits Ed Hollingsworth and Colt Turner were adjusting pretty well. "JA" was doing a good job with the passing game and Grant Sims especially liked the receiving more than the blocking when running the wishbone.

We were in a meeting with the quarterbacks and receivers, reviewing film of a scrimmage. We stopped the film and I related the story to Colt of a high school receiver at Stuart, Ed Sanders, who was there when I was a manager. I said, "Colt, you have been use to being the fastest and in high school they would give you a lot of space. Now you're going to have to use some steps to one side or the other and learn the moves. Then you can get some separation and room to run."

Colt nodded and I turned to Ed Hollingsworth. "Now, Ed," I said. "You see how you have to figure out where to put the ball so it doesn't get knocked down? It is all about doing the little things correctly."

The opening game at Southern Cal was right around the corner. One thing Coach Bryant stressed was that we wouldn't get beat from not being in shape. Our work from spring practice carried over real well. We prepared both drop backs and roll outs because Cal had a really good defensive front and if we had trouble blocking them straight up, we could roll out and get more time.

Be Prepared

Coach Duncan and I prepared our game plan for yardage and distance and he was noted for scripting his first few series ahead of time. He said, "Bob, I like to be proactive instead of reactive. I want them to deal with us and if we are doing something really well we will just wear their butts out with it."

I had my first quarterback meeting set for Thursday morning at seven. Danny O'Keith had me a box to go from Shipley's for my guys and they didn't waste any time when I told them to help themselves. "You sure know how to get our attention, Coach Hayes," "JA" said.

I let them know that on any given play the next quarterback may have to take charge. "Trust each other and when we meet coming off the field, if you notice something don't hold back. That is why this is a team game. There is no "I" in team."

I reminded them that Coach Duncan would call the plays down to me and we would run or signal them in. Bobby Joe was to have his helmet in hand because he was the next to go in. I told them, "Guys, I keep notes, by quarter, and I make a note on all the plays. Then on Monday night we'll review them. It may be things from carrying out fakes, not seeing a receiver, or technique related. Just like in practice if I don't like something any of you are doing, I will bring it to your attention on what we want you to do."

When I looked around I could see that some of the guys looked surprised by this, some of them looked scared. I tried to ease their minds: "I realize there are times you may have your vision blocked, and there are 60,000 plus in the stands, and more on TV, and you see a receiver wide open and then you can't find him to save your neck. That is why we can look and review the plays together. Bobby Joe and Ed you two will be with me and we'll talk things through as we go."

As usual Coach Bryant had us well prepared. "JA" comes out throwing with the Trojans, cheating their safeties up, and we took a 14 point lead to the half. "Coach Duncan, I usually get too conservative in the second half but keep firing at them," Coach Bryant said. He called for Colt and said, "Son, back up three yards deep in the end zone and then I want you to be moving up when you catch and look the ball in. That'll give you some extra momentum."

Southern Cal kicked off, to start the second half, and Colt followed instructions as he caught the ball at the goal-line. He then blazed through the holes made by good blocks. The Trojans only saw the back of #80 going toward and across the goal-line. Jeff kept them off balance with good accurate passes and Alabama beat the #2 pre-season ranked Trojans 31-17.

Our charter flight approached the runway in Tuscaloosa at about four am. There were a lot of bright lights at the municipal airport. It turned out there were more fans at the airport to welcome their team than we use to play in front of at NE Alabama. We walked down the steps of the jet into a sea of cheering fans and I look over to Ed Hollingsworth and said, "This is what I told you about representing the whole state."

"Heck, Coach, there aren't this many people in Canton. I am so glad to be here now."

After our Sunday evening Coaches' meeting I asked our offensive GA, Jay Godfrey, to stop by my office. I told him my story about marking the plays that give our defense problems with the scout team. I advised him to put an extra pen in his pocket and put an asterisk by the "good" ones. I asked him to start putting those "good" plays in a notebook and to make me a copy of them. "That's a good idea, Coach," Jay said. With this resource of a variety of plays, we continued to make progress.

With a good and veteran offensive line "JA" was doing a super job. Bobby Joe had been able to get into a few games and we would have liked to red-shirt Ed if we didn't have any injuries, meaning no playing time. I did like Ed's progress as our season progressed, and it would be difficult to make a call if "JA" went down. Colt Turner had already shown us why Coach Bryant was so high on him.

The Stuart Rebels were off to a good start with Quint leading the way. They were at 4 and 1 and they had beaten Dalton. He told me, "It's just like you stressed in the camps to stay away from chances and take care of the ball. That's been working real well for me."

I smiled and asked, "Are you coming down to the Tennessee game this week?"

"Bob, you think it is about time for me to get a sideline pass?"

"Quint, as long as you tell Mom to bring Coach Bryant's oatmeal cookies this time."

Quint smiled. "I'll drive her crazy with reminders and we will see you Saturday morning."

The week went well and quick. I couldn't wait to find out what all Quint laid on Mom as he came in with a double batch of cookies and a pound cake. The door to Coach Bryant's office opened and Quint stuck his head out of my office and caught his attention. Bryant said, "Quint, meet me back in my office if you've got cookies this time."

That was all it took to get Quint on cloud 9.

Dad and Doc West came in a couple minutes later, and Mom and Mrs. West were out in the lobby, for now, talking with Ms. Jane. We shook hands and talked for a few minutes. "Doc, I'm gonna need to borrow you in a few minutes. Before it gets too hectic my quarterbacks will be over soon and, Quint, you better have me a few cookies or "JA" will have your butt."

I turned back to Doc. "Doc," I said, "I need you to work on me and "JA." He tells me his hips get tight from pushing off throwing. I told him I had that back in high school and would have a solution for him.

My guys walked in and around go the introductions. I asked "JA" to follow me and Doc down to the training room. I asked Coach Vic Hightower, our trainer, if I could show him something. He said sure and I said, "Coach, this is Doc West he is my Chiropractor from Stuart and longtime family friend. I think he has got the answer for "JA's" little problem."

Doc told "JA" to lay face down on the treatment table and he bent "JA's" knees up. When he did that, the right knee dropped down a couple of inches. Coach Hightower looked on as Doc explained that "JA" had some rotation on his right pelvis and that was what kept the muscles tight. Especially when he tried to push off on throws. Doc had "JA" turn on his side and there was a loud *pop, pop, pop*. Doc repeated this procedure on the other side. Then Doc had "JA" lay back, face down, and he explained that everything was now balanced the way it should be. "JA" stood up with his eyes wide open and said, "Wow, that feels really good. The tightness is gone."

Doc explained to Coach Hightower that the hip imbalance was where a lot of tight hamstring problems came from as well. After seeing that, Coach Hightower said, "I have a couple of other guys I would like for you to check in a bit."

Doc said, "Sure thing, we'll be up front or in Bob's, uh Coach Hayes' office."

After he worked on me we walked back to my office to start our short meeting and to go over changes in our signals. "Coach Hayes, you amaze me coming up with so many solutions," "JA" said.

That comment sure put a smile on the face of Doc West.

I got back and Quint was in with Coach Bryant for a few minutes. As they walked out, I heard, "Sure thing, Coach," and I saw eyes as big as saucers. "JA" managed a thump on the back of Quint's head as they shook hands. "JA" mentioned that Quint had gotten larger, and I warned him not to compliment Lil' Brother too much. I asked Quint, "What info did Coach give you?"

"Tarver has this big, 6'3" linebacker named Winston Bennett who is fast and even returns kicks. Scares the crap out of you being the quarterback but Coach says to run right at him and use a few traps to help negate his speed. Coach Sloan may think I am crazy but when I tell him those ideas came from Coach Bryant he will have a different outlook." Quint grinned and continued. "He also said with the open week that you two may be able to make it up for the game."

Coach Bryant walked by and heard us talking and said, "It looks like I may have to, Son. The way these quarterbacks seem to think my cookies are for them." All the quarterbacks around started to wipe their mouths clean.

I looked at the play list Coach Duncan had put together and we went over which calls and signals they looked to get.

On this day Tennessee was over-matched and our keys were right on the money as were "JA's" passes. Both Grant and Colt caught a deep ball, each for a touchdown. Bobby Joe was able to play the fourth quarter and got a score himself. It was very good to keep your reserve ready and to give him some actual playing time. If you scored with the second team, so be it. They had earned their chance just like all the rest.

Keep All Your Players Ready

Coach Bryant had a hectic schedule. It worked out that on Friday morning we started with breakfast at JT's and we made a path that had us stopping at four other schools, to meet with coaches, on the way to Stuart to see Quint and the Rebels take on Tarver and Winston Bennett. While we were driving Coach asked me what I envision of for myself, a little down the road. I said, "I don't want to take a position that won't let me advance further. Offensive coordinator is the usual next step for a QB coach. Not too many get the chance you gave Coach Duncan to go to Division II and then back to Alabama."

Coach Bryant nodded. "I'll be honest with you, Bob. I have had some smaller schools already call me about you. But I wanted to see what direction you might like to go in. Given your background and insight, I know I will have a hard time keeping you around here. But just keep working the way you have. All this is part of the game."

To save time it worked out that Coach Bryant and I were able to stop at home in Stuart for dinner. Something light was Coach's request and Mom had a batch of chicken salad ready. When we walked in Dad was there to greet us and Coach just asked Mom what was for dessert, after his hug. "Bob," he said "Whenever you go to the home of a recruit and the mother offers you up dessert, you always say yes."

Sharon walked in. She hadn't got the memo that we were going to be in town. She had met Coach once before and he said after introductions, "Girl, you make any of those desserts like your Mom and I may just find you a job in Tuscaloosa."

Sharon turned a couple of shades of red.

Dad rode with Coach and me to the game so we could use his parking spot and then sit in the press box which was above the reserved seats. Just before kick-off, we approached the aisle to walk up and it looked like Moses parting the Red Sea. Nobody even knew Dad and I was walking with Coach, as all eyes were on him and he nodded at all the greetings. As we got seated in the press box, Coach looked at me and said, "Bob, this right here, pointing to the fans and at the players, is what makes all of this fun and rewarding."

I agreed with him completely.

The Rebels came right out and did something Tarver hadn't seen all year: they ran right at Bennett. It controlled his aggression and kept him and their defense frustrated to no end. Leading by 10, with 5 seconds left until halftime, the Rebels were about to try a 35 yard field goal and I looked at Coach Bryant and said, "Watch this."

Quint took the snap, put the ball on the tee, and then whirled back around as Bennett leapt high into the air to block the kick. Lil' Brother lofted the ball to a wide-open tight end for a touchdown. Coach Bryant said, "How did you know that was coming, Bob?"

I said, "It pays to have a quarterback holding, and it was the perfect time. Plus I just know Coach Sloan."

At the start of the fourth quarter we shook hands with all in the press box, sign a few programs, and made our way to the car. We timed it for Quint to see us and we got to shake his hand standing next to the fence. On the way back Coach dozed off, while I drove us home. The sweet smell of oatmeal cookies filled the car.

Quint called me early on Saturday morning after he and Dad had breakfast at Paul's Diner. "What did coach say about our game?" he asked.

"He liked the way the Rebels got after Tarver and you made some good throws. It looked like you and Coach Sloan took his advice and y'all stuck with your plan pretty well. I have to admit that I called the fake field-goal pass when you broke the huddle."

Quint said, "Yeah, I guess I have a lot to learn about setting up an offense. I would have never thought we could run right at them. I talked to Bennett after the game, he's huge, and he is looking forward to being down in a few weeks for a visit. He liked it when I told him you and Coach Bryant was at the game. I told him to let me know and we would try to hook up when he comes down."

"That's a good little brother. You'll make Coach glad with that and make me look good."

My first loss on the staff came the following week at Penn State. Even though it was a huge game, we had our TV games already set. It was hard for Coach to keep his cool after we got hit with a barrage of holding calls and still we just lost 17-13. The toughest calls to stomach were when our back-side tackle got flagged for holding when we rolled the opposite way with relative short patterns. We moved the ball well but penalties and a couple of bad breaks sealed our fate. A call at the end of the game was made against Grant for stepping out at the back of the end zone and a photographer's view didn't yield the same result. The reporters were trying to bait Coach Bryant into criticizing the calls, but he didn't fall for it.

It is Not Going to Change the Outcome

We rolled real well for the rest of the season and took care of our rival, Auburn, in fine fashion, to end the regular season 9 and 1. "JA" did a super job with the offense and also with not getting hurt, so we did get to red-shirt Ed Hollingsworth.

A week later it was announced that Alabama would face Nebraska in the Sugar Bowl. We had only a month to prepare to play some big fellas. I saw them play Oklahoma and I knew there was a lot of work ahead.

In our first offensive meeting, Coach Bryant stood up at the end of the table and said, "Coach Duncan, I'm gonna give you and your coaches a little breather. Don't try to come up with too much. We're widening our splits a little more and running the ball right down their throats. They won't know what hit them and our 'little linemen' will be the stars."

Then Coach Bryant looked at me. "Coach Hayes," he said. "It will be like what we saw up at Stuart watching your Rebels."

By opening our splits we don't allow the bigger guys to control the space at the line of scrimmage. Our faster linemen would make good and quick blocks and our backs would have a field day. Now I just had to convince "JA" of this plan of attack.

Classes had just ended and we gave the players a little break. Our first group meeting was for eight am and I met our quarterbacks for breakfast in the dorm cafeteria. We sat down and Bobby Joe said, "Coach Hayes, I was looking forward to some Shipley's treats to be honest with you."

I laughed and said, "We will save that for a couple of days."

Then I got down to business. "Here is what we have. JA you are going to have the opportunity to show how smart you are and demonstrate being a field general out there. We have thrown for more yards than the last three years combined. But, being in charge of the offense is what it is all about." I gave them Coach Bryant's plan and explained how simplicity can be so effective.

We showed up in New Orleans and worked on more fundamentals and drills than anything. Coach Bryant told the players, especially being on the road with some free time, to "show their class and not their ass."

Talk about hitting the nail on the head. The Sugar Bowl committee did something they had never done before. The Alabama Offensive Line was name the offensive MVP. Nebraska could really have used some of Doc West's adjustments because they were getting cricks in their necks watching our running backs zip through holes and having a field day running past all of those big Cornhuskers. The final score was 31-7.

In the fourth quarter Bobby Joe was running the offense and "JA" told me that if his chance in the NFL didn't pan out, he'd take a spot on my staff any time. He said, "I was put back thinking we might be in trouble when I heard Coach Duncan was coming in. Then he brings in this young pup to tell us how to do our job? Well, I admit I had my doubts. But, Coach Hayes, you kept your word of telling us what to do and not making us look bad, and I know you held back a few times with some of my idiot mistakes." He looked me right in the eyes. "I really appreciate that," he said.

Quint walked up then and "JA" tried to put him into the game. "Coach Hayes," he said, "this little guy has been fun to be around, as well," and he rubbed Quint's head. He said to Quint, "You keep paying attention to Coach Brother and you'll do well. He tells me you had a good year yourself."

"Just County Champs, no SEC or Sugar Bowl," Quint said as the clock winded down the last 30 seconds.

We got back into Tuscaloosa after a couple of days to return calls and to try and wrap-up the past season. I was at my desk when Jane beeped me and said that there was a Ms. Elliott on line one. "I'll take the call," I said with a smile on my face.

"Bob, this is Lynn." We exchanged greetings and asked each about the holidays. "I watched the Sugar Bowl and the announcers were talking well about the young coach. At the end of the game, they showed you talking with #10 and Quint got in the picture also."

I was a little glad, then, that we were talking over the phone. She couldn't see me blush. "Well," I said. "I was glad everything fell into place and we didn't get embarrassed."

"Now," she said, "don't start getting too much like Coach Bryant this soon."

We both laughed and I told her that we were able to attend a game in Stuart which was fun. I said, "I may have a little time in-between recruiting, you know any high school linemen up that way?"

"No, Bob, but I did go to a couple of home games this past year at UK."

"Let me know come next season and I'll hook you up with Coach Clark and he will set you up. He was Stew's coach at NE Alabama and played ball at Kentucky."

She had to go then. Would've, could've and should've entered my mind once again.

Ms. Jane walked by my office and said, "That reporter had a nice voice."

"Don't start that up," I said. "She's just a girl from Stuart I haven't seen in over a year."

"Coach Hayes, I do have a person of interest working in the administration department you might want to get in touch with."

"Jane, I must be behind on bringing you some treats from Shipley's. Talk like that and I will get you a key made for the front door there."

Before I left for the day I touched base with Jay Godfrey, our GA, and set up to meet the next morning for breakfast at JT's. We talked about the year and when we got back to the office we spent time going over the plays he had checked for us during the year with the scout team.

I said, "You know, Jay, most of the so called trick plays work because of the timing of them. I'll give you one instance Coach Duncan and I used at NE 'Bama. Our punter had good speed and we were close to midfield and had fourth and 4 to go. We tried to get the defense to jump and took the 5 yard penalty. We then ran the punter, off the fake, for a 20 yard gain and went on to score."

Jay nodded. "I see what you mean and we just didn't have to use many this past year, which was good."

Timing Is a Key Ingredient

We had our first full staff meeting just before our players returned from break. Our secondary coach, Jim Davidson, had taken the defensive coordinator job at Tulane. It was a common step in the natural progression of moving up.

"Coaches," Coach Bryant said, "we have just lost a lot of strong factors to our team. We've got some good 'pups' in training but we are going to have to work the hell out of them this spring for us to have a chance come fall." He explained that some, by the end of the season, think it will be easy. A lot had been home for a week and their friends had really built them up and made them think real highly of themselves. Coach closed by saying, "In your individual meetings we want to let them know what we are facing and we want the ones ready for the challenge. If they ain't up for it their ass'll be gone. It's better they bow out now than come fall."

Last Season Is History and It Can Only Be a Lesson

The next morning I stopped by Shipley's to see Danny Donut and we got to chat a bit. He liked the change in offense and the young, Colt Turner. He said Colt gave us some breakaway speed, the sort of thing the Tide hasn't had in a few years. I got a few cinnamon twists for Ms. Jane as I head out the door.

As I walked in to our offices and delivered my treat for Jane, I asked about her friend at the administration office. "Jane, I actually have a weekend off. Could you see if she has some free time?"

Jane smiled and agreed to talk with her friend.

After a little while Ed Hollingsworth came in to meet. We discussed the previous year and the good changes we had made. "Ed, I told you when we first met you would get the opportunity to represent a lot of people. You are about to get that chance."

"Coach Hayes, Jeff was good at telling me details of workouts and to be ready mentally."

"Yeah," I said. "'JA' was correct. We're going at spring 100% and everybody will be live once we start practice. Coach Bryant told us we have got to get some people ready because finishing second in the country was last season. We lost three of the five MVP's from the Sugar Bowl and you know Coach Ryan has his job cut out for him and the linemen."

I let Ed know that he had to improve with his reads and decision time. He said, "I remember having a few balls picked off in some early scrimmages last fall. Like you told me, the game gets a lot faster."

"Ed, if you pay attention to detail and work on the little things you will be able to slow it down a bit. Just like knowing Colt, to your right, is running a 12 yard hook, don't start starring at him as soon as you start your drop back. Just keep working on the small stuff and don't get ahead of yourself."

As Ed left Jane walks by and said her friend doesn't have plans for the weekend.

"What's her name?" I asked.

"Scarlett Evans," Jane said and handed me a phone number on a piece of paper.

The next morning Bobby Joe Stevens settled into the padded chair across from my desk. We talked about his filling in on the games last year and doing a good job of not making mistakes. I said, "You've got the experience and we're going at spring practice 100%, meaning full contact for everybody. You gave me great effort last year and boosted our over-all confidence."

He said, "Coach, I appreciate the work you have put in for us and your style. I didn't think I had a chance to play when we made the change but you gave me some new skills I didn't know I had in me. Whatever becomes of the result of spring with Ed and me I know it will be fair."

"Bobby Joe, I had a guy move in on me in Stuart. But I hung in and was a part of a state championship team. It's something I will have forever, just like this past SEC & Sugar Bowl."

Scarlett Evans answered the door at her small home and my first thought was, I will be bringing Jane Shipley's treats for awhile. We did the small talk and I let her pick out where to eat. With all the football the past few years, I know I don't run the risk of running into an old girlfriend no matter where we go.

Conversation and dinner, at Dexter's, was going real well, I thought, until we got up to leave. "Oh hell," Scarlett said.

"Oh hell, what?" I asked.

Up walks a guy, about 6'6," and I recognized him as Jasper Higgins. He was the starting middle linebacker for the New York Giants, and a past player at Alabama. "Excuse me a minute, Bob," Scarlett said.

After a moment she came back and told me that she hated to cut our date short but something was up with the two of them and needed to be resolved. Would've, could've and, shut up, I thought.

The next week, I was going over my list of recruits scheduled to come in this Saturday. Jane came by and said, "I'm sorry, Coach Hayes. I didn't have a clue."

"At least the food was good," I said, laughing.

Coach Bryant walked in my office and asks me about Winston Bennett and I let him know he was supposed to be coming Saturday with Quint for the Kentucky basketball game.

"Good deal," Coach Bryant said. "What is your take after talking with Bobby Joe and Ed?"

"Coach, we may have us a good 1-2 punch if we need a change of pace. If Ed continues to improve he can be a special player and I think he learned a lot last year."

As the week went on, I got an interesting call. Coach Clark, Athletic Director from Kentucky, called and asked me to have dinner with him on Friday evening, when he comes in with the team. It was good to see him and he liked the progress we'd made and was impressed with the way our offense performed. He said, "Bob, I am going to be honest. If we struggle this upcoming season we'll be up for changes and I hope you'll talk with me. I keep up with who is doing what and who I think we'll work well together."

I was a little stunned, but I tried to keep my cool. "Sure thing," I said, "but I need a favor."

"Shoot," he said.

"When we play up there, basketball, will you have a couple of tickets available for a friend?" Coach said, no problem, and I wrote down Lynn's name and her address at First Commonwealth Bank. Then Coach Clark wished me well and asked me to say hello to everyone in my family. As he walked out I wonder just who he might have me working under at Kentucky as an offensive coordinator.

Later in the day Quint called about coming down, with Winston Bennett, on Saturday. He said, "Bob, what if we came on Friday afternoon?"

I explained about meeting Coach Clark for dinner, since he was coming with their team, and I said that I would be on the lookout for a spare room in the dorm if a couple of players were out for the weekend.

Quint told me that Winston was so excited he was going to bring a pen to sign now.

I laughed and said, "Just remind Mom for the snacks and his verbal okay will do for now."

Quint picked up Winston, which was about a twenty minute detour from the route he would normally take, and on to Tuscaloosa they traveled. They talked about classes and Winston noticed the sweet smell of oatmeal cookies in the back seat. "Quint," he said "You take your own snacks with you when you be traveling?"

"Nah," Quint said, "those are for Coach Bryant."

"You're damn kidding me. I know your brother is coaching there but having cookies for the Man is awesome."

Quint explained how Coach had taken a liking to Mom's treats and how it helped keep him out of the doghouse.

Winston was impressed. He said, "That was some nice words they were saying at the end of the Sugar Bowl game about your brother. I thought I saw your face and then I guess ABC was smart enough to cut away at that point."

"Winston, you know the walk is getting longer back to Tarver, don't you?"

They laughed a bit and, then Quint revealed the secret. He said, "I hate to admit this but I was down at the Tennessee game and Coach Bryant called me into his office. He had seen some film of you, yes he was impressed. He was the one that suggested we run right at you."

"It caught us off guard," Winston said. "Most teams try to run away from me, but we have good pursuit and are able to shut them down. I guess if y'all had made the play-offs, you would've been calling Lombardi."

"Coach Bryant will do just fine," Quint said.

They pulled in at Bryant Hall and I was in my apartment about to get dressed when they knocked on my door. "Hey guys," I said, "come on in."

I looked at my watch and said, "Quint, I see you found the gas pedal with your driving."

"Well," Quint joked, "it was all downhill."

We talked a bit and I walked them over to have dinner with the rest of the players. Bobby Joe saw Quint and gave him a thump on his head, saying it was from "JA." Winston got introduced and they joined Bobby Joe for dinner. Dinner was barbecued ribs and pork chops.

I got a call and Coach Clark let me know I should just meet him at Dexter's around 7:30. I managed a room, down the hall, for Quint and Winston. I told them they were under curfew and they believed me.

I walked into Dexter's and scouted the place, looking for Jasper and Scarlett. I was relieved that I didn't see them. The hostess said, "Coach Hayes, would you follow me please?" Don't even think that thought.

I greeted Coach Clark and we had our small talk and he asked if he was that hard to find sitting there. I filled him in on my last dinner date, which brought some chuckles. He said, "Bob, from everything I have seen with our football program, between us, I don't see a lot of improvement coming. That means I may get another chance to put together a new staff—what've got now has been a lot of the same. We brought in some good coaches, but all continues to fall short."

I said, "Coach Clark, most of your recent head coaches have been around before and, if it doesn't go well, they will just blame it on being a basketball university and they will settle in with a coordinator job someplace."

"Good point" he said.

"I don't want to give you too many of my secrets, but I see some big voids—I've been keeping up with you there."

"Like what, for instance?" he asked.

"Well," I said, "you aren't getting your own in-state top players. Your left fielder on the baseball team was a quarterback. I know the running back at both North and South Carolina came from Kentucky."

Coach Clark nodded. "It's true," he said.

"Then," I went on, "Coach, ask yourself if you really see the passion? Since you've been there, do see anyone doing the things, like you used to do, like the kidney pill at NE Alabama?" I looked at him. "To this day," I said, "I remember every word of the talk you gave about whipping UT-W's butt the next year."

"Bob, I agree with you 100%. You keep doing the job you've been doing for Coach Bryant and the rest will fall into place."

"Coach," I said, "I'm not pushing for anything now."

We talked a bit more and we broke it off before we got over-served with after dinner drinks, which would make for some headlines.

After dinner, I talked with Quint and Winston and asked them to meet me at my office about nine am. Close to that time, I was looking over a list of recruits I was to meet, when there was a tap on my office door.

"Come on in," I said expecting the two younger guys, but instead I heard a deep voice saying, "Coach Hayes?"

I turned to look up and saw Jasper Higgins standing there. The lump in my throat grew big in a hurry. He said, "Coach I wanted to apologize for cutting into your plans with Scarlett a few weeks ago. It has been some time since we broke things off and I was to meet her and get a few things. She just had the dates mixed up and my time gets limited."

"Ms Jane tried to explain and, you know how little free time we get, but I understand."

Jasper said, "I felt bad after she told me who you were. If there is anything I can do just let me know."

"Well," I said, "Jasper there is one thing." Just as I said this, there was a buzz on my line. I told Jasper my brother and a linebacker recruit was about to walk in. "I know they would like to meet you," I said.

Quint and Winston walked in and their eyes grew big immediately. Jasper stood up and shook hands with them both. "Winston, Coach Hayes was telling me some good things about you, and I would love to see you wearing that Crimson and White—hopefully #47. It was sure a good number for me when I was here."

Winston said, "I will take any number I can get. I love watching you play your game, Jasper."

"Thanks, Winston," Jasper said. "Quint, I hear you'll be next in line to play."

"I have had a couple of good brothers ahead of me, but any place will suit me," he said.

When Jasper was about to leave, he shook my hand and told me to keep up the good work. "Call on me at any time, Coach Hayes."

Then a deep loud voice said, "Who is trying to get out of here?"

"Hello, Coach Bryant," Jasper said, getting a bit of a hug with his handshake.

I saw saw Wilson looking looking at Quint. He said, "This is too cool."

After another moment Jasper said goodbye and waved to all of us. Coach Bryant looked at Winston, extended his hand, and said, "Nice to meet you, young man. I feel a little bad that you have had to put up with Quint. He better have something for me from his mom."

We all laughed.

Guys," he said then, "walk down the hall to my office where we will have a little more room."

We walked into his spacious office. The first thing you'd notice about his office was a couple of his hounds—tooth hats on his rack. We all looked up at then before we took a seat. "Winston," he said, "we were able to come up to yours and Quint's game against each other and we liked what we saw, in that game, and all year."

"Coach Bryant," Winston said, "that was not one of my better Games."

Coach Bryant shook his head. "Son, you had great effort and, with a little bit more technique, you would have had a better outcome."

"Coach, I'm sure glad you didn't show him anything beforehand," Quint said, laughing.

I asked Winston how he has liked what he has seen around the campus and how he liked everything else.

"Coach Bryant," he said, "I have already found out, the hard way, with just a little advice, that I can't beat you. So, I am ready to join you if you'll have me."

The two shook hands and Quint said, "By the way, Coach, here is your batch of cookies that Winston got to smell all the way."

Coach Bryant smiled. "I told your sister, Sharon, I would have to find her a place down here if she cooks anything like your Mom."

We talked a minute more and I walked them down to Coach Rich Alford's office, Line-backers Coach, to talk and get acquainted.

In the packed basketball arena Alabama pulled off an upset of #2 ranked Kentucky, who was in the Final-Four the previous year. Quint and Winston had a very full day. Winston said, "Coach Hayes, I couldn't have asked for a better time. Everyone has been great and meeting some of the players, along with Jasper Higgins, was too special."

"Thanks, Winston. We're glad you have liked everything and we're glad to have you coming onboard."

"I didn't know getting your butt kicked in a game could be this beneficial," Winston said and we all laughed.

Our spring practice went well and, even with a lot of full contact scrimmages, we got through it without any major injuries. Coach Bryant explained to the players that more injuries occur when not going at full speed. None of the guys were going to dispute it with him, anyway. He had a main point to get across: "Winners know how to practice."

Winners Practice Hard

Ed Hollingsworth and Colt Turner turned out to be a good tandem working together. Ed's stronger arm utilized Colt's speed and ability to make cuts; they were a potent duo. With our lack of experience regarding the offensive line we added more to our roll out package to give our quarterbacks more time to throw.

To give an example, in practice Ed and Bobby Joe were both rolling out and getting a few balls tipped. We lined up and called a roll out right and I told Ed to back out of the way and I'd complete the damn pass. "Full speed I yell."

This had our defensive ends smiling and talking. I took the snap, rolled right and started to throw. The defensive end jumped up to block himself another pass. Instead I pumped fake and put the ball into Colt's hands for a completion. "That was a good leap there James," I said slapping him on the back.

"Aw, Coach Hayes, that wasn't cool."

"James, with your height, don't go for the fake because most all of the time that's what it'll be."

"Quarterbacks remember what it was like playing in your back yards? The same fakes work just as well, if not better up here."

Know How to Play the Game

This spring game was different than the previous year. For the first half both Coach Bryant and Coach Duncan wanted to see how Ed could handle actual game situations. In our meeting setting up the game plans, we had to be open with both offenses to give equal time to our quarterbacks. We let them know we wanted to see the little things.

On the second drive, Ed had his offense, Red Team, moving down the field with a good mix of run and pass. They got to the 12 yard-line with first down. An inside trap play netted 3 yards. The next was a roll right to aim for Colt running a curl pattern inside of the defenders. Ed took the snap, rolled right and the safety darted over in front of Colt. Seeing that Ed pumped a good fake and reversed back to his right and spotted Brad Holmes, tight end, who did an about face and made the catch for the touchdown. It was a perfect example of our egg package, at its best, and there was no panic. I looked over to Coach Duncan, who was looking at Coach Bryant, nodding his approval.

"What just happened, Ed?" I asked as he came off the field.

"Coach, I've seen so many quarterbacks who try to force the ball, throw it away, or take a sack. But, working on the egg deal felt as comfortable as any play, and did you see the jumps with the pump?"

"That's why we practice it, Ed. Just be smart out there."

After a good effort from our players, they began to understand what they could do with consistent hard work. With the way Ed Hollingsworth stepped up, we were going to have him starting. Coach Duncan and I have had this episode in the past at NE Alabama when Mitch Fontenot came in from LSU to take over for Senior to be Ralph Maddox.

We sat down with Bobby Joe to explain our decision and told him that we will need him ready for our team to be successful.

An Honest Explanation Can Go a Long Way

After our meeting there came a voice, "Hold on Coaches." It was "JA," Jeff Austin, who had become the second round pick of the New Orleans Saints. "I've got to give you two a lot of credit and especially seeing Ed know what to do on that touchdown pass. That's the first one I've seen where he didn't panic. That's why I mentioned you both a lot in my interviews after the draft. You come in here, out of high school, thinking you are smart but you really don't have a clue."

We talked a bit longer and "JA" said he was going to be around and had already agreed to work with our camp. He said, "I can't wait to put some work on Quint when I see him."

"'JA,'" I said, "I appreciate your efforts with 'Lil' brother. You pick on him all you want."

The camps and summer work seemed to go well. For Coach Bryant we were getting the perfect coverage from the sports magazines. With the loss of a lot of seniors we were not highly ranked and given low expectations coming in to this season. Changing offenses last year caught a lot of Teams off guard and they would be ready for the Tide this year: those were the remarks and analysis from the so-called experts.

As the opening game hosting Georgia Tech approached, the routines, repetitions and work go according to plan. It was good to see our players had the preparation and the willingness to take on the challenge. Winston Bennett had a spot on the coverage teams and back-up outside linebacker to utilize his speed.

The Crimson Tide handled the Yellow Jackets, to the tune of, 27-10. Ed Hollingsworth only had 1 pass picked off due to a deflection and showed he belonged. Using his speed, Winston made 4 tackles on kick-off coverage.

We played at Tennessee and the Vols were playing good ball. Just before half, we drove into field-goal position and the clock wound down to 3 seconds before a time out was called. We sent on the field goal team at the 27 yard line. Coach Bryant gave me the nod and Coach Duncan agreed. The fake and pass from third team quarterback and holder, Wayne Simmons, to tight end Brad Holmes worked perfectly for a 14-3 lead.

Going into the locker room at half I looked at Winston Bennett and asked, "You see that play before?"

"I liked being on this side of it better and I bet Quint takes credit for the play."

The Vols were giving Colt Turner a lot of room to make sure to not get beat deep. After I noticed this, I said, "Coach Duncan if they are going to give us the 6 to 8 yards on our quick out let's do it a few in a row. We'll let Colt catch and run out, catch and run out and then catch and turn it up the field." We instructed Ed to get the ball out fast and Colt to do his deal.

We hold and got the ball on our 25. The first play was a run left to get the ball to the center of the field. The next play was a quick out to the right and first down to Colt stepping out. Next play the duo gained 7 yards. The third play Colt stopped about 2 yards from the sideline, cut back to his left. Those watching the game on TV could probably hear, "Whoa Nellie," coming from broadcaster Keith Jackson. Colt then dashed past the safety and #80 to "take it to the house." 'Bama went up 21-3 and Coach Bryant holds true to the idea of the first five minutes of the second half being so important.

It's Okay to Take What They Give You and Then Take a Little More

In the middle of October, Alabama was ranked # 4 at 6-0 and Kentucky sat at 2 and 4. The off week came at a good time. Quint and Coach Sloan had the Rebels at 6 and 0.

I got a good lesson about how to get the players' attention and how to show them a coach means business. On Tuesday of the off-week, being 6-0, Coach Bryant put our team through full contact scrimmages. "Guys we ain't good enough to rest on what we have. If we sit idle we'll get passed by in a hurry," he told them.

In the next game Ole Miss hoped that Alabama would be too rested, but instead they caught a case of 'whup ass to the tune of 35 to 10. It was funny to see the looks on some of the players' faces when a reporter asked them about the rest during the off week.

Stuart hit a bump and fell to 7 and 1. They blew out their final two opponents but just missed the play-offs and Quint learned the meaning of would've, could've, and should've. He had been visiting a couple of other colleges. His 5'10" height kept the major schools at bay, but he was getting the rumor about going to NE Alabama, to possibly play for his brother Bob—their new, young, head coach.

Homecoming games could be very tricky. Too many people bought into the fact that you brought in a patsy team, rolled over them like an off week, and everybody gets to play. This year came a little school, Southern

Mississippi. They were a scrappy team with some talented players. They got players from all-over and played with a chip on their shoulder because some of them were passed up by the schools, like us, that they play.

The game was just hard played and there were not a lot of extra breaks for either side. We were up on the Golden Eagles 20-17 with two minutes left. A tipped pass fell their way to gain a first down on a fourth down pass. With five seconds left in the game they opted to try a 51 yard field goal to salvage a tie. It would have been good from 60 yards out and the game ended, tied at 20-20. The Sunday headline read, "Tide loses 20-20"

Take the Bitter with the Bitter, Again

We finished off Auburn, again, and ended the regular season, 9-0-1. We waited on the fate of the USC and UCLA game to see if we had a chance to play for a National Championship. USC pounded the Bruins to stay undefeated and was to take on once beaten Ohio State in the Rose Bowl. Alabama got the Orange Bowl to face Oklahoma which sat at 10 and 0. Dejected in one sense but a good showing and win over the Sooners coupled with a loss by So. Cal would have been our dream scenario.

We had a few regular days of no meetings which allowed us to get organized and ready to start our bowl preparation. On Tuesday, though, I got a call. "Coach Bob?" the voice on the other line asked.

"Hey, Coach Clark," I said. "I recognized your voice."

He said, "Can you meet me at the Birmingham airport around six pm in the coffee shop?"

"I don't see any problems with that. What have you got?"

"As you know, finishing 4 and 6 does not bode well for our current staff and program. I want to run a few ideas by you and let you know what I'm thinking before we start anything up here."

I made the fifty minute drive and saw Coach Clark in a back booth at the coffee shop. We shook hands and talked about a couple of our games. "Bob," Coach Clark asked, "what did you have to do with the fake field-goal against Tennessee?"

"Well," I said, "when Coach Bryant and me went to see the Stuart and Tarver game. Coach Sloan pulled that before half and Quint lofted an easy touchdown pass just like Wayne did to Brad. We started using our third quarterback as holder at the start of the year for that very play."

Coach Clark laughed and then his face got serious. "Okay, now," he said, "enough of the small talk. I have a short list of coaches I want to bring up to Lexington. I know for sure I would love to have you as my offensive coordinator. I know it depends on the possible head coach. Both of the two on my list are defensive coordinators. We actually have some talent but it's just not used wisely."

I nodded. "Who are the two, if you don't mind me asking?"

"I sort of wanted to hold off until I knew for sure, but I trust you, Bob. One is Mike Holland from Virginia and the other, the one who I have heard mentioned most around the board, is John Sargent of Georgia Tech."

I nodded. Those were certainly names I was familiar with.

Coach Clark went on: "Bob, what're a few things you can bring to the table real quick?"

"Like I have told you," I said. "The best talent in Kentucky has got to want to come to your program. I also think there is passion lacking: you have to have the passion to succeed. People need a fresh outlook and not a lot of the same old stuff."

Coach Clark started nodding. "I agree with you completely. He turned his head and looked out at the coffee shop. "When I get back, I'll call Coach Bryant and try to borrow you for a couple of days. I'll be giving you a call and we'll send our plane for you."

"Coach Clark," I said. "I'd appreciate it if this could be kept quiet. I can't make a decision until after the Orange Bowl."

"I appreciate your honesty and your integrity, for wanting to be with your team. I look forward to having you up."

We shook hands and I thanked him.

He nodded again and added, "Also, be thinking of a couple of assistant possibilities."

I made the drive back to Tuscaloosa. As I was thinking about the two coaches, I thought about how my quarterbacks have handled Tech the last two years. Also, Mike Holland at Virginia hasn't won anything special. I would look at my overall scope and go at this alone before asking Dad. Well, I thought slowly, I guessed if Coach Bryant trusted Dad, I might just run a few things by him, too.

I talked with Mom for a few minutes and asked if Dad had fallen asleep watching TV. She laughed. "Not yet," she said and handed him the phone.

"Hey, Dad," I said, "I thought you may have been watching TV with your eyes closed as usual."

Dad laughed. "What you have going this week?" he asked.

"Just some catch-up work," I said, "but I had an interesting meeting a couple of hours ago. I met Coach Clark at the airport in Birmingham and he wanted to know if I was interested in becoming the offensive coordinator at Kentucky."

"Coaching under whom?" Dad asked.

I told him the top 2 and was surprised with the reply.

Dad said, "I think you may have as much talent and ability, even given your age, than those two."

"Thanks, but for an SEC position, don't you think that may be a stretch?"

"It may be, but be thinking about who you might hire yourself. I imagine you will have major input."

"Hello," said the voice on the other line.

"Lynn, it's Bob Hayes, if you remember who I am. Are you free for a few minutes?"

"I'm not that that old yet," she said.

We talked for a bit about how time goes by faster and faster.

"Lynn," I said, "I wanted to get your advice on something. I'm sure you'll understand that this is confidential. I may be asked to be the coordinator at Kentucky. I met with Coach Clark earlier and he may fly me up in a day or two."

"Oh," she said and she paused for a long moment. "I met Coach Clark. He brought those basketball tickets to me himself." She paused again. "Well, Bob," she said. "It would be a good step forward, wouldn't it? Of course, I say that not knowing the particulars."

I laughed. "Lynn, that sounds like advice from a banker."

She laughed, too. "Bob," she said, "I am a banker."

"Well, that's true," I said. "But what I want to know is, what do people think about the football up there?"

"Oh, I don't know," she said. "There hasn't been a lot to get excited about since I have been up here. Knowing what it was like at Stuart with the championship year gives you a good insight."

"Lynn," I said, "do you have plans this weekend?"

"No," she said, without hesitating, "and if I had plans I would break them."

"That was a charming reply," I said. Then I added, "I'll call you as soon as I find out something."

There were a lot of possibilities involved and I had to figure out how far those possibilities would reach. After that call my phone rang and it was Quint.

"Bob," he asked, "do you know a Coach Anthony Metz?"

"Yeah," I said, "he played quarterback at East Carolina and has been an assistant. He'd been to a couple of the meetings here. We talked for a spell, he seemed nice. If I'm not mistaken, he's just a couple of years older than me."

"Well," Quint said, "he may be the offensive coordinator at NE Alabama. A couple of other schools who have been calling the most seem to always be everybody's homecoming opponent and that's not good. Bob you have been mentioned some about coming to NE Alabama, but I haven't really asked."

"Well, Quint, I talked with Coach Clark, and don't say a word, but I may be talking with Kentucky." I paused. "No matter what I decide I don't want it out until after the Orange Bowl."

Quint was silent on the other end of the line.

"Quint," I said, "NE Alabama with a passing offense may fit you real well."

I joined Coaches Duncan, Ryan, and Robbins for breakfast at JT'S. We were going to try and beat Coach Bryant with the theme against Oklahoma. "When I watched part of the Texas game, their defense seemed to rely on speed. Their ends just blew by the tackles and the Texas quarterback panicked some in the pocket," Coach Duncan said.

"I'll keep that in mind with Ed and Bobby Joe, to get a good deep drop and take a couple of steps up. Then they should have a clear pocket to throw from. Coach Ryan, your linemen can use their quickness to let them take themselves out of a lot of plays," I said.

"With faster backs, I'll make sure the receivers are coming back to Ed to give him a better target. Bob, after that some hitch and go's should be there."

Coach Ryan threw in some draws and screens and our attack seemed to be set.

We got to the offices and Jane said Coach Bryant was waiting for us. "Okay," he said, "Coaches, what have you got?" He looked around at all of us.

"Don't look at me that way," he said, "I was about to walk into JT'S and saw you in there and I didn't want to shake anything up."

Coach Duncan explained our attack plan and Coach Bryant, for once, agreed. "Let's start working on the finer points," he said.

We started to walk out and Coach Bryant asked me to stay a minute. He said, "I just got off the phone with Coach Clark at Kentucky. I gave him permission to talk with you this weekend. Bob," he said, "make sure it is what you want and that you like what they offer you. I know you have exceeded my expectations and helped to bring us up from potentially mediocre seasons here."

"Thanks, Coach, but your guidance sure makes it easier and your talent doesn't hurt either." That brought a smile to his face.

Then I said, "I told him no matter what it won't be made public until after the Orange Bowl."

"I like how you think of the rest, Bob, and that means a lot."

I returned the call to Coach Clark. Their plane would pick me up this afternoon, Thursday, at four in Tuscaloosa and I would meet with him Friday morning. Then I would meet their board for lunch. I let Coach Clark know that I had dinner plans for Friday night, so I could find out a little more about Lexington. "No problem," he said.

I dialed the number for the First Commonwealth Bank and luckily I caught Lynn Elliott on the phone. "Hey, Lynn, it's Bob."

"You mean, Coach Hayes?"

"Enough of that," I said, laughing. "They are flying me up there this afternoon and I'll be at the Downtown Hilton. I'll have meetings with Coach and then lunch with their Board tomorrow."

"Wow," she said. "That's a great place and only a block away from me. I have a couple of meetings as well but I'll meet you in the lounge at about 5:30. I have been reading about the search for a coach. Your name hasn't been mentioned for head coach but it has as offensive coordinator."

Visions of grandeur danced around in my head—about Lynn and not the coaching position. I had those visions with Scarlett, too, but they got squashed in a hurry. I have always had those visions about Lynn, ever since early in high school back in Stuart. They were yet to be squashed.

Coach Clark's assistant, Miles Staten, met me with the plane at the Municipal Airport. He extended his hand and said, "Coach Hayes nice to meet you. No disrespect but you are a young one."

I shrugged. "Well," I said, "you gotta start sometime."

Coach Clark met me at eight am for breakfast. I had time to read a couple of the sports pages and they were leaning heavily toward Coach Sargent of Georgia Tech. We got back to his office and I said, "Let me have what you've got."

"Well, Bob, with what you have done in a short time at NE and Alabama, developing the quarterbacks, has been tremendous. I have talked with Coach Ken and he assured me you can put a game plan together just like y'all were working on for Oklahoma. The Board hasn't been happy with some of the recent hires. These coaches just seem to enjoy being in the SEC."

"Coach, I have been thinking about this since we talked down in Birmingham. I feel with a good change of pace, the players will come when you have something for them here at Kentucky. I just know you aren't getting them doing what you've been doing."

"You're right Bob and just what would you tell a kid, from say Frankfurt?"

"Coach, it gets a little simple. I show them what we are going to do for them with education and I would offer them the chance to put Kentucky football back on the map. Then I'd probably pull out my map of Kentucky and point out that the University of Kentucky is for the whole state. If they want to play for the city of Louisville then so be it. But at Lexington they will represent the State."

I paused for a moment. "Coach," I went on, "before I meet with your Board, I want to ask you a question that is on my mind. I think it's kind of a serious question."

"Okay, Bob," Coach Clark said. "Let me have it."

"Coach Clark, are you solid on Coach Sargent?"

"The papers think so, but not entirely."

"Well, I know one thing: over the past two years, my quarterbacks wore his ass out. I know I was with Alabama, but I have confidence in my ability and if I took the coordinator job under him I think I would have my doubts."

"Okay, Bob, but I know they will question your age and inexperience."

"You won't find a lot of blemishes on what I have done so far. I know the lessons I learned from you, Coach Bryant, and Coach Duncan have been super. Show me which one of your finalists can give you that."

"You have a good argument there, Bob. Who might be a couple of hires for you?"

"I know you hate the school, but Gary Patterson at UT-Winston is a dang good coordinator and was all SEC at Georgia. Bobby Snead, your all everything wide receiver is blowing up scoreboards in the Mississippi delta. Wes Roberts is now coaching defensive ends at Auburn. I have a few others, too." I took a deep breath before I went on. "Coach, if you want to win and create some change then you have to show some courage. Hire me as your new head coach."

"Bob," he said, "you have just given me something I wasn't sold on. But, when I think about it, I can't find a single weakness in it. I'm going to let them change their mind-set before you talk with them. I'll be interested to see what you offer the board."

Coach Clark walked in and, after about 15 minutes, called for me to enter and do the introductions. I started by telling the board about the same thing I had just told Coach Clark.

"Ladies and gentlemen, I really like to answer people's questions because I can be a lot more specific and to the point when asked. I learned that from our high school team doctor at Stuart, Doc West. He was our Chiropractor. First I want to give you some insight so you will know what questions you may want to ask."

"When the players come here and spend their time and effort they need to get something that is worth more than what they put in. I have checked with all the top companies and found out, no matter who you know, they can't talk to you without a college degree. Some may get lucky every now and then but we have to look at the other 99%. When they leave here with that diploma and the lessons they learn at this University, they will be ready for their future. The 1% may get an opportunity to play in the NFL or have a rich uncle somewhere, but that's just 1%." I looked around at the board members. It seemed like they were listening.

I went on: "A lot of the players only get shown the football aspect but we will have the very best in education opportunities with tutors and study hall. My players will attend class and they will know every professor's name. I don't care what Baptist church some of the guys went to, but they won't be sitting in the back of the class here. They'll know that if myself and my staff didn't think they could play we wouldn't be having the meeting with them."

The board looked stunned. This was my chance, though. I kept talking. "Yes, Coach Hayes is young, but he knows where he is going and what can be the very best for the University of Kentucky. My talent level wasn't quite there to excel in the game of playing football. I promise you I know what it takes to succeed. I am a teacher first. I believe in showing my players "what to do" instead of talking or yelling if they screw up. You won't have to worry about background for Kentucky football. I know Coach Bryant won here when he was young, Coach Clark was all-everything here and this school needs a fresh start to get something great. A fresh start will help bring more enthusiasm and a little of 'what the hell is going on,' a positive shock to the system. When I got here, I talked to a resident of Lexington and asked about Kentucky football. Do you know what she said?"

I paused and looked around, but nobody answered my question. "She said, 'There is just not anything to get excited about.'"

After I finished speaking, I didn't answer as many questions as I thought I would. One lady looked at Coach Clark and asked about a couple of things I learned from him. I reminded them that he knew you had to beat the best in your league to make an impact. For us it was UT-Winston. I let them in on the kidney pills and peeing orange, which brought some laughs. I told them how he always knew what to say, especially when he declared that we would beat their butts the following year. I reminded the Board that we did beat them.

Know Your Commitment

Another question was from Mr. Hickman, Chairman of the Board of Trustees. "Bob," he said, "what is a specific new element you will bring in?"

"Mr. Hickman, when we played Nebraska last year they had been a so-so team for a few years. I talked with Coach Moe Bradshaw, offensive coordinator, and he related the best thing their program did was to hire a strength coach to monitor the players' development and have access to a regular chiropractor to work with their staff to help the players. I know the benefits of the chiropractor from my home town in Stuart: Doc West is the high school team doctor and good friend. I plan to add both to get this program developing faster."

After that, I thanked them and Coach Clark said he would meet me back in at the Hilton about an hour later. Miles drove me back to the hotel and asked me how it went. "Well, they may have gotten more than they thought. I guess I have to leave it at that for now."

Coach Clark walked into the lobby. We took a seat and grabbed a drink. "Bob, you impressed the hell out of me. I thought more about your comments with Coach Sargent, nothing against him personally, and I let the Board know after your talk I am behind you 100%. Now then, we didn't cover the topic, but a few brought up the concern of having a young bachelor as head coach."

"Coach," I said, "when are they going to decide on the topic about me and the position?"

"I told them we would talk and the Board will meet again at 9 am tomorrow."

I almost laughed. "Well, hell, so what you're saying is, if I was married I would get the job?"

"Yes, Bob, that would seal the deal for sure. The fact that you weren't married was a concern and some wanted to think on it tonight."

I knew then what I would do. "I'll give you a call before eight am. Better yet, just come by and we will have coffee in the morning. By the way, how were they on keeping it quiet until after the Bowl game if they approve me?"

"I told them it was a testament to your character and commitment."

We shook hands as quite a few thoughts started to fill up my head.

I had time to freshen up and change before I met Lynn Elliot downstairs. The timing was pretty good as I saw her walking in the door as I left the elevator. We hugged and smiles painted our faces. We sat and ordered cocktails. I asked her to decide what we'd have. She said, "How about a Southern Comfort manhattan on the rocks?"

"Make that two," I said and then turned to her. "I'll see your level of expertise."

We talked about what had been going on and how we both had been way too busy with careers, putting our personal lives aside a bit. I looked around the lobby and asked Lynn if she was dating anybody.

"Not steady," she said. "Why?"

I related the story about Scarlett Evans in Tuscaloosa and we both agreed how fun blind dates can be. The drink was nice with a sweet taste and I filled her in about my hankering for Shipley's to satisfy my sweet tooth.

"Okay, Bob, enough of the small talk, what the hell went on today?"

"Lynn, as I talked at breakfast with Coach Clark I realized we have beaten Coach Sargent in the past two years. As I started talking to the Board, I let them know if they want to win I would be the man for the job."

"Wow, I thought you were talking about the offensive job?"

"I think I was at first, but I felt this morning, with Coach Sargent being a defensive coach, I would be too limited on what I wanted to accomplish. We have a good thing at Alabama, for sure, and some talented players. Coach Bryant had told me to make sure I get what I want. He told me not to settle for a position."

Lynn looked excited. "How did that fall into place with the Board?"

"Coach Clark said he was real surprised and liked what I had to say. He liked how I presented what could happen here for UK."

I started to fill Lynn in with all the details, but suddenly I stopped. "Does this bore you?"

She looked surprised. "No, Bob," she said. "Actually, it intrigues me."

As I tell her the rest, she said that, with my background at Stuart, and my family, it doesn't surprise her at all.

"Lynn I have another question. Is the steak house in here a good place to eat?"

"I hear good things about it, but I am too anxious to get away from the office usually. I've never stuck around to try it."

"Well," I said, "let's go in and have dinner."

Dinner went well and we talked about high school and going out a few times. "It is unique, Lynn, that when I signed at NE Alabama you joined me for dinner. Then you were at the West Marion Diner when Coach Duncan asked me to join him at Alabama and here we are discussing the Kentucky job. I almost kept looking around to see if I see any brothers or sister around since I am here with you."

We laughed and finished off a good steak and shared a dessert.

"At least we have some things in common," Lynn said. "The way a lot of this has developed and," she grinned, "we both like food."

"Well, let me ask your thoughts on a subject," I said. "What are your honest thoughts about a relationship?"

She looked at me, a little stunned it seemed.

"I mean," I said, "a relationship with me."

She laughed. "I know that, Bob." She seemed to think for a minute. "I have been busy and now I'm a vice-president. I have a career I have been working on and because of this, I foresee there has to be some give and take with me in a relationship. But, if you can deal with that and this is the right thing, I'm in."

Then Lynn asked me about some of my thoughts. She said, "So many couples spend so long planning out ordeals that the trial and error part can really lessen the sizzle. It is kinda like coaching—they don't give you the championship and then see how the season plays out."

"That is a point I have never heard," I said, smiling.

"We've been out a few times over the years and we did have a great good-bye kiss in Birmingham. You have been my favorite. I loved watching you at pep rallies back in Stuart and seeing you in class. But our timing has never been the best."

"Well," she said, "Why didn't we go out more in high school?"

"I don't know. I worried too much about what others would do and you were off and on with Chris Cooper. At our small school you hate to get someone mad at you. But, as I recall, we talked a lot and was always around each other. Just look in our yearbook of the photos of us together."

She nodded.

"Lynn, I've had a lot of overwhelming thoughts in the last few hours. I am going to go for broke, here. After My meeting with Coach Clark he said I pretty much floored them with my plans and ideas. He said a few wanted to think over the situation tonight about hiring a young bachelor as their head coach."

"There's nothing like a little pressure with a situation," she said.

"That is my point exactly. Given that, Lynn," I reached forward to about a foot away from her, and I started to stutter. "Uh, uh, how would you like to be the wife of the head coach of Kentucky?"

She paused for what seemed like an eternity and stood up.

When she stood up I panicked. I was sure she was about to run off. I stood up to be polite, and she walked over and planted a big long kiss on my lips.

I laughed. "If this is maybe then I can't wait for yes."

"Bob," she said, "I have always enjoyed being around you and with you and your family. I only foresee great things happening and, as I told you a bit ago, if it seemed right I was all for it."

She looked me in the eyes and said, "It seems right to me."

A little later we both said, "What a day!"

We sat closer together, ordered another round, and Lynn said, "I know my holiday plans just changed. I was planning to just go back to Stuart and do nothing."

"We'll go over some of that tomorrow. I am supposed to meet Coach for coffee here at eight in the morning."

We got our drinks and toasted ourselves. Then I asked, "What next?"

"Maybe we should work on the yes part," she said. "Check please!"

I met Coach Clark and the waitress had a pot of coffee waiting at our table. "Any second thoughts, Bob," he asked.

"Coach, I may have set a record of pulling out all stops."

Coach grinned. "I can't wait to hear this."

"You remember the young lady you brought the basketball tickets to?"

"Yeah, Lynn. She has done some refinancing for me and a few others since then."

"Great. We met for dinner last night and she is to become Mrs. Lynn Hayes."

"Now how did you pull that off?"

"That's a long story," I said and I couldn't stop myself from smiling. I wished then I had a saying which meant the exact opposite of would've, could've, and should've.

"Well Bob," he said, "With that, I'm going to go ahead and say 'glad you're here with us.'"

We discussed keeping wraps on this until after the Orange Bowl. I would be calling and getting my coordinators. I'd have all that in place the first week of January. "I need the names and numbers of all the top high school players you've been talking with. If you have a few, on the fence, then ask them to wait till the announcement," I said.

"That sounds great and we'll fly you up here after the Orange Bowl game for the press conference. We'll get this horse to running." Coach smiled. "Bob," he said, "with all the thoroughbred farms up here you will have to get use to all the horse references."

Coach said the meeting might take an hour and I called Lynn and asked her to meet me at the athletic offices around 9:45.

We walked in to the meeting and after greetings Coach Clark said he had an announcement: "I'm willing to put the rest of my career on the line now: I'm going to introduce to you our new head coach at the University of Kentucky, Bob Hayes."

A few looked up then and Coach said, "By the way he is now engaged and plans to be married soon. You will get to meet his bride-to-be in a bit. She is a vice-president at First Commonwealth and they had dated back in high school in Alabama. Any questions?"

Mr. Jefferson Talbot, President of the University said, "Bob, if this is any indication of how fast you get things done, then we are ready to buckle up and hang on. Welcome to Kentucky!"

He then walked over and we shook hands while the remaining members applauded. I went around shaking everyone's hand. "Coach," I said, "see if Lynn is just outside while I hold my breath to make sure she hasn't run off."

The door opened and in walks Coach. There was a long pause and my heart just about stopped. Finally, there was Lynn, grinning.

I laughed and said, "That was not funny, you two."

The introductions went around and before we dismissed, I let them know how important it was to keep this under wraps until after the game.

I said, "We want to do this with class and the right way. That is one thing you'll get from me and my staff."

We planned for Lynn to drop me off at the airport for them to fly me back to Tuscaloosa in about four hours. Miles had a list of names and numbers for me. Lynn drove us to her house. She was glad everything worked out with the Board. "What are your first thoughts about a wedding?" I asked.

"Bob, you are the one shooting from the hip and it has gone well so far. When I called Mom I actually heard the phone drop," she said, laughing "The the not telling anybody is what got her the most."

"You said you were going to get back there on the 23rd. We have practice that morning and we could have a quiet little "I Do" at one of our houses on the 24th and let the parents know we would plan a larger reception in a few weeks."

Something occurred to me and I said, "Have you ever been to Miami?"

She shook her head.

"Instead of flying back to Lexington, I would like for you to come and meet me down there for a few days, since you'll be my wife, for the game and Coach will have us flown back to Kentucky for the press conference."

"That should work well. I'd like to be able to hang by a pool in late December while you do your stuff."

With a lot of work in progress, I was flown back to Tuscaloosa. I got to the office and as I walked down the hall Coach Bryant waved me in. "Bob, I had to be out. What was your decision?"

"Coach, I followed your advice about not settling for a position that just sounds okay. I figured since we had beaten Coach Sargent a couple of good times, I was not sure about being his offensive Coordinator. I told Coach Clark if they wanted to make real progress, they should hire me as their next head coach."

"Bob," Coach Bryant said, very surprised, "what were their first concerns?"

"You may not believe this but some of their board members were wishy-washy about me being single. So I got engaged and will be named their new head coach after the Orange Bowl."

Coach Bryant looked worried and then he started laughing. "Did you just go up and pick any girl up and propose?"

"There is a girl I went out with in high school that is a VP at a bank up there. I think we've just have had some bad timing because of our careers. We talked and she thought it felt right. I think it would have happened one way or another."

Coach shook his head and said, "I am not the least bit surprised. I knew you were capable and I don't look forward to playing you in a few years."

"Don't start that already, Coach."

"I made it clear that it wouldn't be released until after the game."

"I appreciate your integrity and the work you have done for me."

We shook hands and I told Coach, "I've got work to do and I won't be letting you down."

He smiled. "If you need any help with assistants or anything, you just let me know."

Practice went well and Ed and Bobby Joe did a good job of moving in the pocket and making their throws. As before, we had our players working on a lot of fundamentals, which helped to keep their focus in check.

My phone calls to Gary Patterson and Bobby Snead worked to my good and both made plans to come on board with me. I tracked down Pat Byrd, who was coaching quarterbacks at Memphis State and he agreed to join me as well. I advised Gary and Bobby to look for their other position coaches. I told them we'd meet on them January third in Lexington.

I was headed to Stuart for Christmas when I realized I was getting married in the morning. I walked in to the house and Sharon and Mom were sitting in the kitchen. "Do you have a clue how hard this is, trying to be secret?" Mom said, walking over to hug my neck. She said, "From what I remember Lynn is a nice girl and being bank VP is not bad either."

"The head coach of the Kentucky Wildcats," Quint shouted loud, walking into the room. We greeted each other with a hug. I congratulated him, also; he had just signed a scholarship with the Owls.

Dad made it in and with his hug, I knew how special it felt for him.

After that, I made a call. "Lynn, do you have time for dinner," I asked.

"Yes, I'm at home," I said. "Plus the plans are still on from this side. Well, the yes part carries a lot of weight. Okay, I'll see you in an hour."

The plan went off without a hitch. I told Brother Barnhill, our preacher, that he had to keep this quite until after the bowl game.

I got back to Tuscaloosa and practice went well. We boarded the charter flight for Miami and among the coaches we discussed different situations we may face. Being at the Sugar Bowl last year has really helped Ed to understand the high profile and magnitude of this game.

It felt good to get through with practice, get back to our team hotel and have Lynn there. She had a genuine interest in football and more so now than ever. Coach Duncan stopped by to meet Lynn since he was the only other coach who knew. I reminded him that she was the one at the West Marion Diner when we met about going to Tuscaloosa. Coach reminded her it was good she had some time off. He said, "Lynn, we are going to do our best to send Bob and you off to Kentucky in fine fashion with this game."

The Tide kicked-off and Winston Bennett made a hard hit that set the early tempo. When the offense took over we peppered them with short, quick throws, and moved down the field. Colt ran an in and out pattern to the corner and Ed laid it right into his hands for the first touchdown.

Our defense was onto their option game and our mixing it up got them frustrated. They rushed and we dropped it off in short throws for big gains. When they blitzed, Ed picked it up and hit our short receiver. At halftime we were up 21-3. Coach Bryant told Coach Duncan to come out firing like we did against Tennessee. When you aren't used to losing, you can get out of your plan in a hurry.

Going into the fourth quarter Ed Hollingsworth set an Orange Bowl record with his fourth touchdown pass, to Brad Holmes, as Alabama went up 35-10. With 10 minutes left in the game, after a first down running play, Bobby Joe was sent in to finish out the game and his college career. Ed got a huge standing ovation on his exit. With about five minutes left in the game the NBC announcers were looking for something to talk to the viewers about and they got their topic. Unbeknownst to me, while sending in plays and talking with Ed, their cameras were zooming in on us. The announcer says, "This is an example of class on behalf of Coach Bryant for giving us this breaking information. This young man in your picture, Coach Bob Hayes, shown now with his MVP quarterback, will officially be named as the new head coach at the University of Kentucky tomorrow during a three pm press conference,. Coach Hayes will become the youngest head coach in college football. He follows in his dad's footsteps, Paul Hayes, who was a top high school coach at Stuart High School in Alabama for 18 years." The announcers laughed. "The Wildcat is out of the bag now," they said.

THE REST WILL BE HISTORY

In his second year at the helm, Coach Hayes led the Wildcats to victory in the Peach Bowl. It was Kentucky's first bowl game in fifteen years.

Gary's Gems

Within the stories you just read are pieces of knowledge that highlight specific learning moments. By touching on these "gems," you will have a list to remind you of each specific moment when these pieces of knowledge were applied. This list can also make the knowledge available for you, allowing you to apply the lessons to your own circumstances.

One thing Coach Hayes learned was to take aspects from a bevy of activities and sports and apply them to other areas where they could increase his advantage. Some are very self-explanatory and others may take a thought or two. Hopefully you will recall some of the situations when they were used and mold them to fit your own specific endeavors.

PART I

- We learned to watch games: We didn't just watch the ball. You learn by watching how the best athletes play their position.
- Learn and know the rules: Rules can be your friend and they are there to protect the game.
- To win it takes everybody playing together: There's no I in team. Everyone has to function together as one unit.
- Know when to use a specific play: At times it can be risky, but know what advantage you are looking to gain.
- Learn or have a specific system: By doing so all the players know what to expect and this makes playing together better.
- Know how to ask a question: Be specific about what you want to learn or know from a person.

- Learn from a lot of examples: By watching different techniques you can mold what fits you or a player to best suit them.
- Learn from your mistakes and be able to handle criticism: There will always be many doubters and "Monday morning QB's."
- Have a game plan and stick to it: Don't let yourself be caught off-guard. You may have to make adjustments, if the opponent makes changes, but keep focused on what you know how to do.
- Give credit where credit is due: It may come from a manager, assistant, or spouse, but let the person know they made a difference.
- Don't retaliate in anger: The officials/refs seem to always catch the second player and then you hurt your team. You can look for payback the right way.
- Practice with a purpose: Wasted time slows down teams a lot. Organize your activities so you can cover more in preparation.
- What it boils down to are the little things: Making the right steps, putting the correct foot forward, holding the ball just so, get your shoulders square—the list can seem endless. Pay attention to proper procedures.
- Protect your players and don't air out your dirty laundry: A coach should take the blame for the loss and credit his players with a win. Keep your differences inside the locker room.
- Review the proper fundamentals and don't keep making the same mistakes: Adjust your focus. Remember that you can't keep doing the same thing and expect different results.
- Most defenders almost always go for the first move: By knowing this you can have the opportunity to make something out of nothing and not get too risky.
- Practice your special plays: In the backyard you can make them up. By preparing, you get the timing right and can be effective.
- Look for specific player's tendencies: You can look to see if they make moves the same way, lead with a certain foot, or take a stance to dictate a certain move. Scouts are people trained to do this.
- Be careful talking in public: So many times players and coaches will spout off dumb quotes only to give the opponent extra incentive. Think before replying.
- IT is a team game: Play together as one and the results will become easier to obtain.

- Jumping rope is one of the best overall agility exercises: Look for techniques to enhance ability and agility. Some of the routines can be real simple.
- There is a proper place and time for everything: Do things the right way and if something goes awry then work together to correct it.
- Be careful doing outside activities: Don't get stupid trying to show off, get injured and hurt your team. "I'll show them" usually backfires.
- It is great to have passion for the game at any level: By knowing the game and the effort desired a player can elevate their game to a more positive level.
- You have to have desire and preparation to go along with emotion: Just yelling or delivering an emotional speech won't get it done if you haven't put in the time to be ready to play the game.
- Practice game situations: In doing so you won't get caught off-guard as much. Then you can be at the right place at the right time.
- Always coach from the positive and let players know what you want them To DO: A lot of times the mind doesn't differentiate between the positive and negative. By knowing what you want to do a lot of mistakes can be eliminated.
- Be careful trying to steal signals: A simple change can backfire on you. Tendencies are one thing. Be aware people are going to be watching.
- Control your expressions: If a player or team is getting the best of you then don't advertise it. Make the proper corrections and, "don't let them see you sweat."
- A little gamesmanship can work real well at times: Within the proper confines, keeping the opponent guessing can be a real advantage.
- Winning is the bottom line: It's what you play for. You may not win all the time. 100 % of all games will have a loser, barring ties, but that doesn't mean you have to like it.
- A little encouragement can go a long way: Getting behind and supporting a player will by far beat berating them.

PART II

- Know the strength of your teams: This allows you to properly prepare for an opponent and be able to make adjustments to give you the best chance to succeed.
- Take advantage of your opportunities: Sometimes an opponent will allow certain factors to happen. Make the correct call and be prepared.
- Be ready for your chance: You have to prepare "as if." Then you can step up when timing is everything. I saw my older brother get inserted into the first game of his freshman year, after being the fifth team quarterback, and he started every game the next four years for Jacksonville State University.
- What you do can speak a lot louder that what you say: Leading by example is a true test of character.
- Knowing the rules can be a big advantage: Alignment, possession and other aspects, like a tackle eligible in football, can be utilized with a little know how.
- Don't panic: Just because you can get down doesn't mean you're out. A lot of teams can spring a surprise on you. Take stock into the situation and make good decisions.
- Speaking with conviction and getting right to the point can work wonders: Don't "beat around the bush." Be precise and know what you're talking about.
- Know how to set up your special plays: It doesn't have to be complicated. By preparing, knowing the timing and feature of what you want to do sets the play into motion.
- Sometimes you have to take the bitter with the bitter: A ref's blown call, a bad bounce, and the list goes on. Try your best to not get into those situations where one aspect can mean the outcome. But, yes, "it" happens.
- A little motivation can go a long way: Some just need a little "positive" reinforcement and presented properly it can work wonders.
- Commitment is crucial from all involved: At times you can only be as strong as your weakest link. Everyone needs to be on the same page with the same plan.

- Don't let your players get complacent. Competition is a vital element: If you don't perform properly there is usually someone more than ready to take your place. Thinking you have it made is an accident waiting to happen.
- It really helps to learn from others: Most are eager to help and welcome the chance to display their skills and knowledge. You will sharpen your skills when you show others as well.
- Sometimes things don't go your way: Preparing properly will help you overcome adversities. It goes back to not panicking in difficult situations.
- Try to make the best of all situations: When your back is against the wall then use that wall to push off of and come back stronger. Look ahead and anticipate what may happen.
- Have a good outlook for your team: Review and know what you are looking forward to. That will create more positive opportunities.
- It pays to be ready to play: Getting complacent will lead you to a cliff. Nothing runs on automatic, as in just going through the motions.
- Always look for positive changes: They don't have to be monumental but improvement can always be obtained.
- Try to visualize the "what if:" In doing so you will stay ahead and can anticipate your opponent's next move.
- Have a goal but know when you are ready for it: All teams want to go undefeated to start. There will be factors that can limit your expectations. Try looking ahead and gaining valuable knowledge and experience. Learn the lessons well.
- The proper process will produce more results: Do not get sloppy with the details of preparing which will give you the best opportunity for success. As before, pay attention to the little things.
- Know how to prepare for the conditions: The secret lies not in having the will to win, but in having the will to PREPARE to win. Be ready for sudden changes AND expect the unexpected.
- You have to have emotion, you can't fake it: False emotions fade in a hurry and take the steam right out of you. Focus on the task and know you are doing it for the right reason.
- Championships live forever and they are worth the effort: Whether it's youth baseball, or the Super Bowl, all players remember hoisting the trophy with their teammates. The work ethic to get you there is rewarded and appreciated.

PART III

- Coach proper procedure and technique: Sometimes you can get lucky in situations and things go your way. Most of the time the correct instructions will win out and help to achieve greatness.
- A lot of time players hate it when the coach is right: That's about 100% of the time (even if he is wrong). You also need make sure players believe and trust their coach.
- Just keep working as hard as you can: Don't slack off or the momentum will fade. If things are not going well, look to see where you can get better.
- Learn good fundamentals for all type of situations: Most of your top players and teams do things the right way. They know the little things matter and prepare.
- Be open to ideas and suggestions and don't let ego get in the way: Whether it is simple or something major, don't think you know it all. Change is all too common in athletics.
- What works for one may not work for another: There are countless examples of different styles athletes utilize which suit only them. They may have a physical characteristic to allow them a certain kind of control. Be consistent in doing what you do.
- Know what to say so you won't be taken the wrong way: Do not rush too quick trying to get a point across. A little thinking can go a long way toward not getting your foot stuck in your mouth.
- Know when an opportunity presents itself: Be prepared so you do not spend all your time wishing you had done something else. Hindsight can be 20/20, but with preparation you will feel you are doing the right thing in the present.
- Self-help techniques save a lot of future mistakes: Taking time out to visualize what you are trying to accomplish can be a major factor with achievement.
- Sometimes you never know people's situations: Motivation comes to people in a variety of different ways. Struggle may have been one person's background and taking things in stride suited another. A kid may have had an All-American dad showing him how to throw and another may have not even grown up with a dad at all.

- Hard and good work can create opportunities: Putting forth your best, at all times, can make all the difference. Then you will be ready for your chance.
- Coaching is about the players: Say "my teams have had 200 wins," not "I have 200 wins." Do things for the right reason.
- The first five minutes of the second half in football are usually the most important: The tone gets set for the rest of the game. Then the one on top can manage and dictate the events.
- Don't blame your players: Coaching is about responsibility and taking care of the ones putting out the effort of performing. Mistakes will be made and coaches need to find the best ways to make sure they do not keep happening.
- Know all the aspects of your plays: In doing so you can come up with different options that may get presented with efforts by your opponents. "If they do that, we can do this."
- Have measuring sticks to gauge your progress: Stats can help. Watch to see how some players are attaining what they have been working on and the efforts they are putting in.
- It helps to be precise: "aim small, miss small." Trying to do things the right way will help to avoid costly mistakes in critical situations.
- Learn to watch and apply: By paying attention to how things are done the right way, you can take what others do well and mold it to fit your situation or team.
- 4 P's (Proper Procedures Produces Profits): Work to do the right things at all times.
- Don't forget where you came from and remember your friends: Loyalty means a lot. The people who have stood behind you at all times are invaluable. As you move forward remember that there are a lot of people who helped you to get there.
- Be careful about burning bridges: Know the people who have helped and don't get foolish thinking it was all just you.

PART IV

- Ask what questions they may have and you can give a specific response: This will allow you to hone in on the response people are looking for. Otherwise you could talk for an hour and not answer their questions.
- Be prepared: No matter what you are about to endeavor, preparation is the key.
- Keep all your players ready: Whether you use different units or teams they have to be ready to perform. Then the ability to step up when called upon is available.
- Once it is over nothing is going to change the outcome: Whether it's good or bad accept it and move forward. See what you can learn and grow with the experience.
- Timing is a key ingredient: In sports or relationships timing is such a critical element. A great plan or action can go bust if applied at the wrong time.
- Last season is history and it can only be a lesson: Review and move on to the next challenge. This will allow the future to be brighter.
- Winners practice hard: Thinking you are good will get you slammed in a hurry. Working to prove your mettle will stand up to the opposition.
- Know how to play the game: Know the total aspects of your sport. Many avenues will open up when you apply them. You will be glad you did.
- An honest explanation can go a long way: Some players think they are doing the right thing. Coaching requires getting into the finer details of the game, where you can use the aspects in other phases of the game and in life. Most players do not have the coach's experience and, because of this, positive communication is priceless.
- It's okay to take what a team is giving you and then take a little more: If a team's trying not to get beat deep then throw short passes down the field. Patience really helps and mistakes can be avoided.
- Know your commitment: If you are in for the right reason, the ride will be smoother. Try to not settle for a position but look for the opportunity you envision or can see yourself becoming part of.

Then you can make all the contacts and preparations to become the successful coach/person you want to be.
- The most intangible aspect between success and failure lies within the human heart. You must believe you can make it and strive at all times, no matter the circumstance. There are over a thousand reasons for failure, but yet, not a single excuse.

TRIBUTE

There are three coaches and a group of 'mates I have to give a special mention to.

Being involved and around sports all of my life, I've realized that there are many attributes and characteristics each coach is able to share and personalize. From midget football to the NFL, from little league to the majors and beyond, coaches are truly special.

E.C. Wilson coached at Glencoe High in Alabama for eighteen years starting in 1949. He helped build a solid and stable program that was the focal point of the whole town. Coach was always present through the good times and the bad and his family's friendship was and has always been very special. He won his last game at Glencoe coaching his older son Dale and my older brother Kenneth. His youngest son Nathan and I were the managers.

Lyle Darnell took over and raised the Glencoe program to championship status winning the 1973 2-A title, to date the only one in school history. Coach Darnell had a plan and gave his players the mentality and discipline to know they could get the job done. Coach Darnell was special because he was my coach and also my younger brother Ed's.

The football field at Glencoe High sports the name "Wilson-Darnell Stadium." Both men are members of the Alabama High School Athletic Association and Etowah County Sports Hall of Fame.

This next group is special because as a member of this team each gets to proclaim they were a State Champion. Going 13-0 and winning the championship game on the road captivated the special season. The whole town of Glencoe deserves credit for the part they played, along with the band and cheerleaders. Just being a part of this team was special.

The players: Mile Holmes, Jeff Davis, Doug Prater, Gary Lett, Phillip Spann, Mike Marker, Larry Nabors, Barry Dunston, Willie Davis, Hal Smith, Billy Towe, David Burgess, Kevin Colvard, Gene Richey, Alan Norton, Randy Phillips, Chris Norton, Terry Chapman, Dennis

Daugherty, Steve Davis, Donald Lancaster, Frankie Hubbard, Mark Walden, Jerry Lewis, David Holmes, Lex Clowdus, Dennis Robinson, Steve Brown, Robert, Noah Larry Hale, Daryl Reid, Mike Link, Greg Davenport, Don Richards, and Johnny Watson.

The assistant coaches: Jimmy Champion and Charles Tucker.

The team doctor: my dad, M.G. Lett

COACH PELL

Coach Charley Pell was a special person. His life and attributes are the inspiration and backbone of *SIDELINE*. After playing one year of high school football in Albertville, AL, he was a member of both sides of the line for Coach "Bear" Bryant at Alabama and his first National Champions of 1961.

In 1969 Coach Pell became the youngest head coach in college football at that time. He took over a struggling program, at Jacksonville State in Alabama, with a budget of about $40,000 total. He found a way—with determination and an unrelenting work ethic—to go from 3-6 to 10-0 in the first two years. As head coach at Clemson, he led them, in his first year, to their first bowl game in seventeen seasons. The pinnacle was the best turn-around in college football history: taking the University of Florida program from 0-10-1 in his first season to 8-4 and winning the Tangerine Bowl the next. The Gators have never looked back since, setting the course for their success. When NCAA sanctions were brought up, Coach Pell didn't try to pass the buck and took the blame himself. That is integrity.

My older brother was the starting quarterback at Jacksonville State for Coach Pell during his first three years, and I was on the sideline as a ball boy for all the games. I got to see firsthand Coach Pell's intensity and leadership. These qualities were truly special.

In 2001, while battling cancer, which would win out that year, Coach Pell was able to visit the teams where he had coached. He spoke to the players about the values, purpose, and education each player got the opportunity to obtain because of football. The crowning part was Coach Pell sharing his relationship with Jesus Christ.

To give you an example of what a coach can mean to his player's, the following was written by Mike Cundiff who played during Coach Pell's first stint as a head coach. Mike shared this at the 40 year reunion of the Gamecocks undefeated 1970 team.

COACH PELL

He'd block you in the shoot and when you got up he'd say, "Now, by God, that's what I want each and every day." Coach Pell was tough as hell.

(Coach would get down and block you full speed, him in coaching attire & you in full pads.)

On a hot crappy day he'd yell, "All up." As we gathered around he'd say, "All non-scholarship take it in. For the rest we'll see who really wants to win." Coach Pell was tough as hell. (All on scholarship would line up on the goal line and we'd do 100 yard stop and go's until someone would quit)

He put the ball on the one yard line, 99 yards away. "Five times we'll score without a mistake, or we'll be here all damn day!" Coach Pell was tough as hell.

(Full scrimmage with no substitution where we had to score five times without a single mistake. It took two hours.)

We'd drill and scrimmage and run and hit, until we felt no pain. When we thought we'd got through it, he'd yell, "Get dressed, we're going out again." Coach Pell was tough as hell. (He sent us in after a two hour scrimmage and after twenty minutes came in and had us get dressed and go back out for another hour)

In '69 I recall, the Greyhound schedule was on the wall. Three roomies I had all took flight, sneaking out in the middle of the night. Coach Pell was tough as hell. (The bus schedule was posted in the basement of Salls Hall for anyone who wanted to leave.)

In that first year an open date, we thought. But at chow that night, on Saturday eve, he stood on a table and with a shout, "Full scrimmage, 8 a.m. no one leave." Coach Pell was tough as hell. (We had an open date in 69 and everyone thought we would have Saturday off. Coach thought different.)

And on that silent bus at Troy, he said with pride and brass, "One year from this night, you'll see, we will whup Troy's ass!" Coach Pell was tough as hell. (And we did. 55-10, 'nuff said)

In just one year we'd come, from 3 and 6 to 10 and 0. He'd kept the faith, made us winners, and took us to a bowl. Coach Pell was tough as hell.

Yes, Coach Pell was tough as hell, but I loved him. He was our Coach you see. He's someone I'll always admire. He is someone I'll never forget. He'll always be a part of me.

Coach Pell was tough as hell, but I loved him.

Mike "Tubby" Cundiff

Acknowledgements

When #80 looks the ball in, after the kick-off, on the goal-line, he weaves his way in and out of holes for a 100 yard touchdown return. To accomplish this it takes the other 10 players doing their job—to open up those lanes to make the play successful.

It is the same with *SIDELINE* that my special team members stepped up to the task when I called upon them.

Mrs. Ward Pell, wife of Coach Charley Pell, gave her valuable time to provide knowledge and information that only she could give. The time we spent talking about such a special era in our lives was truly memorable. Mrs. Pell demonstrates with her continued ties to Jacksonville State University how special Coach Pell's first head coaching job really was.

Thanks to Facebook I was able to connect with Rex Stanfield who is a graduate of Glencoe High School. Rex has recently published two outstanding books, *BAIL OUT* and *STIMULUS*, and both are a joy to read. Rex was gracious enough to share some of the more intricate attributes and details of writing and coordinating a story to be told.

Another name surfaced from a Facebook connection, a person who was also a graduate of Glencoe High. Rita McMahan teaches English and Composition in Chelsea, Alabama. She really thought I was joking when I first asked for her help starting this project. Her professionalism and expertise has been very insightful and much needed.

June Clark, my aunt and her son/cousin Robert have been my sounding board and have given me a lot of encouragement and guidance.

Rounding out my special team is captain, wife of 23 years, Angela. She has provided valuable insight for all of my professional articles and made sure I crossed my t's and dotted my i's. Angela even knew what I was supposed to be thinking and what I meant to say, in most cases.

Be on guard, for the next book, *OUT OF THE ROUGH*.